Saving Grace

by

H.P. Munro

About the Book

When Charlotte Grace left Grace Falls at the age of seventeen, she swore she'd never return. More than twenty years on she still regrets breaking the heart of her first love. Reaching a crossroads in her life, Charlotte has started to merely drift along.

Erin Hunter has spent a lifetime recovering from having her heart shattered by the person she trusted most. Taking shelter in her home town and her career, she's avoided relationships.

Neither woman ever thought they'd see each other again. They didn't count on Grace Falls. The quirky town's charm pulls people in, and if the town isn't enough, its residents are more than willing to lend a hand.

Celebrate a return to Grace Falls.

Acknowledgements

So it's been a while!

The story outline for this book started in December 2013, before I'd even published Grace Falls.

I can blame no one and nothing on the time it's taken. I'm tardy and undisciplined.

However, there are a number of people that I have to thank for their encouragement, support and guidance.

First thanks go to my book (#wine) club for their initial enthusiasm which had me start to write this story. In particular, thanks to Karin who read it in installments and continued for almost three years to harangue me for the next chapter. That woman has commitment!

Thank you to every family member, friend and reader who have asked on my story's progress. I eventually finished this just so you'd stop asking.

To Jenny for sitting with me in December 2014 and working out a schedule for me to complete, edit, and publish the book in 2015... I eventually followed the plan this year.

A huge thanks to Clare Lydon for reading the first draft and pointing out all my bad habits. To be fair none of these had anything to do with my writing, but I'm grateful regardless. In all honesty, Clare has been a great support and her guidance has been invaluable.

Another vital part of the support I received came from Cindy Rizzo, thank you for pointing out where my Scottishness got in the way of a book set in Alabama.

I don't have enough words to thank my friend Fiona H. She reviewed the book many times along the way and I could not have completed it without her suggestions, and advice. In addition, her demand that I change the title of the book to 'Saving Grace' from its working title was the right one. Her approach to the title change was just to stop calling it anything else until I submitted to her will...it took a whole three days. (I was proud of holding out that long).

To the final readers Jenny, Lyn and Fiona MacG. Thank you for pointing out all the things we didn't spot...hope you got 'em all!

Finally, thank you to my wife...for pretty much everything.

For Jane

Contents

Prologue

1982

Charlotte changed quickly, pulled her auburn hair back into a ponytail and secured it with a rubber band. She folded the lemon-colored dress her mother had made her put on and carefully placed it in her hiding place. She looked down at the overalls she'd slipped on. She was getting too tall for them now, and they sat above her ankle bone. Huffing, she rolled them up so they didn't look as ridiculous. She would have to see whether Matt Sullivan would trade another pair with her soon. Pulling on a pair of worn sneakers, she finally felt like herself and set off skipping into the woodlands for the day's adventure.

She was almost at her favorite place beside the creek when she heard another voice. She walked on her tiptoes, trying not to make a noise as she got closer to where the sound was coming from.

You had to be careful in the woods, there was always the chance of hunters. Stronger than the fear of getting shot, was that if she did she'd have to explain to her mother why exactly she was wearing overalls and sneakers, particularly ones that belonged to 'that Sullivan scamp,' as her mother referred to him.

"Being a big sister sucks. Play with your brother. Take your brother with you when you go out and make sure he doesn't fall in the creek...again. Like I can stop that happening!"

Charlotte watched intrigued as a blonde girl in red overalls, who looked to be of a similar age to her, sat on a rock appearing to have a somewhat animated, if one-sided, conversation with a toad.

As if sensing she was no longer alone, the blonde girl looked up slowly, her hazel eyes scanning the trees. "If that's you, Sam, I'm not playing with you, and I'm going to kick your butt for running off like that."

Charlotte stepped out from her hiding place. "I don't know who Sam is, but it isn't me." She grinned and tucked her hands into the bib of her overall.

As she got closer Charlotte saw that the girl's lips rose up at the edges, making it look as though she was smiling before she actually was. It made Charlotte want to smile even more.

"Sam's my brother," the girl replied. "Who are you?"

"Charlotte Grace."

"Can I call you Charlie?"

Charlotte shrugged. She'd never had a nickname before and nor had anyone ever dared to shorten her name either. "Sure. What's your name?"

"Erin Hunter and this is Elliot my toad."

"Pleased to meet you, Erin and Elliot."

Charlotte beamed showing the large gap where her front teeth should have been. "You new here?"

Erin nodded. "We moved here last week, from St Anton," she said, referring to Grace Falls' closest neighboring town. "You one of the Grace Falls' Graces?" Erin picked up her toad and set it on her lap before motioning to Charlotte to sit down beside her.

"Yup, my..." Charlotte paused and started to count on her fingers, before giving up with a shrug. "There're a lot of Greats in there, and I can never remember, but the town is named after my"—she waved her hand as though rounding her forefathers up—"grandfather."

"Cooool! Wish I had a town named after me."

Charlotte scrunched her face up in thought. "How 'bout we call this rock after you? Erin's Rock." She patted the stone beneath her.

Erin's face lit up. "That's so cool! Do you want to hold Elliot?" She didn't wait for an answer before she plonked the toad onto Charlotte's lap.

"I've never been this close to a toad before." Charlotte inspected the toad on her lap almost as intently as it inspected her.

"I've got loads of animals." Erin's chest puffed up with pride. "My daddy says that maybe I can be an animal nurse when I'm growed up."

"How old are you?"

"Seven, but I'll be eight real soon."

Charlotte sat up straighter. "Me too."

Their conversation was interrupted by a boy's voice shouting Erin's name.

"That's my brother Sam. He's five and a big poop-head." She giggled. "I'd better go. I'm meant to be looking after him." She slipped off the rock, retrieved Elliot from Charlotte's lap and tucked him into the bib of her red overalls.

"Nice meeting you, Erin." Charlotte slid from the rock and brushed dust from her lap.

"Nice meeting you too, Charlie." She skipped off, but before exiting the clearing she turned back and kissed Charlotte's cheek. "See you tomorrow?"

Charlotte nodded quickly and patted the stone affectionately. "I'll be right here, on Erin's rock."

Chapter One

2013

A small envelope appeared at the bottom of the laptop screen.

"You have fifty-five unread emails in your mailbox. Do you ever look at your emails?" Molly shouted to Charlotte, who was attempting to draw out her coffee making in the hope Molly would forget her latest grand idea.

"The majority of them are crap," Charlotte shouted back. "They're either telling me I've won a lottery I haven't entered or have had a security breach on a bank account I don't have. Or they're trying to sell me blue pills for a condition I've never experienced and that I'm not likely to!" She grinned as she reentered the room and placed a mug of coffee in front of her best friend.

"Have you heard of spam filters? Honestly, God only knows how you managed to get where you are, being so freaking disorganized," Molly chided. "However, you have me, and I'm about to get your life on track. Well your love life anyway. I have given up on you and a career."

Charlotte rolled her eyes, waiting for the onslaught that was likely to follow. However, Molly was far too caught up in what she thought was her best idea yet to chastise her further.

"Right, we have to fill in your details to register and then select a picture where you look half decent. Then we sit back and wait to see what little fish bite."

Charlotte's head was still reeling slightly from being woken up by Molly at half past seven on a Sunday morning. A time which previously Molly knew existed but had little experience of, especially since she'd been out at a work party the previous night. However, last night Molly had been introduced to Glen. A gorgeous looking, wonderfully funny, and successful man brought to the party by one of Molly's workmates. Who, after several glasses of pinot noir, admitted she'd met Glen online. Once Molly realized that her perception of online dating was out of date, she started to think it would be the perfect solution for Charlotte and her empty black book.

"Okay, surname, Grace. Forename, Charlotte. Age..." Molly cast a surveying eye over Charlotte who, dressed in blue checked pajama bottoms and a white vest, was curled up on the sofa opposite attempting to transfer the warmth from her mug into enough energy to go for a shower.

"You could probably pass for forty," Molly surmised.

"I am thirty-nine you cheeky—!"

"Exactly." Oblivious to the offense she'd caused, Molly continued completing the registration form. "Occupation? There's no point going into the whole story. You want to make sure someone replies for the right reasons, not because you're loaded."

Charlotte sighed. She missed the buzz she got from running her fitness centers and heading up her own business. It had been a year since she'd sold her LifeFit gyms. A move prompted by the news of her father's death. News which hadn't come from her mother but from an old friend back home who'd tracked her down after thinking it odd she wasn't at the funeral. In some part of her, Charlotte knew her business achievements had been a way to try to make her father proud of her again, and his death forever removed that possibility.

She'd grieved for the loss of her parents years ago. However, the news reawakened old pains, and her thirst to succeed became a victim of her past. A past she kept bottled up and hidden from the life she'd created away from Grace Falls. As a result, her parent company, Elliot Enterprises, had been almost dormant ever since.

"You still with me?" Molly waved a hand to get her attention. "What do you want for occupation? Oh, actually, I know what'll get the juices going. Personal Tennis Coach." Molly typed the words as she said them aloud. "Location, Manhattan. Okay, now we have a little blog thing. How about...former professional tennis—"

Charlotte interrupted immediately. "I don't think you can honestly say professional." Charlotte absently rubbed her right knee, as she often did when she thought about that period in her life.

"You got a scholarship to college. That's payment for playing."

Molly looked over at Charlotte and smiled before continuing to type purposefully.

"Former professional tennis player, looking for a lady who likes movies, good food, great company and can match my active lifestyle, or is at least interested in the massages that follow!"

Charlotte shook her head, but she decided not to get into it with her. She knew once Molly left, she'd be accessing the website and removing the profile anyway. So she was content to let Molly have her fun.

"So, Miss Grace, now for a picture where you look hot." Molly hauled herself out of her chair and onto the sofa beside Charlotte. She flexed her fingers and clicked on the photo folders. Charlotte saw the cursor hover over the folder marked 'Tina.'

"Do not delete that."

"But why?" Molly practically wailed. "Seriously, for six years she made your life a misery. She's eroded your confidence so much that even now, after two years since you found her in your bed with that slut, you've only been on a couple of dates." Molly adopted her best mafia voice. "Let me take out the trash, boss."

"Leave it, I'll delete it when I'm ready."

Grumbling, Molly shook her head and moved on to the folder marked 'Holidays.'

"I know just the picture. The one I took of you when we were in Whistler last Easter, and you were mocking my Terminator protective pants." Molly searched the folder until coming upon the image she wanted.

In the picture Charlotte was resting in one of the bars at the bottom of the slopes, after a morning snowboarding. Sitting back in her seat, with a white long-sleeved base layer outlining her athletic figure, her sunglasses were pushed up into her auburn curls, which framed her face. She was smiling broadly into the camera, with a smile that reached deep into her green eyes.

Molly looked at the picture she'd chosen and smiled as she attached the image onto Charlotte's profile. Before Charlotte could object she hurriedly selected a couple more where Charlotte looked like an all-action kind of girl, but one who would equally want to snuggle up and enjoy a glass of wine and a movie.

"Right, we're ready to go. Time to sit back and wait," Molly said with a satisfied tone as she clicked the mouse emphatically to activate Charlotte's profile.

Chapter Two

"I bring coffee and pastries from Ruby's."

Erin Hunter looked up at the sound of her assistant's voice. "Is my Monday going to be so bad that you have to fill me with goodies from Grace Falls' premier coffee house?"

Cindy screwed her face up as she placed the coffee cup and Danish in front of her boss. "Your first appointment is Emmett Day."

Erin closed her eyes and ran her fingers through her short hair, trying to regain the serenity and sanity she'd had before finding out how her day was going to begin. This would mark Emmett's third appointment this month. Thanks to Doctor Maddie Marinelli's approach to Mr. Day's legendary hypochondria, he'd switched his attention from his own health to that of his aged basset hound Buster.

While Erin, like all in Grace Falls, was thankful they now had a permanent doctor in the clinic, she could quite cheerfully throttle Maddie now that her patience was being tested so regularly by Emmett.

"How many of Alex's pastries did you buy me?" Erin finally opened her eyes to glare at Cindy.

"Three."

"This is probably going to be a four pastry kinda day."

Cindy suppressed a smile. "On it, boss lady!"

Taking a huge bite out of the pastry, Erin moaned in pleasure. "And keep the coffee coming," she yelled after a retreating Cindy, who held up her hands in acknowledgment. "And if you fancy going to Sully's bar and putting a drop of Irish in it, I wouldn't complain," Erin mumbled, taking a deep breath and preparing for her first appointment.

∞ ∞ ∞

"I can categorically tell you Buster doesn't have myxomatosis Mr. Day." Erin attempted an upbeat smile, as she held the thirteen-year-old hound's chin.

"Well, how do you explain the swelling around his genitals then?" The old man huffed, nodding his head in the direction of Buster's backend.

Erin flashed a look of apology at the hound, who just stared back with a look of resignation on his hangdog face. She placed an exploratory hand between his hind legs and sighed.

"Emmett, his balls have always been that size. I know this because I've handled his balls more often than I've..."—she paused. Emmett Day did not need to know about her testicle handling history, so she switched what she'd been about to say for a more PG-version—"had hot dinners."

Remarkably, she managed to ignore Cindy's snort. "For his age, he's doing great." She carefully lifted Buster from the examination table, grunting slightly as she put him down. "He could do with losing a few pounds, but aside from that he's great." The dog shook, in an attempt to right his fur after the lift, causing his long ears to clap loudly. "Aren't you, Buster?"

The old dog stopped when he heard his name and looked up at the vet with doleful eyes. His tail started to wag back and forth a few times until the effort seemed too much and he lay down on the floor.

Emmett Day gave Erin a disbelieving look but took the dog's leash that she held out to him.

"Well, we'll see," he muttered, as he pulled on Buster's leash in an attempt to get the old dog back on his feet.

"I'm sure I'll see you again soon, Emmett," Erin said sweetly, motioning to Cindy to accompany him out of the clinic.

"You want me to lock the door?" Cindy whispered as she passed. "Stop him from coming back in."

Erin gave it a second's consideration. "Push the sofa in front of it too, just to be sure," she replied with a wink.

14

Chapter Three

"Okay, so I've narrowed it down to a couple of suspects," Molly announced, as she flung her purse onto Charlotte's chair.

"I know I've been out of the dating game for a bit, but I'm pretty sure referring to potential suitors as suspects isn't the done thing!" Charlotte smiled at Molly.

She would never admit it, but ever since Molly decided to create her own version of The Bachelorette, using Charlotte as the dating bait, she'd felt a little excitement ignite inside of her.

Molly scrunched her face up. "Whatever." She flipped open Charlotte's laptop and flopped onto the sofa beside her. "I've been chatting online with a couple of them today, and I've screened out the ones I think might be slightly unhinged."

"Did you actually do any work today?"

Molly snorted, then rather sheepishly glanced sideways at Charlotte. "I'm your friend, I would do anything for you. Besides, I'm also your lawyer, so I billed Elliot Enterprises for the time."

Shocked at her friend's impudence, Charlotte shook her head. "You're very lucky I love you."

"So the one I thought sounded most promising was the girl called Sarah. I told you about her on the phone last night."

Charlotte frowned as she tried to extract the details of Sarah from those of the twelve other women that had responded to her profile. She and Molly had sat on the phone for an hour and a half looking at the responses and deciding on who to pursue.

"Was she the photographer or the bar owner?" Charlotte scooted closer to Molly to look at the details on the screen.

"The photographer. I've been...well, you've been"—she corrected—"flirting with her all day. We...no, wait, I mean you, chatted about your love for extreme sports, and she said with your eyes she'd be into extreme anything." Molly grinned proudly at her friend.

"Well, I am pretty gorgeous and an awesome flirt." Charlotte smiled. Her head shake as if she were in a shampoo commercial made both of them laugh. "So, what else did she say?"

Molly clapped as she saw a flickering envelope from Sarah in Charlotte's inbox. "Well, she told me she was going to send an email through with some more photos as she didn't think her profile one did her justice and whoop, heeeeere it is," Molly sang as she pointed to the envelope on the screen.

"So? Open it already. See what she's sent." Charlotte was suddenly nervous. Was she about to see a picture of the woman she was going to fall in love with and who would finally exorcise the ghosts of her past? She quickly shook her head. She was putting too much pressure on the situation.

Molly clicked on the envelope and opened the attachments.

"Ohmygodohmygodohmygod...what did you say to her?!" Charlotte screamed at Molly.

Molly sat with her mouth wide open and her eyebrows somewhere near her hairline. She opened and closed her mouth a couple of times, but nothing came out.

"She's naked, Molly...Naaaaked. Nude, as in no clothes and...and tied up. With handcuffs!" Charlotte's head snapped back and forth from her friend to the screen. "What did you say to her that made her think she should send me porn shots of herself?"

Still sitting staring at the screen but finally able to speak, Molly shook her head as she waved her hand over the image on the screen. "Seriously, it was all strictly PG flirting, I swear. I didn't encourage her to...to do this!"

"Please close the picture. I think we can strike Sarah from the list." Charlotte felt torn. She wanted to laugh at the situation, but was also acutely aware of being disappointed that her dream of a future girlfriend had turned into a naked dominatrix with... '*were those nipple clamps?*' she wondered as the image disappeared from the screen. '*Not going to disappear from my brain though. Nope that's going to stay for a while and not in a good way,*' she thought. She was brought out of her reflection by a snort of laughter beside her.

"What are you laughing at? This is not funny. Okay, no, it is." Charlotte allowed herself to join her giggling friend.

"I was just thinking a couple of things she said make far more sense! Whatever you do, don't open the picture titled, 'water sports.' I'm guessing she wasn't talking about snorkeling."

Charlotte flung her head back and guffawed loudly.

Ten minutes later both women sat on the sofa, Molly still chuckling softly and Charlotte hiccupping every so often.

"This is interesting." Molly sat up straighter as she looked at the laptop screen.

"Please no more and delete that damned profile. If I'm going to date then I'm going to date via traditional methods. Oh, God, my stomach is aching."

"No, nothing like that." Molly shook her head. "You've got an email from a Virginia Grace."

Charlotte stiffened at the mention of the name. "Delete it please."

"Is she a relative? You have relatives?"

"She's my mom."

The admission was barely above a whisper but Molly heard it. "You have a mom?"

Charlotte gave her a look hovering somewhere between frustration and bemusement. "Did you think I was a pod person? Of course I have a mom."

Molly shook her head quickly. "No, it's just, you've never said a thing about your family. God, I don't even know where you come from."

"A little town, nowhere special. Delete the email, I'm not interested in what she has to say and stop reading my emails." Charlotte shook her head, making her curls bounce manically. She jumped up from the sofa and started to pace.

"Charlotte, please will you sit down. You're giving me neck strain with all the back and forth," Molly said as she rubbed the back of her neck.

"I can't believe she's trying to contact me."

"Maybe it's something important?"

"I doubt that. My father died a year ago, and I only heard about that from someone else back home after the funeral happened. If she couldn't be bothered to contact me for that, then I don't think I will ever be interested in what she has to say." Charlotte winced at the memory.

Molly hesitated for a moment as her growing curiosity almost overtook her loyalty to her friend. However, with a sigh, she clicked on the delete icon. "You've got another email from a Ruth Campbell? Do you know her?"

"What did I just say about reading my emails?" Frowning, Charlotte sat down and took the laptop from her friend. "First my mom and now Ruth. Something must be happening," she mused as she opened the email and started to read.

Hey Charlotte, hope you're well and still happy in the big city. Thought I'd drop you a line about what's happening back home. I'm good, chasing after Ben – who's one now (where'd time go??) and is keeping me busy.

Peter is okay. The garage is still keeping him busy enough to keep a roof over our head and food on the table. Sully is still dating my sister (Don't say a thing, I'm still working through it). Teddy still hates you for beating her in the county tennis championship. Alex and her doctor (Maddie) are now living together, which means I have to sell my mama's place...Grrr (actually, wait, that sounded weird. Maddie's not actually Alex's doctor, she's her girlfriend. The story of how they came together is kinda cute but too long to get into here).

Sam Hunter is still trying to get into the Winter Olympics doing some biathlon thing, which means not only is he skiing everywhere (on wheels!) but he's shooting up a storm too. Peter had to yell at him yesterday for practicing at the garage...beside a propane bottle!

I know you'd never ask, but Erin seems good.

Charlotte stopped. She'd found herself smiling as she pictured the faces from back home, but that final single sentence had her reeling. She was used to sporadic email updates from Ruth during the past year, and although unwilling to be honest with herself, she actually looked forward to reading them. However, just seeing Erin's name in type brought back all the feelings of hurt and guilt from when she'd last seen Erin more than twenty years before.

She shook her head trying to rid her mind of the memory of Erin's tear-stained face and started to read once more.

Anyway, I wanted to let you know that Grace Falls' 150 year celebrations are next month, and it'd be nice if the one Grace that's left - that folks actually like - was here. Your mother is still as popular as ever, you'll be pleased to hear - I typed mama at first, but it didn't seem right to call her that. I could almost feel her glaring at me, so I changed it! On the mother front, I may or may not have inadvertently given the dragon (that felt infinitely easier to type than mama!) your email address. I was hormonal when she asked me. If she hasn't/doesn't email you then I didn't. If she has then I'm sorry. Anyway it would be great if you were here to celebrate with us. You really should think about coming home. It's time Charlotte.

"Bad news?" Molly asked gently.

Shaking her head, Charlotte closed the email. "Nope, just news." She placed the laptop onto the sofa, rose with a sigh and headed towards the kitchen. "I'm getting some wine; you want some?" she called over her shoulder.

"Yes please."

"White or red..." Charlotte slowly lowered the two bottles of wine in her hands as she reentered the room and spotted Molly with her laptop. "Please tell me you're not doing what I think you're doing."

"That depends. What do you think I'm doing?"

"You're reading my email after I told you not to...twice!"

Molly sheepishly closed the laptop. "Okay, yeah I'm totally doing that. I'm sorry, it was an asshat move."

"It totally was."

"Still love me?"

"You've been downgraded to tolerate," Charlotte replied, annoyed with her friend.

"If I order pizza with extra anchovies even though I hate them, could I get an upgrade?"

Sighing, Charlotte shook her head. "You really do push your luck. Order up and I'll consider moving you back up to like."

Chapter Four

*E*rin raised her head at the timid knock on her office door. A broad smile appeared on her face as she recognized the blonde hair peeking around the edge.

"Jessica Milne-Sullivan, what can I do for you on this fine Friday?" She rose from her desk to meet the young girl.

"I was wondering if I could take Cooper out for a walk?" Jessica looked over towards the dog bed in the corner where Erin's cocker spaniel lay lazily surveying the humans who had interrupted his afternoon snooze.

"Sure you can. Just give me a second and I'll go get his leash." Erin paused as she went to leave the room, then returned to her desk and made sure her computer screen was locked. The whole county knew well enough not to leave Jessica unsupervised with internet access, and Erin didn't want to face the wrath of Jessica's mother, Alex, if the youngster repeated her previous exploits while on Erin's computer. The stories of horses bought on eBay as well as her escape to San Francisco the past year was the stuff of legend in Grace Falls.

"I wouldn't have done anything, Doctor Hunter, honest." Jessica knelt down to give Cooper some much-appreciated attention.

Erin smiled. "I'm sure you wouldn't, just give me a sec." She wandered out into the reception area to retrieve the leather leash she'd dumped on the desk when she'd taken Cooper out earlier.

"You lock your computer?" Cindy asked, without looking up from her own screen.

"You know it!" Erin grinned, scooping up the leash and bumping Cindy's chair with her hip. She returned to the room to find her dog on his back enjoying a five-star belly rub from Jessica.

"Here you go." She clipped the leash to Cooper's collar and handed it over. "Don't have him out any longer than an hour and don't let him eat anything from your mama's coffee shop."

Jessica nodded as she took the leash. "Promise I won't."

"And don't leave him alone in your yard or he'll try and dig up Buttercup again," Erin said, referring to Jessica's deceased rabbit of gigantic proportions, as she followed her into the waiting room. She smiled as she watched Jessica speaking to Cooper the entire way. However, the smile slid from her face when she spotted her next patient.

Standing in the reception, a vision in a pink suit and pearls, her hair as white as the Persian cat in the carrier balanced on the reception desk, was Virginia Grace.

"Why, Jessica Sullivan, how are you? You sweet thing," Virginia said with her patent fake politeness.

"I'm very well, Ma'am. Thank you for asking." She waved a hand towards Erin and headed towards the door. Turning before she left, Jessica screwed her face up. "Mrs. Grace, I know I have a pretty long last name, but I'm not in favor of people shortening it. My name is Jessica Milne-Sullivan." She gave a sweet smile to the older woman before slipping out of the vet's office leaving Erin and Cindy chewing on their lips trying not to laugh.

"Well, I never. But what can you expect with her parents,"

It took all of Erin's effort not to roll her eyes. "There's not one damn thing wrong with any of her parents, and I'd say she showed you the same amount of respect you showed her."

Virginia glared towards the vet. Her mouth twitched as though preparing to lambast Erin. Meanwhile, Erin glared straight back almost willing her to attempt it. Finally, Virginia thought better of it and gestured towards her cat. "I'm afraid that my Persian pussy Pearl is losing hair."

It was a challenge, but Erin managed not to react to the gurgling noise now coming from behind the desk. Virginia glanced in the same direction, and the sound quickly became a cough.

"Excuse me, something caught," Cindy mumbled, unable to raise her eyes from her keyboard.

"Why don't you bring Pearl through to the exam room so I can take a look," Erin said smoothly, deflecting attention away from her assistant, whose shoulders were now shaking uncontrollably.

Virginia brushed past Erin leaving the cat carrier on the desk for her to take through. Erin gave up the fight and let her eyes have free reign as they rolled at Virginia Grace's notorious rudeness and sense of entitlement.

"If you haven't heard anything in five minutes, come in 'cause I've probably killed her," Erin whispered to Cindy as she dutifully lifted Pearl's carrier.

"On it," Cindy replied with a shaky voice.

"So, you think that Pearl has been losing hair?" Erin entered her office and placed the carrier on the examination table.

"Have you become deaf or just as stupid as that brother of yours?"

"Sam is not stupid, and neither am I. I just want to check the facts. Is the hair loss in one area or just generally?"

"Generally."

"Okay." Erin's professionalism took over from any ill feeling she had towards Virginia Grace. She lifted Pearl from the carrier carefully as the cat was known for being almost as ornery as its owner. If she managed to get out of the appointment with only a few claw marks from either, she would count it as a victory.

"Well, hair loss can be related to parasites, an allergy or it could be emotional."

"Are you saying my cat either has fleas or is stressed?" Virginia's voice rose. "Is this what my family paid out on your education for? For you come out with that bullwacky!"

"It was the Grace Falls Foundation that paid for my education, and I no longer have a debt to the foundation, as well you know."

Virginia's face reddened at the comment. "And who do you think funds the foundation?" she huffed loudly. "I have no idea what my late husband, God rest his soul, thought he was doing writing off the remainder of your school loans."

"Perhaps he felt guilty. An emotion I'm not sure you're familiar with," Erin murmured before raising her voice. "I think it better if we focus on Pearl's treatment rather than go over old history. I'd like to take some samples just to rule out any parasites. For the next couple of days you should also put her on hypoallergenic food to rule out an allergy. Can you hold onto her while I get some equipment?"

She turned and walked towards her cupboard. It was only as she reached for the handle that she realized her hands were shaking. Ever since she was a child, she could remember Virginia treating her family as 'less than,' and that disdain had only worsened after what happened with Charlotte. However, Erin was no longer a child or a scared teenager, she was a woman now, and Virginia Grace only elicited anger from her, not fear. She'd collected a scalpel and a glass slide when Virginia spoke again.

"Have you spoken with Charlotte recently?"

The sound of breaking glass filled the room as the glass slide Erin was holding slipped out of her hand into the sink. It wasn't just the casual question that threw her but also the change in attitude. The sharp tone was replaced by an almost

21

desperate breathless voice, quite unlike anything that Erin heard pass Virginia Grace's lips before.

"The last time I spoke to Charlotte, I was seventeen, and you were there," Erin stated, not turning to face Virginia.

"I thought that maybe—"

"No," Erin interrupted as she selected another slide. "It was made quite clear to me that I wasn't to contact her again, and I haven't." She turned to face Virginia. "Now let's get these samples shall we."

∞ ∞ ∞

As she closed the door behind Mrs. Grace, Erin slumped against it. Her energy had seemingly left the building with the older woman, leaving her drained.

"Did you both survive?" Cindy put the lights out and picked up her purse.

"Barely," Erin replied, still somewhat frazzled from her run in with Virginia.

"Sully's?"

"Oh God yes!" Erin grinned, opening the door and sweeping her hand for Cindy to pass. "This has been a tough week, starting with Emmett Day and ending with Virginia Grace. I must have been really evil in a past life."

The walk to Sullivan's Sports Bar was just enough for Erin to clear her head and as a bonus rescue Cooper before he managed to eat his body weight in 'sell-your-mama' muffins, as her brother called them, from Ruby's Coffee Shop. In Sam's opinion, one bite of the latter and you were likely to consider the former.

They slipped into the bar and motioned across to Sully for a couple of drinks. Before they'd even completed the wave two beers were placed on the bar in front of them.

"I heard you had a visit from Persian pussy Pearl and Miss Vagina, I mean Virginia," Sully said grinning.

Cindy sprayed beer across the counter. "You are a complete bastard, Matt Sullivan. You deliberately waited until I took a drink."

Sully shrugged. "Why would I do that? Makes more work for me." A large guilty smile adorned his handsome face as he wiped down the counter. "You okay Erin?"

"Nothing I haven't handled before," Erin replied with a cocksure grin of her own. However, the tone of Virginia's query about Charlotte was still lingering in her mind.

They went across to their usual table in the corner and sat shooting the breeze while keeping half an eye on the baseball games playing on the various TVs positioned around the bar. They were on their second bottle when Ruth arrived, pushing a basket with dollar bills in it under their noses.

"You playing tonight?" she asked, referring to the tradition of betting on the point during the Doc's radio clinic that Mack, the town's nurse, would let rip at Gregor White and his hemorrhoids.

Erin looked around the bar, then into the basket. "You just started collecting? The pot doesn't look too big tonight."

Ruth shook her head. "Nah, I've been around already. Seems like there were some pay issues with the lumberyard this week, so money's a bit tight for some folks. You'll play though?"

Erin tossed a couple of tens into the basket for both herself and Cindy. "They're obviously missing your organizational skills, Ruth." She smiled as Ruth nodded in agreement. "I'll take one-minute forty-four. How 'bout you?" she asked Cindy.

"Fifty-four seconds," Cindy said absently, tearing her eyes from one of the TV screens.

Ruth laughed. "You say that every week and you haven't won it once."

"Yeah, but I started with it. So now I'm stuck with it." Cindy sighed, finishing her beer. "Another?" she asked Erin, who nodded. "Can I get you anything, Ruth?"

"I'm good." She watched Cindy depart then turned her attention towards Erin. "I heard about Virginia's visit. You okay?"

"Yeah, I'm okay. Like I said to Sully, nothing I haven't dealt with before," Erin replied with a wry smile.

"Did she mention Charlotte at all?"

"Wow," Erin muttered. "For twenty-two years people have avoided saying her name in my presence and in the space of a couple of hours I hear it twice and once from her mother of all people. What gives?"

"Virginia cornered me last week when I was out with Ben and gave me this big speech about how she hoped I'd fair better in the mother department than she did."

The incredulous noise Erin made echoed into the neck of her beer bottle.

"I know!" Ruth acknowledged. "Damn near shocked the hell out of me," she admitted with a laugh. "She just sounded sad...No, it was more than that. She looked defeated."

Erin nodded. "I had a similar thing with her earlier. She was like a different person when she asked after Charlotte."

Ruth snapped her fingers. "Exactly! Which is why...in my defense...when she asked, I gave her Charlotte's email address."

For the second time in as many minutes, Erin was surprised. "You're still in contact with Charlotte?"

"Course I am. She's still a friend."

Erin blew out slowly, processing this new information. All the years that had passed and Erin had never realized anyone was in direct contact with Charlotte. She'd assumed when Charlotte hadn't attended her own father's funeral that the desire to be cut off from Grace Falls, and all those in it, was complete. A myriad of questions started to form in her mind until she remembered Charlotte had made the decision about Erin not being part of her life. The questions slowly dissipated never to see the light of day as Ruth continued.

"After her daddy's funeral last year I wanted to make sure she was alright so I got Jessica, oh don't tell Alex that I let her use the internet, by the way, I got Jessica to track down an email address. That kid seriously scares me sometimes. I watched everything she did 'cause I still have visions of her doing something like in that Mathew Broderick film in the eighties when he almost caused a nuclear war.

"I'm the only one she keeps in contact with"—Ruth placed a hand on Erin's forearm—"and even then I'm not sure that's really a conscious decision of hers. I just bombard her with emails every now and again. More often than not I don't get a response."

"It's fine. You don't have to protect me. I'm a big girl now, and that was all a long time ago. Water over the falls."

"Seems like everyone employed at the lumberyard hasn't been paid full wage this week," Cindy commented, sitting down and passing Erin her beer.

"Probably some computer error somewhere," Ruth surmised. "Let's just hope Jessica hasn't got anything to do with it, 'cause Alex would have her strung up." She slapped her hands on her thighs. "Well, ladies I will leave you for the moment. Remember, clear eyes, full hearts..." She waved the basket under their noses and returned to the bar to wait on the radio clinic starting without waiting on their response.

"Can't lose," Erin finished absently, her mind still replaying the conversation with Ruth.

***

Ruth gazed down at her sleeping son as she pushed the stroller through the gates of the lumberyard. She was half-tempted to wake the little Nighthawk just to give him a taste of his own medicine. Her son's proclivity for sleeping all day and keeping her and her husband, Peter, awake all night had taken its toll since his birth.

The sensible part of her just sighed contentedly and smiled, the sort of smile she swore blind before Ben's birth would never feature on her face, but had since come to accept. She was now a doting mom. A doting mom whose interest was piqued by the news from the lumberyard.

The supposed wage slip up would never have happened on her watch. For all her love of motherhood, she was still the same woman who had worked alongside James Grace, making sure his grand ideas actually had plans to back them up. While he shook hands and played the good ol' boy with buyers, she'd been the one to follow through on those deals.

She walked through the yard silently taking stock of what she saw around her. Standards had definitely slipped since James' death. Ruth never worked with the man Virginia Grace hired to run her husband's business. However, she'd heard stories about him and not one of them was flattering. If Ruth believed half of what she'd been told, his attitude towards safety was at best blasé, and at worst downright dangerous. Worse still was that it would appear James Grace's business strategy had been ditched, and the yard was no longer operating in the ripped timber market or following the sustainable and responsible felling plan.

She reached the small office, already looking forward to catching up with Chip, the foreman. He'd worked for the yard since Ruth was nothing more than a sparkle in her daddy's eye. Despite their obvious age difference, she and Chip worked well together. Their love for the yard and respect for James Grace had bound them together.

Ruth hesitated at the door. Raised voices boomed out from inside the building. She turned her head to hear better and listened to Virginia Grace in full attack mode.

"I have no interest in what went wrong. I'm telling you to fix it. My reputation does not need to be tarnished by your inability to manage money. If people start thinking we are unable to afford to pay wages my standing will be affected, and I will hold you personally responsible. So unless you want to spend the rest of your life flipping burgers, I suggest you do what I'm paying you for and get this sorted. And take a shower, you smell like you slept in a distillery."

Ruth gasped. Not wanting to be caught eavesdropping, she quickly pushed the stroller back the way she came. She managed to turn about and slowly walk towards the office as if arriving, just as the door flung open and a determined Virginia Grace flew out of it. The look of fury melted from Virginia Grace's face upon spotting Ruth, only to be replaced by the blank mask of faux serenity she wore as a matter of course.

"Morning," Ruth said jovially, hoping to give no indication of what she'd just heard.

"Ruth Campbell," Virginia trilled. "Perhaps while you're visiting you can give Mr. Ford some assistance on how to run a lumberyard." She waved a gloved hand back towards the office where an enraged looking Brett Ford stood boring holes into the back of Virginia Grace's head.

"I would have thought a lumberyard would be dangerous for a child," Virginia remarked, picking invisible lint from her sleeve as she glanced into the stroller. Her face softened for a moment as she regarded the sleeping child. "He's an attractive child. You know you really are fortunate he got the Campbell features and wasn't blighted by the Anderson nose."

She considered Ruth's face. "Your more robust face seems to cope with it, but your poor sister has more delicate features which seem to be rather overpowered by it."

Before Ruth gathered enough of her wits to formulate a response, Virginia swept off.

Brett Ford slammed the office door leaving her standing alone in the center of the lumberyard tentatively touching her nose and wondering what having a robust face meant.

Chapter Five

Charlotte dragged Molly's legs off the sofa, earning a groan of displeasure from her friend. Molly lay with a cushion covering her face recovering from a hangover after an impromptu girls' night that consisted of old musicals and wine. The consumption of the latter resulting in her passing out on Charlotte's sofa.

Charlotte's phone lit up alerting her to a text. Seeing it was from Molly's sister, Joanne, she opened it wondering what could be so important so early on Sunday.

Is my lazy ass sister with you? I've been calling her since 7! If she is, tell her brunch 10:30 usual place...you come too.

Before she could tell Molly, her phone buzzed again. This time it was a text from Joanne's partner Ellie.

Sorry for early morning call! Joanne's wired. She's wedding planning...you've been warned!

Charlotte laughed as she read the message. "Molly, your sister is going into meltdown again. We're meeting her and Ellie for brunch, I think Ellie needs our help."

Molly groaned. "What's with her and this Goddammed wedding. She's flown aircraft into Iraq and had things fired at her." She removed the cushion from her face. "Don't ever mention that in front of mom. She doesn't know, and her blood pressure is only now back to normal with Joanne flying commercial. If she can do that, why the hell is her wedding throwing her into a tailspin?"

Charlotte smiled as Molly started to head-butt the cushion.

"It's her wedding, that's the difference. I'm going to shower. You are not allowed to touch any communications device belonging to me. Are we clear?" Charlotte warned her friend. She was still smarting at finding Molly reading her email from Ruth the previous week.

She'd spent a lot of time trying to forget Grace Falls and those she left behind. The last thing she wanted or needed was Molly getting curious about her background and starting to ask more questions than she had already. Molly's muttering followed her as she left the room.

$$\infty \quad \infty \quad \infty$$

"Remind me again. Where are we up to with the wedding plans?" Molly asked as she and Charlotte walked towards their favorite coffee shop.

"This is your sister's wedding; you should be paying attention." She grinned at Molly's rolled eyes. "I'm not sure. I think we've narrowed it down to three possible venues. But to be honest, I've taken the nod and smile approach ever since the dove conversation." Charlotte grimaced at the memory of that debacle.

"Oh lordy, I'd forgotten about that." She smiled at Charlotte as she pushed open the door of the coffee shop. "Assume the brace position as we encounter bridezilla."

As they entered the coffee shop, they spotted Joanne and Ellie hunched over a coffee table strewn with papers. Joanne was gesticulating wildly while Ellie looked on with a mix of bemusement and fear.

Charlotte looked at Molly and pursed her lips. "Okay, you be the advance party. I'll get us something to drink. I think this could be a long one!"

Molly took a deep breath and walked over to the table. Almost immediately Ellie leaped up to engulf Molly in a bear hug.

Charlotte stood at the counter waiting, smiling when her usual server turned around. "Hey, Jen."

"Morning, Charlotte. You may have your work cut out this morning. They were standing outside waiting for me to open up. I think Joanne's lost it."

"I'd gathered as much. Can you really take your time with our coffees? I'd like to stay in my happy place for as long as I can," Charlotte whispered behind her hand.

Jen laughed and started to make two Americanos. "These are on the house since I reckon with Joanne there you're probably going to be buying enough of these today to keep me in business. Drink plenty of water too. I can't cope with you both wired to the moon as well."

Charlotte thanked Jen, took a deep breath, and headed over to her friends. "Hey, Joanne." She greeted her friend, who held up a hand in acknowledgment while still studying the folder in front of her. She shared an apprehensive look with Molly, before turning her attention to Ellie. "What's up, Doc?"

"So how is our favorite loafer?" Ellie stood up to embrace her friend.

Charlotte scowled at the description. As she opened her mouth to complain she was stopped by Joanne waving her hands in the air.

28

"Yes, yes, we all know you're still taking some time out. However, meantime I'm planning a freaking wedding here people. Are you bringing anyone?" She scowled at Charlotte. "Because that will entirely screw up my seating plan."

"Sweetheart." Ellie sat back down and patted her fiancée's arm affectionately "You're going to have to breathe 'cause you're gonna die if you don't."

"Yup 'cause I am sooooo close to killing you right now." Molly sipped her coffee, throwing a sickly sweet smile towards her sister.

"Okay, so now that we're all here." Charlotte raised her voice with false cheer and clapped her hands in an attempt to diffuse the situation. "What do we need to do?"

***

After three hours of sitting looking at seating plans, eight cups of coffee and only a bagel for sustenance, Molly felt like she would never be able to sleep again. If she did close her eyes, she would still be able to picture the damn seating plan causing all the issues. "I'm sorry, but I'm not getting the problem here." Molly rubbed her eyes.

"It's the six degrees thing." Charlotte nudged Molly, hoping that it would be enough for her to leave it before Joanne's blood pressure hit records level.

"Six degrees? Is Kevin Bacon coming to your wedding?" Confused, Molly scanned the seating plan again in case she'd missed the opportunity to sit next to someone famous.

"No Kevin Bacon is not coming to our Goddamn wedding," Joanne yelled, thumping her fist down onto the seating plan in front of Molly.

"Okay, no more coffee for the crazy lady." Charlotte smiled at Joanne as she reached over to rub her friend's back and remove the coffee cup from her grasp.

"It's the ex-law that Joa...we"—Ellie hastily amended when she spotted Joanne's glare—"thought should be in place with the seating plan. No table to have more than two exes and if we can, make sure there have been at least six partners since they were together."

"Oh, okay 'cause now it makes sense and doesn't sound crazy." Molly's tone dripped with sarcasm.

"It's Celia that's causing the issue. She's been around...a lot!" Charlotte looked closely at the table plan. "How 'bout there?"

Ellie looked at where Charlotte was pointing. "Oh, we are not putting her next to my Aunt Adrienne."

"What? She seemed like an open-minded woman. She was friends with your gay grans," Charlotte said, recalling when she met the woman at Ellie's abuela's funeral the previous year.

Grinning, Ellie nodded. "She is open-minded, but she's also in her nineties. So no, Celia is going nowhere near her."

Charlotte sat back and threw her hands up in defeat. "Why don't you just put her at the table with Molly and me? That's a pretty safe one!"

"Hmmm." Molly winced. "Maybe not so much our table." Her head snapped back in surprise as the three other woman at the table spun around to face her.

"Whaaat...Molly Parsons, have you been holding out on me?" Charlotte looked incredulously at her best friend.

Molly shrugged as she sipped her coffee. "It was no biggie." Seeing the looks around the table, she narrowed her eyes. "What? If my best friend and baby sister are lesbians, why shouldn't I give it a whirl? Besides, I just had a pasta night at Joanne's birthday party last year."

"Okay to hell with the wedding plans. I want dirt, and I want it now." Joanne smiled as she swept the seating plans to one side and planted her elbows on the table cupping her face as she stared directly at Molly. "Pasta night?" she asked with one eyebrow cocked.

"You know, straight until wet." Molly waved her hand in the air dismissively.

"Spaghetti," the three women shouted at Molly.

"The term is spaghetti, not pasta." Ellie picked up a crumpled napkin and threw it in Molly's direction.

"I can't believe this happened a year ago, and we're only finding out about it now." Charlotte shook her head in astonishment.

"Yeah well, we've all got our secrets, Charlotte," Molly replied pointedly.

An expression of anger flashed across Charlotte's features as she rose from the table. "I'm going to use the restroom."

Ellie watched her retreat, then turned to Molly. "Okay, I'm confused. What was all that about?"

Molly looked over her shoulder to check Charlotte's departure. Then weighing up whether to say anything further, she finally sighed and spoke in a low voice. "You go running twice a week with her, how much do you know about Charlotte from before she started LifeFit?"

"Nothing other than her losing her tennis scholarship when she injured her knee and had to drop out of college. That's it now that I come to think about it." Ellie looked surprised at the admission. "She doesn't talk about herself much."

"Well apparently Miss thing there comes from a town that's named after her, and she has a mom there...and friends!"

"Wait, she comes from a town called Charlotte?" Joanne wrinkled her nose and looked at her sister in confusion.

"No Grace Falls, Alabama," Molly corrected.

"Well, now I know you're talking crap." Ellie shook her head. "She's not from Alabama. She doesn't even have a Southern accent."

"Maybe 'cause I've worked hard to get rid of it."

The three woman gasped in surprise and spun in their seats towards Charlotte who stood with her arms crossed.

"Did it ever occur to you that I don't speak about where I'm from because I want to forget?"

Molly closed her eyes and swallowed hard at the hurt and disappointment in her friend's tone. "Charlotte, I am so sorry. It's just that it feels like something important to you happened. I'm your friend, and it suddenly seems like I don't know who you are."

Charlotte nodded, reflecting on Molly's words. She sat down and crossed her hands on the table. "Okay, what do you want to know?"

"Who is Erin?"

Charlotte gave them a small smile. "She was a girl on a rock with a toad."

"So the toad was called Elliot?" Molly tugged on Charlotte's arm as they walked back to Charlotte's apartment. "As in Elliot Enterprises? You're telling me you named your company after a toad?"

"He was a good toad."

Charlotte grinned. She'd been worried sharing even a tiny portion of her history with Erin would be too painful. However, she had to admit just talking about her childhood with Erin put a spring back in her step.

It had been a calculated move on her part. There was no way Molly would leave the subject, so she'd given her something she was comfortable sharing. Hoping it would be sufficient, she could then leave the more deeply rooted wounds alone. So far her plan had worked.

"What I don't get, is why you left home and haven't been back in over twenty years, and you don't speak to your mom or this Erin?"

It would appear the plan had worked up to a point.

"There's a lot more to it, and I'll be honest with you a lot of it still hurts today. So I'm not keen to go dredging up those memories."

Molly shrugged. "You know before when you didn't share it was okay, 'cause I didn't know what I didn't know. But now I know—"

Charlotte's growl was enough to stop Molly from continuing.

"Okay, I'll let you off the hook. But I do think you should talk about it at some point."

"For me, or for you?" Charlotte gave her a sideways glance.

"Me of course!"

Laughing, Charlotte laced her arm through Molly's. "I promise if I ever feel like telling you the tale of how I came to be, you will be the first to know."

"Well alright then." Molly grinned, tugging Charlotte closer.

Chapter Six

*E*rin yawned and stretched, enjoying the tension in her muscles before the blissful feeling when she released them. She'd had a fitful night's sleep. Her brain taunted her with memories of Charlotte as well as her more recent conversation with Virginia Grace. Rubbing her eyes, she padded down the stairs and into her living room, pausing at the sight that greeted her.

Her brother was completing squat lifts, which given her brother wasn't unusual. The fact he was doing it in her living room with Cooper draped around his shoulders was; however, something new.

"Hey, Cooper, you've got a Sam on your belly." She gave her dog's head a ruffle.

"Mornin', Sis," Sam said brightly, continuing to bob up and down barely missing a beat.

"Mornin', Poop-head."

It wasn't something she was particularly proud of, but for some reason, she returned to childhood behavior when in the company of her brother. "You want some breakfast after you've finished whatever the hell it is exactly that you're doing with Coop?"

"I was waiting on you getting up so thought I'd have a workout." His answer made it seem as if it was the most obvious thing in the world.

Erin gave him a look that Sam would likely swear he'd first seen on his mother's face.

"And you decided that lifting my dog onto your shoulders and squatting up and down was the way to go?"

"I need to build up my thigh muscles." Sam shrugged, which was made difficult by the twenty-pound dog now dozing on his shoulders.

"Put him down." Erin pointed at the floor.

Huffing, Sam lowered himself down to his knees then gently extracted Cooper from his lofty position. The dog shook and gave Sam one last look before trotting off upstairs to make the most of the warm bed recently vacated by Erin.

"Will you help me?" Sam pouted his lips and fluttered his eyelashes pitifully.

She sighed seeing her relaxing day disappearing before her eyes thanks to the six foot of lean muscle her parents saw fit to give birth to.

"What do you need? I'm not climbing on your shoulders so you can squat," she said hastily, seeing a gleam in her brother's eye.

"Relax, I'm going for a long run, and I could do with some encouragement."

Erin held her arms above her head. "Yay, Sam. Go do it!"

"Funny lady," Sam grumped. "Go get a cup of coffee, so you're in a better mood, then we'll head out."

$$\infty \quad \infty \quad \infty$$

The coffee helped. However, whatever positive effect it had disappeared when she saw what was parked in her driveway.

"Why is that golf cart here?"

"Well, I thought you could drive it while I run alongside."

Erin shook her head, but seeing her brother's pleading look, she gritted her teeth. "Fine, but you are taking me to Sully's for dinner tonight."

"Absolutely." Sam dragged his finger across his chest in a cross. "Promise."

An hour and a half later, Erin took pity on him and eased her foot off the brake. She turned in her seat to look behind the cart, where a sweat-laden Sam was pushing the cart along. "Not much further now, Poop-head, soon be back." She could hear her brother swear at her under his labored breath. Tutting she added pressure back onto the brake. "So I'm guessing next time you decide to take this out you'll be checking that the battery is fully charged?"

Erin grinned as she steered the cart down the street. Spotting a couple of figures on the sidewalk, she yelled back at her brother. "Mush, Sam, there's Alex and Maddie. Step it up a gear." She lifted her foot off the brake, and the cart shot forward almost causing Sam to fall into a heap.

"Hey, Alex, Maddie." She leaned out of the cart and waved at them.

The two woman stopped and turned. She could see Maddie laughing as they approached.

"Didn't think I'd see that thing again," Maddie said, indicating to the cart.

"Yeah, I'm betting Sam started regretting it right about thirty minutes ago." Erin jerked her head back towards her brother, who managed to lift his weary head up in agreement.

"How's things?" Alex asked. "I heard Virginia Grace was in the vet's office yesterday."

Erin winced as she heard her brother mutter 'sonofa' under his breath. She hadn't had a chance to tell him about yesterday yet, and she could imagine the conversation she would be having with him later would be less than entertaining.

"Yeah, she was her delightful self as ever," Erin said, hoping Alex would drop it.

"She is a joy to behold that's for sure." Alex nodded in agreement. "I heard she's been trying to get in contact with Charlotte. I wonder if she's trying to get her back for the anniversary?"

Erin could practically feel the anger rolling off her brother when he spoke.

"Well, I hope that Charlotte Grace has the sense that she was born with, and doesn't come back where she's not welcome."

Alex cocked her head to the side thoughtfully. "I don't know about that Sam, I always got on alright with her."

"Yeah sure you did," Sam said sarcastically. "You know as well as I do Charlotte Grace got on with those that she wanted something from. She was self-centered and manipulative, and our town is better for her leaving it."

"Jeez, Sam, tell us what you really think." Maddie looked at Sam in surprise.

Erin stared impassively at the steering wheel during her brother's rant. It wasn't anything she hadn't heard him say before, but all the recent talk of Charlotte had left her feeling more exposed than she'd felt in years.

"Try and make sure you don't overdo it, Sam. It's my day off, and I'd like to spend it with Alex, not doing CPR on you." Maddie gave Alex's hand a tug. "We should let you get on."

Alex waved her free hand. "See you later. Erin, you should pop into Ruby's soon so we can catch up."

Erin nodded numbly. "Will do."

As Alex and Maddie, walked on Maddie put her arm around her girlfriend's shoulder. "So Charlotte Grace, wasn't she the one you almost..." She let out a two-tone whistle. "On Ruth's mom's bed?"

"The one and same," Alex said laughing.

"So what in the hell did she do to Sam? I've never seen him get angry before, never mind whatever that was."

"Oh that's easy." Alex leaned further into Maddie's one-armed embrace. "She broke Erin's heart."

∞ ∞ ∞

"Why didn't you tell me?" Sam yelled, slamming the front door of Erin's home behind him.

"Why should I?" Erin yelled back. "What business is it to you if Virginia Grace brings her cat into my surgery?"

"Because it's never just anything with her. There's always another reason or motive. Where the hell do you think Charlotte learned it from?"

Erin raked her hands through her short hair, leaving it sticking up at odd angles. "That's not fair, Sam. Charlotte's not like her mama," she said, lowering her voice.

"No?" he replied, with a penetrating glare. "So I'm just supposed to forgive her and her bitch of a mother for what they put you through?"

Sighing, Erin put her hands on her brother's shoulders. "That's just it, Sam. It happened to me. Not you. Me. I don't need you to pull the protective brother routine. I can't be hurt by Virginia Grace anymore."

"And Charlotte?"

The simplest of questions. However, there was no simple answer for Erin on the subject of Charlotte, and she wasn't sure there ever would be.

"I haven't seen or spoken to Charlotte since..." She closed her eyes and swallowed. "I'm not who I was then. I'm a big girl now, and I've moved on and so should you."

"You've moved on?" He walked over to Erin's bookshelf and pulled out a copy of Doctor Dolittle.

She shook her head. Sam knew exactly what he was doing.

"You sure you've moved on?"

"Please, Sam, don't." She followed him, her fingers twitching as he held her most cherished possession.

He held the book up by its cover, allowing the pages to fan out. Photographs fell from their hiding places. He bent down to retrieve one and held it up. The picture was of Erin and Charlotte smiling for the camera, their arms around each other.

"I'll believe that you've moved on when you actually do, Sis." He placed the book gently down and pulled a shocked Erin into his arms and held her tightly. "I know you loved her, but she left you without a second glance. She doesn't deserve for you to keep pining after her. You are wasting your life on what never could have been."

Erin immediately started to protest. She wasn't pining, but unbidden tears began to form in her eyes. She chewed on her lip, trying to stop herself from crying, but Sam's soft pleading broke something in her. She sobbed gently on her brother's shoulder.

"She said we were unbreakable."

Sam rocked her gently. "She was only half right. You are. She was the weak link."

Erin's sobs gradually lessened. "You're still a poop-head," she muttered into her brother's wet shoulder.

"And you're still annoying." Sam laughed and held her tighter.

"You also smell. Something awful." Erin wrinkled her nose and pulled out of her brother's embrace.

"Yeah well if someone hadn't had her foot on the brake, I wouldn't have had to work so hard to push the damn cart home."

Erin grinned sheepishly, her eyes still watery with tears. "You saw that huh?"

"Oh yeah, and just so you know, you're buying dinner at Sully's."

Later, when Erin was on her own, she picked up the Doctor Dolittle book. Her eyes scanned briefly over the written inscription on the inside cover. She sighed and laid it on the coffee table. Picking up the bundle of photos of Charlotte she kept stored within the book, she began flicking through them. Their childhood and teens played out through the half dozen photographs now worn at the edges. She thought back to what she'd said to Sam about Charlotte and her being unbreakable, and laughed softly at the memory it conjured up.

It had been 1984, an Olympic year. The year Sam started his fascination with all things snow, and she'd had her own obsession. Thanks to the summer Games she'd taken to going everywhere with a backpack on with sticks threaded through the straps, pretending it was a jetpack.

Her family had been in Grace Falls for two years, during which time she and Charlotte had formed a close friendship. Each day they would meet at Erin's Rock and play together. They built hideaways, fought dragons, and made shooting noises that no doubt scared half the wildlife in the woods.

However, that day when she'd gone to the rock Charlotte didn't appear. Erin knew better than to go to the big Grace house to look for her. So with a disappointed shrug, she switched on her jetpack and swooped her way towards town.

She was running along the sidewalk when she spotted Charlotte standing outside Ryrie's Store. Her auburn hair normally tied back into a ponytail was loose around her shoulders, and where the light caught the blonde streaks that appeared in the summer months, it almost shone in the sun.

She was wearing a short white dress with white ankle socks and pristine white sneakers. Erin was used to seeing Charlotte in dresses since she wore one most every day to school. But to Erin when Charlotte was dressed that way, she wasn't her Charlie. Her Charlie was the one that wore Matt Sullivan's old jeans cut off into shorts and a bartered for T-shirt from Peter Crawford. The Charlotte standing in front of the store didn't belong to Erin, and she felt sad.

She looked down at her own attire. Her T-shirt had a muddy paw print from her run-in with a neighbor's dog and, much to her dismay, the summer sun had failed to join up the freckles on her arms to give her an even color. They just stood out against light brown skin instead of her usual pale color. Her shorts had grass stains on them that no amount of washing could remove. Her skinny legs had various cuts and bruises that seemed to appear without her being conscious of them, and her sneakers were without laces, as she'd used them to twine the sticks together to form the handles of her jetpack.

When she looked up, she saw two green eyes, full of happiness at seeing her, staring back. She skipped over to Charlotte.

"Hey, Charlie. I waited, but you didn't come. Do you like my jetpack?" Erin gave a little twirl, showing off her handiwork.

"Yeah, it's cool. I'm sorry, but I wasn't allowed out." Charlotte threw worried glances over her shoulder as she spoke.

"It's okay." Erin shrugged. "You gonna get out later?"

Before Charlotte could answer, a woman dressed in a lilac suit appeared out of the store. Erin wrinkled her nose at the waft of strong perfume that accompanied the woman. She wasn't sure, but the woman was either Charlotte's mom or the Queen of England. Either way, she fought the urge to curtsey.

"Charlotte, who are you talking to?"

To this day, Erin was unsure where the courage came from, but under the icy glare of Virginia Grace she'd stuck out her hand in greeting and announced her name.

She had to check her hand to make sure she didn't have poop on it or something equally disgusting because by the way Mrs. Grace looked at it, you would have thought she was handing over a pile of it. She took her hand back with a shrug and went back to holding the controls of her jetpack.

"I see you've met our resident Doctor Dolittle."

Erin turned towards the friendly voice and smiled at Ruby Gale. The town's nurse put a comforting arm around Erin's shoulders. "This little one can charm the birds from the trees, literally. What you got with you today?" she asked Erin.

"Just Baloo, he's in my jetpack." She wriggled around until she could put her hand into the backpack and secure the small field mouse that'd been happily asleep in its cozy burrow. "You want to hold him?" She held the mouse out to Charlotte.

Virginia Grace moved quicker than Erin thought possible as her arm shot out catching Erin's forearm. "She doesn't want to touch it; it could be riddled with diseases."

38

Erin brought her hand back and rubbed the spot where Mrs. Grace had caught her. She looked over towards Charlotte, who'd yet to speak since her mother's arrival, and now had a look of horror on her face. Erin felt Ruby move from her side to stand between her and Virginia. She only made out half of what Ruby said to Mrs. Grace, something about hands, but whatever it was Virginia Grace's face drained of color, which given the layers of makeup on her face was a feat in itself.

It was only years later when Erin heard Ruby giving Matt Sullivan and Peter Crawford a ticking off for damaging something with their horseplay, that she understood what Ruby said that day. Being a relative newcomer to Grace Falls, Erin never had the phrase said directly to her, not that she would ever have given Ruby cause to. But many a resident of the town had heard the words 'These hands were the first to touch you, and they'll be the first to put you back in line.'

Ruby turned back to Erin with a broad smile on her face. "Now, young Dolittle, my granddaughter, and grandson have just moved here"—The smile on the older woman's face wavered slightly, but she seemed to rally herself with a nod of her head— "and Lord knows they could do with a friendly face right now. So why don't you come on over and play with Alex and Alan. You'll take right to Alan, 'cause we all call him Bear." She turned back to Charlotte and her mother. "Charlotte, you're welcome to come over too."

Virginia opened her mouth to speak, then seemed to change her mind about whatever she was going to say. Instead, she smiled a smile that reached nowhere above her lips as she thanked Ruby for her offer, but explained she was just taking Charlotte to St Anton for a tennis lesson.

"See you later?" Erin whispered hopefully to Charlotte when Virginia Grace turned to leave.

Charlotte glanced in her mother's direction making sure she wasn't paying her any attention before nodding quickly, turning on her heel, and skipping to catch her mother.

Ruby looked down at Erin and shook her head. "That girl is going to cause you nothing but trouble, little 'un. I hope you know that."

Erin shrugged. "She's my best friend."

Erin sighed as she slotted the photos back into the book. She mused that had she paid more attention to Ruby Gale's warning that day she wouldn't have had her heart broken into a million pieces years later. But then, for every time that Charlotte allowed her mother to ride roughshod over her, there were the sweet times when it was just them.

Hours after she'd run into Charlotte in town, she found herself back on their rock waiting for her. Knowing for some reason Charlotte would appear. She hadn't to wait very long before Charlotte arrived, out of breath and still wearing the outfit she'd had on earlier.

"I knew you'd be here," Charlotte said with a grin.

Erin shrugged as if it were nothing.

"I'm sorry about what happened earlier, my mama is…" She screwed her face up as she tried to explain her mother. "Well, she's hard to get along with." Charlotte frowned, dissatisfied at the description which failed to capture her mother entirely. "My daddy says that he doesn't think she likes anyone very much." She giggled as she repeated her father's muttered comment, made when he didn't think anyone was listening.

"You hurt my feelings." Erin tucked her head against her shoulder and crossed her arms.

Charlotte rushed forward and pulled Erin into a tight hug. "I'm sorry, I would never want to hurt you. You're my best friend." She let go and stared into Erin's hazel eyes. "I know, we'll make a signal so that even if my mama doesn't let me speak to you, you'll always know that you're my best friend forever."

Erin's spirits perked up. "Like a bat signal?"

"Exactly." Charlotte nodded. Her forehead crinkled as she thought hard about what the signal might be. "I know!" she yelled, jumping up and down with excitement. "You know how a chain has links, and they go together?"

Erin nodded, jumping in time with her friend.

"Well, we're like that. Two links that make a chain." Charlotte clapped her hands together. "It's perfect. So our signal is this." She made a loop with her thumb and forefinger and placed her other thumb and finger through it, closing the chain.

Erin copied the signal. "Like this?"

"Exactly like that. This is our signal. That no matter what, we're unbreakable."

Erin felt a warm tear trickle down her cheek at the memory. She looked down at her hands in her lap. She'd no idea when during her reminiscing it had happened, but her fingers were now looped through each other making a chain.

Chapter Seven

harlotte exhaled in frustration when she saw the incoming call to her cell was from Molly. She swiped the screen the answer the call. "Where are you?"

"I need to know that you're not going to hate me."

Charlotte looked around the busy restaurant they were due to meet in and frowned. "Have you got held up at work? It's a Friday. Even lawyers are allowed a little fun on a Friday." She could hear Molly take a few deep breaths before answering.

"Not exactly."

Charlotte's frown deepened at Molly's words.

"You see, you know how you told me to delete your profile and cease and desist from all online dating activity?"

"Mmmmm?" Charlotte could feel her temper start to flare at what she anticipated was coming next.

"Well, I didn't exactly delete it...or stop. In fact, I got chatting with a lovely woman. Her name's Sophie, she's an accountant, and she should be sitting at the bar wearing a red dress."

The line was dead before Charlotte could respond. She looked at her cell phone and growled. "I am going to kill you, Molly."

Scanning the bar, she saw a woman with short dark hair wearing a red dress, her eyes nervously darting around the room until they settled on Charlotte. Plastering a smile on her face, Charlotte walked towards the bar. "Hi, are you, Sophie by any chance?"

The woman looked relieved. "Yes, and you'll be, Charlotte?"

"I am. Look there's something you should know, I—"

"It's okay." Sophie placed a hand on Charlotte's forearm. "Your friend Molly came clean. I know it's not been you that I've been chatting to."

Charlotte let out a relieved breath. "Oh thank God. I was wondering how I was going to explain why I had no idea what we'd spoken about."

"Well now that's out of the way we can spend the time getting to know each other a little better," she said, her eyes blatantly roaming up and down Charlotte's slender frame.

Suppressing the need to gulp, Charlotte sat down and waved the bartender over to order.

∞ ∞ ∞

Charlotte tapped her fingers waiting on Molly picking up the phone. Before Molly even had the chance to utter a greeting, Charlotte spoke.

"Molly, you in danger girl."

"I am? Why? How'd your evening go?"

"Really lovely."

"Really? That's great."

"Yeah, we had a few drinks and then stayed for dinner. The conversation was flowing. The food was lovely. Sophie was great fun, and we had a lot in common."

"Why do I hear a but in there somewhere?"

"Well I like big butts, and I cannot lie."

Molly snorted. "Okay, out with it. What happened?"

"Remember that time you set me up with the woman with narcolepsy, and she kept passing out during dinner?"

"Yes."

"Well, that was a better date!"

"Why? I thought you just said you had lots in common."

Charlotte laughed without humor. "Oh we did, in particular, we had Tina in common. During a chat about disastrous relationships, Sophie mentioned a woman she'd slept with, who told this sob story about her partner not understanding her or fulfilling her needs as she was more interested in work than her. Imagine my surprise when Sophie casually mentions that the poor woman who sought solace between her legs was in a relationship with someone who owned a chain of gyms!"

"Oh God, I am so sorry. I would never have—"

"I know." Charlotte ran her hand through her hair in frustration. "Now will you leave it alone? I think we've proven that your record as Cupid is flawed."

"Absolutely, no more I promise."

"You have your fingers crossed don't you?"

"Err...Nope."

Charlotte laughed as she hung up the call, knowing her friend was lying. She'd deliberately kept her tone light in an attempt to hide from Molly how unnerved she'd been when she realized the connection with Sophie.

Although it had been two years since she'd ended things with Tina, she'd spent a lot of time reflecting on why she'd allowed herself to settle for that relationship. Finding Tina with another woman in their bed hadn't been a revelation. Charlotte had been aware of her cheating for years. It was only the fact she no longer had plausible deniability about it that resulted in her kicking Tina out.

That was the reason she'd spent hours in therapy, to understand why she'd allowed herself to be used in that manner. In the end, it hadn't taken a therapist to work it out, Charlotte knew the reason...Erin.

The guilt she felt over leaving Erin and cutting off all contact was still as fresh today as when it happened. The wounds were still there, raw and angry, and nothing she'd done since had come close to soothing them.

The music on her iPod changed and Cyndi Lauper's 'Time after Time' started to play. She picked up the remote to change the song as was her habit. The tune held too many memories, and the words were too close for comfort most nights. However, tonight she paused. Tonight she would allow the memories to come.

"You are going, and I won't speak to you about this again." Her mother rose from her chair and walked towards her.

"But I don't want to go to a different school. I want to go to school with my friends." Tears flowed down Charlotte's reddened cheeks. Her mother's unexpected announcement had shaken her to her core, and she'd spent the past hour pleading with her mother to change her mind.

Virginia shook her. "You are a Grace. You are not one of these town children. They are not your friends. When you're older, they will no doubt be employees. You need to recognize that you are above them. You will go to this school, and you will learn your place. Then you will go to college, and we will find you a man we think suitable to take over the business affairs from your father."

Charlotte's twelve-year-old brain almost melted as her mother casually laid out the plans for her future, as if she had no say in the matter. From an early age, she'd accompanied her father to the yard and listened intently as he explained the family business. When he decided to expand, she'd stood proudly beside him while the first hunting lodge was built. It had always been a thought of hers that she would be the one to take over from her father, and that was why he was investing such time in her, showing her each process at the lumberyard in painstaking detail.

"Did you hear a word I said?"

Her mother's voice interrupted her train of thought and brought her back to her current plight. She was to be sent to a different school than her friends. As far as she was concerned, there wasn't much else her mother could say that would inflict as much pain.

"I said, they've given us a list of the things you're to take, so we'll need to go shopping as their winters are nothing like ours."

Charlotte blinked in confusion. "What do you mean their winters are different? Where am I going to school?"

Virginia Grace huffed irritably. "Massachusetts. I knew you weren't paying attention."

Charlotte felt a lump form in her throat. She thought the pain of going to another school was bad enough when she thought it was another school in the county. Now the realization she was going to be sent across the country was almost too much to bear. She looked at her mother with all the pain in her heart visible on her face.

"I hate you, and I will never forgive you for this." She spun on her heel and sprinted from the room before her mother had a chance to respond.

Her only desire had been to get out of her mother's presence, and she ran without thought. However, she wasn't surprised when she found herself at Erin's Rock. Sobs racked her body at the realization she wasn't going to be able to spend time here with her friend.

She'd no idea how long she'd sat on the rock shielding her face as she cried, only that at some point a white rabbit was placed on her lap and freckled arms encased her in a tight hug.

Chapter Eight

"Good afternoon everyone and thank you to Miss Roosevelt and all of you for letting me come to your class to speak to you today." Erin looked at the expectant faces of Grace Falls Elementary School's third-grade class and took a breath.

Animals she was good with, but children were a whole different kettle of crawfish. "So I'm here to talk to you about caring for animals. I've brought my dog Cooper with me today to help out." She looked down towards Cooper, who was laying resting his head on his paws on the floor.

"So first up, how many of y'all have a dog?"

A half-hour later and Erin was completely at ease. Her presentation was over, and she was hosting an impromptu Q&A session with the children.

When Teddy approached her about coming to her class to speak, Erin had been wary on two counts. Apart from Jessica, she didn't have a lot of experience with kids. Besides a conversation with Jessica was like speaking to an adult a lot of the time. The second thing that made her apprehensive was the fact Teddy asked her at all. Despite having known Claudia Roosevelt since they were both kids, Erin always got the impression she'd done something to piss Teddy off, but for the life of her, she'd no idea what it could be.

Seeing Lewis Mack's hand waving in the air, Erin called on him. "Lewis, what's your question?"

"My mama says puppies and kittens come from Virginia. I wanna know whether she's talkin' 'bout Mrs. Grace or the state, 'cause I'd like a puppy, and I need to know who I should be goin' to."

Erin looked at the back of the class where Teddy was perched on an unused desk quietly stuffing the sleeve of her sweater into her mouth. Sensing she was on her own, Erin focused her attention on Lewis.

"Well, Lewis, regardless of where puppies come from, I think that's a question you should be having with your mama, 'cause I'd imagine she'd have an opinion on you having a pet." She flashed a smile at the class, deciding then and there her Q&A

session was over. "I should go let you get on with your studies. Thank you again for asking me."

She grabbed Cooper's leash and made a quick exit while the children clapped their appreciation. Once outside the classroom door, she started to laugh loudly, stopping when she heard the door open and close beside her. Teddy stood in the corridor her eyes glistening with tears of mirth.

"Oh my God, how did you ever keep a straight face?" Teddy asked between peals of laughter.

"I just kept thinking about what would happen if Lewis ever asked Virginia Grace. Mack would have a heart attack. I'll tell you this though, it was damned hard!"

"But it would almost be worth it to have seen both their faces. I should get back in and start getting them packed up. Thanks again." She shook as if to compose herself before disappearing back into the classroom leaving Erin standing in the halls of the elementary school she'd attended, still giggling.

She could almost visualize ghosts of the past and hear their voices echoing down the halls. Marion Mack, or Marion Sinclair as she was then, her hair a mass of thick dark curls sticking out in various directions, standing with her hands on her hips as she dictated to everyone within earshot. Matt Sullivan and Peter Campbell horsing around with Bear Milne. Hovering close by were Alex Milne, Ruth Anderson, and Claudia Roosevelt. The twosome of Ruth and Teddy had enveloped Alex when she and her brother moved to Grace Falls, in the summer following their mother's death. As ever, standing next to Erin was Charlotte, surveying all that surrounded her with the composure that seemed inherent in the Grace family.

Cooper's impatient nudge to her leg brought her back to the present day. She scanned the corridor once more, the color and images in her mind replaced by reality.

The bell rang loudly as she stepped out into the sunshine. She spotted Alex standing with Mack, waiting for their children's exit from school. They usually let the kids make their own way home. However, comments about Alex and Maddie's relationship had flared up again. Although Jessica was able to rise above it, Lewis, Mack's son, in his self-appointed role as her protector found himself in trouble again for replying with his fists.

Alex was immediately on her knees to greet an equally excited Cooper. "Hello, handsome," she cooed rubbing his ruff. "Have you enrolled in school now too?"

"We were just doing a talk on pet care." Before she could say anything to Mack, Jessica and Lewis appeared at her side.

"Hey, Mama." Jessica knelt down to join her mom with Cooper. "We learned lots today, and I got to show the class how to make Cooper sit and lie down."

"Did you?" Alex watched her daughter warily, knowing today's lesson would no doubt lead to a 'wannadog' campaign for the next few weeks.

"Oh, Dr. Hunter." Jessica squinted up into the sunshine. "I sorted Lewis out. He knows now it's vagina and not Virginia."

Erin looked at a shocked Mack and Alex. "Thank you, Jessica, that's real helpful of you. Um, Mack, Lewis wanted to know whether puppies came from Mrs. Grace or the state of Virginia."

Mack rolled her eyes, as she pulled her son into an embrace. "This boy will be the death of me, I swear it. I mean could you imagine if he asked Virginia Grace."

Alex snorted. "Oh, I would have paid to have seen that." She stood up, frowning as her knee clicked. "Erin, you want to come over for some dinner on Friday? Maddie is at a conference, and Jessica will be with Matt, so I thought I would have a little girls' night. You'd be doing me a favor; Ruth normally keeps me from going along with Teddy's ideas, but she's cooking dinner for Peter's mama."

Before Erin could answer, Mack was sucking air in through her teeth. "Don't see me going off to New York for some fancy conference, leaving people behind for four days to cope on their own."

Alex flashed a grin at Erin. This was not a new moan from Mack. The small nurse had given Maddie a hard time over her decision to attend an out of state conference from almost the point Maddie spotted it.

"Now, Mack you know it's just 'cause Maddie is still new to being a family doctor, and it gives her a chance to see her folks. You wouldn't deny a girl seeing her mama would you?"

Mack scowled. "You don't fight fair, Alex Milne."

"Never said I did. You're welcome to join us, Mack."

"What! A night with you and Tequila Sunrise over there." She nodded towards Teddy, who was speaking with another parent. "My liver is already aching at the thought of it."

"Well don't say I didn't offer." Alex shrugged and turned to Erin. "I'll see you at seven on Friday."

Erin just nodded as Alex made her decision for her.

"What have I done to piss you off?" Erin twisted in her seat and leaned back so she could see Teddy's face clearly. The swing chair hanging from Alex's porch they were seated on swayed erratically at her movement.

Alex suppressed a groan and sat back on her Adirondack chair.

The night had been going so well. Erin had been thoroughly enjoying herself, they'd had dinner and throughout Teddy was on her best behavior, seemingly putting her stupid ancient gripe to the side.

Then the tequila started.

Erin had been matching Teddy's pace, and along with a pleasant buzz, it appeared tequila brought out her candid side.

"What do you remember of summer of eighty-eight?"

Erin looked at Teddy in confusion, her face not quite managing to assemble itself in the correct formation thanks to the alcohol she'd consumed. She closed one eye to bring Teddy into focus. "Some stuff. Why? Is there something I should remember?"

Teddy's jaw clenched. "County tennis championships. You were calling the line in the final."

Erin's face split into a messy grin. She remembered the tournament.

Charlotte had persuaded her to line call so they could spend time together without her mother becoming suspicious that their friendship continued. It was the second summer since Charlotte had been sent off to school, and although they wrote regularly, vacations were cherished time. It was during this vacation Erin started to notice changes in her friend. Her accent was disappearing as a result of the comments and teasing she'd endured in her first few terms. She'd grown a couple of inches in height, and her body gained curves that Erin's own body had yet to experience. It was the curves Erin noticed first when they met at their rock. During their habitual embrace, Charlotte's body felt different and more importantly Erin felt differently about holding Charlotte. Her face burned, and there was a fluttering in her stomach.

"You don't have to smile about what you did." Teddy nudged her in the ribs.

"I..." Erin snapped out of her reverie and glanced over towards Alex for help, who merely shrugged as if to say she was on her own. "I'm not smiling about what I did 'cause I don't even know what I did!"

"You were line calling, and on match point, you called the ball in when it was out, in Charlotte's favor. I know you two were friends, but I never thought of you as a cheat."

Erin shook her head, unable to believe that this is what Teddy had a bug up her ass about. "Boobs," she said grinning.

Teddy's eyes widened. "I'm sorry?"

"I was fourteen, jammed full of hormones and Charlotte came back from school with boobs. I have no idea whether that ball was in, out, or whistling Dixie when it landed. My attention was on Charlotte." She poked her finger in the air towards Teddy. "Or more specifically Charlotte's boobs."

Teddy pulled herself out of her comfortable slouch. "You're tellin' me that I lost 'cause you were horny?"

Erin nodded laughing. "Pretty much."

Teddy took a deep breath, considering this new piece of information. Decision made, she turned to Erin and held out her hand. "Well, at least I know you weren't cheatin'. Horny I can cope with, but cheatin' was a whole different thing."

Erin shook it. "I'm sorry it cost you the match."

Teddy held the bottle of tequila up to pour more into Erin's glass. "Ah, all water over the falls now."

Alex blinked in astonishment. It appeared with that simple explanation, Erin removed decades' worth of animosity. "So you're both good now?"

"Yup," Teddy and Erin choroused, clinking their glasses together and downing the drink in one.

"So you had a crush on Charlotte Grace?" Teddy's body was now swaying in a different rhythm to the swing seat. "Did you know this?" she asked Alex.

Alex shook her head. "Not at the time, no."

"You're a lousy lesbian," Teddy said and returned her attention to Erin.

"Thanks," Alex deadpanned.

"Welcome." Teddy didn't bother to look in Alex's direction.

Ignoring the chat around her Erin sighed deeply. "I gave her my heart and in the words of George Michael," she slurred, waving her finger in the air, "she just gave it away, and now. Now my brother says I'm emotionally stunted."

Teddy shook her head vigorously. "Pssshhh. You're not stunted, I will tell you what you are." She poured more tequila into Erin's glass, then lurched forward almost landing in Alex's lap as she offered her the bottle.

Alex took it from her and placed it out of sight. "Erin, you are about to hear the Roosevelt theory on relationships."

Teddy waved a hand to dismiss Alex. "Don' listen to her. She's had this chat an' it all worked out for her."

"I'm all ears if it worked for Alex an' she's all loved up." Erin smiled in the general direction of Alex, as she was unsure which iteration of Alex was the genuine one.

"To Maddie." Teddy raised her glass in the air in a toast.

"To Maddie," Erin replied, hitting her glass off Teddy's and frowning as tequila spilled over onto her hand.

"So...wait...was Charlotte your first love?" Teddy whispered.

When Erin nodded in reply, she opened her eyes wide and slapped Erin's thigh. "Well, no wonder then! So here is the deal. Each time you come out of a relationship you have things that will be forever like landmines. When you go into a new relationship, your new love can step on these landmines unwitt...unwittinl...without

49

knowing"—Teddy stopped to check she still had Erin's attention—"an' they can make you behave crazy. Maddie went all the way to San Francisco to get away from Alex here." She waved her drink in Alex's direction, ignoring the daggers her friend was throwing her. "The trick is to know where your landmines are."

"So I have landmines?" Erin looked at Teddy as if she'd given her the key to her happiness. "So how do I diffuse them?"

"Well. See 'cause Charlotte was your first love, your mines are doozies. First love is pure, it's untarnished. You don't protect yourself 'cause you have nothing to protect against. You're a blank field, all ready to be plowed." Teddy stopped and scrunched her face. "That sounded a lot ruder out loud."

Erin sighed and thudded her head against the back of the swing. "It's not like I haven't tried to date. I went a bit wild in college. I was the female Sully of Auburn for a while. Then I had a couple of relationships that lasted longer than an orgasm, but they didn't really go anywhere. I'm not sure I was ready for a full-on relationship then. According to my exes, I was emotionally untouchable."

"Clitoral damage," Teddy said knowingly.

"She means collateral." Alex rolled her eyes and sat forward. "Erin, you have to let her go. For what it's worth I think you won't let anyone in. Not because you're scared to but because your heart is still too full of Charlotte. No one can compete with her because you won't let them even get in the starting blocks."

Erin exhaled loudly. "I'm a complete screw-up. I'm almost forty, and I'm still pining after my teen love."

Teddy gave her a watery smile. "There's nothing wrong with that. I still wish every day that Bear was here, but at some point, you have to live for now. I never thought I would love anyone like I loved Bear but then Douglas came along."

Alex stood up. "Before we get downright maudlin, I'm going to put some coffee on."

Teddy and Erin watched her go into the house.

"So how'd you do it?" Erin lowered her voice. "Move on, I mean."

"I spoke to Bear and told him I had to move on. He don't talk much on account of being dead an' all, but I felt better speaking to him." Teddy stood up and placed her glass down. "You know what I want to do?"

Erin shook her head but stood up beside Teddy. "Nope, but I'm with you whatever it is."

"I'm going to go climb Bear's tree." Teddy climbed unsteadily off of Alex's porch and meandered down towards the tall tree at the bottom of the garden. The tree also housed a platform build by Alex's brother when they were all still in high school.

"I haven't climbed that thing in years." Erin downed the remnants in her glass then followed behind, wondering whether her health insurance would cover her for injuries sustained due to tequila and stupidity.

50

∞ ∞ ∞

When five minutes later Alex appeared on the porch with a tray of cups and freshly brewed coffee, she was surprised to find it empty. She put the tray down and cautiously called out, "Marco."

The direction the distant response of 'Polo' came from could only mean one thing.

"Awwwww shit," she muttered, pulling her cell phone from her pocket. "Matt, can you come over? Erin and Teddy are up in Bear's tree." She grimaced and pulled the phone away from her ear at Sully's swearing. When she eventually put the phone back to her ear, she laughed at Sully's question. "No, you cannot just shoot them out of it! Now get your ass over here and help me." She hung up and trudged down towards the tree.

Chapter Nine

"I can't believe Molly set you up with one of Tina's conquests." Ellie huffed as she ran alongside Charlotte.

Charlotte laughed and shook her head. "I'm not sure Molly can either."

"You okay?"

"It threw me a bit. It started me thinking again about why I let Tina treat me that way, and that started me thinking about stuff from back home. Stuff I've not thought about in years."

Ellie stopped abruptly, almost taking out the two men jogging behind.

"You okay? You pull something?"

"Hi my name is Ellie, and you are?"

Charlotte scowled and jogged on the spot to keep warm. "Funny, I'm not that bad." Seeing Ellie's lack of reaction, Charlotte whined, "Oh my God. I am that bad."

Starting to jog slowly again, Ellie shook her head. "Honey, you really are. That's the first time I've got a response from you that was"—she scrunched her face up, searching for the right word—"honest?"

"You saying I'm a liar?" Charlotte was embarrassed she was so closed off that even the smallest admission like the one she'd just made was enough to shock her friend.

"You know that's not what I'm saying. You're just usually more circumspect with your responses."

This time, it was Charlotte who stopped. "God! Why on earth do you all put up with me?"

Ellie turned back towards her friend and pulled her into a hug. "'Cause you're a great listener and one of the biggest hearts around. We all know you would be there for us at the drop of a hat, just like we'd be there for you if you'd let us."

"Still, Jesus, I am so fucked up."

"Oh please." Ellie smacked Charlotte's shoulder. "Aren't we all?"

"Okay, so new approach. How would you like to go out to dinner on Friday and I'll give you the gory details of my life?"

Ellie groaned. "I'd love to but I'm at a conference, and there's a drinks reception. Why don't you come along? You could pretend to be a doctor, drink some fizz, eat some canapés."

Charlotte's face lit up. "Can I wear a white coat?"

"Nope."

"Stethoscope?"

"Nope."

"You're a real spoilsport you know."

"Yup."

∞ ∞ ∞

"There you are. I've been looking all over for you!" Charlotte arrived at Ellie's shoulder. "Oh God, I'm sorry did I just talk all over you?" Charlotte was horrified she'd interrupted Ellie talking shop with a colleague.

"That's okay," replied the dark-haired woman standing with Ellie.

"I'm sorry." Ellie held out her hand. "I've been really remiss. We're standing here chatting, and I've not introduced myself. I'm Ellie, and this rude creature is a gatecrasher and my friend Charlotte."

"I'm Maddie. It's nice to meet you, Ellie and you too, Charlotte." Maddie shook hands with the women in turn.

"I was just asking Maddie why she didn't sound like she's from Alabama, but hey I guess I shouldn't make any assumptions based on accents." Ellie's smile took the sting out of the rebuke to Charlotte about her own accent's origins.

"You know what they say about asses and assuming," Charlotte responded, capturing a glass of bubbly from a passing waiter. "So where about in Alabama are you not from?"

Maddie took a sip of her wine and shrugged. "Nowhere you would have heard of. It's a tiny town in the middle of nowhere."

"You never know," Charlotte said taking a mouthful of her bubbly.

"Grace Falls."

That same mouthful of champagne sprayed from Charlotte's mouth.

"Jesus, Charlotte!" Ellie glared at her friend. "I'm so sorry, Maddie, I'll go get something to clean you up."

Maddie's shocked expression was matched by Charlotte's. Slowly a look of realization crossed Maddie's features. "Oh my God! Are you Charlotte Grace?" Maddie sodden top forgotten in light of her discovery, she barely noticed Ellie's return with a fistful of napkins. "The Charlotte Grace!"

Charlotte still stood with a stupefied look on her face, observing Maddie's outfit and the mess her reaction had created.

"You know the way you're saying her name makes her sound famous." Ellie handed over the napkins to Maddie.

"Infamous more like," Charlotte muttered sadly.

"You are Charlotte Grace!" Maddie's smile lit up. "Alex will be thrilled."

Charlotte jerked out of her shock at the use of Alex's name. "You're Alex's doctor," she said, remembering Ruth's mention of Alex's new relationship in her emails.

Maddie chuckled as she tossed the now damp napkin onto a nearby table. "Well, I'm the town's doctor really, but I am Alex's partner, yes."

Ellie looked at the two woman with a puzzled expression. "I feel like I'm missing something here. Do you two know each other in some way?"

Charlotte shook her head. "Maddie is the doctor in Grace Falls. Where I'm from."

"Ohhhh, the town we didn't know about," Ellie said, raising an eyebrow and looking at Charlotte. "Well, I think we should go grab a seat and get to know each other a little better."

Before Charlotte could disagree, Ellie caught her by the elbow while hooking her other arm through Maddie's, and led them both from the function room into the quieter hotel bar.

Charlotte chewed on the inside of her mouth while her fingers plucked nervously at the edge of the arm of the leather bucket seat Ellie had deposited her into.

"You're not infamous by the way," Maddie said.

Charlotte lifted her eyes to meet reassuring brown ones.

"In fact in the town where no one has secrets, you're probably the best-kept one. I wouldn't even know you existed if it hadn't been for Alex." Seeing Charlotte frown deeply as she spoke Maddie grimaced. "That was meant to make you feel better. I should stop talking now." She chewed on her lips and turned her attention towards the bar where Ellie was ordering drinks.

"It's okay, you underestimate the power of Virginia Grace." Charlotte was unable to disguise the bitterness in her tone.

Maddie nodded. "I have dealt with your mother, and I'm acutely aware of her abilities." She reached over to place a warm hand on Charlotte's forearm. "I was there with your father at the end."

Surprised at the comment, Charlotte felt a lump rise unbidden in her throat. Unable to stop herself, she asked the question that haunted her the first few days after learning about her father's death. "Did he ask about me?"

"I'm sorry. It was a massive stroke. By the time I saw him he didn't have the ability to speak."

Charlotte nodded and swallowed down the lump as Ellie brought their drinks over.

"So I'm prescribing a couple of stiff drinks to help overcome the shock." Ellie smiled as she placed three high ball glasses of whiskey onto the table.

Forcing a cheerful tone, Charlotte raised her glass. "To bite you in the ass coincidences."

Ellie winced at the toast but clinked her glass against her friend's. Maddie, on the other hand, hooted with laughter as she touched her glass against Charlotte's.

"I think it's something to do with Grace Falls. You think you've escaped, but it sucks you back in."

Charlotte asked after taking a long slug of her drink. "So Alex has a kid with Sully? How'd that happen? Please tell me he didn't get to her too!"

Chuckling, Maddie shook her head. "No, it was all done strictly by not touching boy and girl parts. Don't tell me you're one of Sully's conquests?"

"I would happily tell you that"—Charlotte watched Ellie's response carefully— "but I would be lying." She smiled triumphantly as her friend choked on her drink. "I was trying desperately not to be gay," she said by way of an explanation. "So moving on. Ruth said that Sully is dating Lou?"

"Yeah, it's been a year and both Ruth and Peter are still trying to get their heads around it."

"What about Teddy? Ruth says she still hates me for the county tennis competition."

"Well you're in good company, 'cause she holds Erin responsible for it too. Something about a bad line call. In fact"—Maddie looked at her watch—"World War Three may have broken out at home since they're both round having dinner with Alex tonight."

Charlotte took another long drink. The warmth of it coated her throat as she swallowed. Just knowing where and what Erin was doing created a heat in her that had nothing to do with the whiskey she was drinking. She cleared her throat hoping the emotion she was feeling wasn't apparent in her voice. "So Teddy's with Alex and

Erin? What's Bear doing tonight? No doubt causing trouble with Sully and Peter somewhere!"

Maddie swallowed before sitting forward in her chair. "Bear was killed in Afghanistan over ten years ago. He joined the Marines after he graduated high school and was one of the first deployments to be sent after the attacks."

Charlotte's mouth opened and closed as she processed Maddie's words. Finally, she found words. "Ruth never mentioned..."

Shaking her head, Maddie sat back. "Ruth, Sully, and Peter don't talk about Bear. It's like if they don't speak about him being dead, then he's still with them. Alex and Teddy talk about him more, but the others"—she shrugged—"they just don't. They do still, however, make stupid bets on everything."

Despite her shock and sadness at the news, a laugh bubbled in Charlotte's throat. "He was terrible for making bets. I know it's been a long time, but could you pass on my condolences to Alex and Teddy?"

Maddie nodded. "Of course I will."

Ellie blew out air softly. "Well, my grandma and abuela taught me that at times like this whiskey is required." She smiled softly at the two women looking at her. "So I will go get us some more drinks."

Charlotte watched her friend walk to the bar. The short conversation with Maddie had drained her. For so long her memories and emotions about Grace Falls and all she left behind had stayed locked down. When she felt strong enough to reflect, she would remove a memory almost like a precious stone from a jewelry box and hold it up to the light. Twisting and turning it to elicit every ounce of pleasure she could, before carefully returning it to its rightful position and closing the lid. Tonight the jewelry box had been tipped upside down, and Charlotte was straining to recapture its contents.

It had taken several attempts before Maddie's voice managed to catch her attention.

"Would you like to see a photo of Jessica?" Maddie held out her phone towards Charlotte.

Unsure she could handle a further assault on her memories with photographs from Grace Falls, Charlotte wanted to say no. However, she was also mindful that people are funny about their kids. If being friends with Molly had taught her anything it was, always look at photos of kids and say how gorgeous they are, even if they resemble Sloth in The Goonies. Molly had once made a less than gushing remark about a colleague's baby and found herself suddenly without paralegal support for a month. The other lesson has to do with assuming a pregnancy. Never remark about a pregnancy until it has been confirmed by the woman herself. That misstep cost Molly a tax audit. So it was with Molly's voice ringing in her ears that Charlotte found herself reaching to take the phone.

"Those are from Easter," Maddie said, looking up at Ellie's return.

Charlotte looked at the phone and smiled knowing she wouldn't have to lie. "She's gorgeous." She could see both Alex and Sully in the girl's features.

Maddie accepted a drink from Ellie. "If you scroll left there are more photos."

Her finger hovered briefly over the screen before she replaced the image of a smiling Jessica with a family photo that included Alex, Sully, and Maddie with Jessica. She laughed at the sight of Sully sulking. His face was painted like a rabbit, and he was wearing a set of rabbit ears with one ear flopping down onto his forehead. "Sully hasn't changed much, well apart from the ears." Charlotte turned the phone to show Ellie and Maddie. "They seem bigger than I remember."

"They were only temporary, unfortunately." Maddie grinned. "He bitched the whole day that his face was itching with the face paint. It was only after a couple of hours when we removed it that we realized he was allergic. His face was bright red for days."

Charlotte laughed, then returned to look at the photo. "Alex looks much the same too."

Maddie smiled that smile that people have when they are stupidly in love.

Flicking her finger across the screen, Charlotte changed the image again. This time, a group shot full of faces she hadn't seen since her teens filled the screen. The world seemed to get smaller for Charlotte at that moment. The sounds of piano music, glasses clinking, and general chatter from the bar dissolved in an instant only to be replaced by the sound of her own blood rushing through her ears.

She increased the size of the image, focusing on the face that made time stand still for her over twenty years ago and apparently could still render her immobile now. Her blonde hair was much shorter than Charlotte had ever seen, but her hazel eyes were still as warm as they remained in Charlotte's memory. The small upturn at the edges of her mouth made it look as though a smile was only ever seconds away. Faint laughter lines crinkled the corners of her eyes now, but the face was unequivocally still the Erin that Charlotte had loved. A touch on her arm brought the sounds of the room flooding back, and Charlotte looked up dazed.

"You okay, you look like you've seen a ghost?" Ellie asked with concern.

Charlotte took one more glance at Erin before restoring the image to its normal size and returning the phone to Maddie. "Yeah, I'm good. Sorry, I zoned out there for a minute."

"So are you going to come back for the celebrations?" Maddie retrieved her phone and returned it to her purse.

Ellie looked at the two women. "Celebrations? Is there a party we don't know about?"

With a faint laugh and a shake of her head, Charlotte swirled her whiskey around and watched as the legs of the liquid slowly meandered back down the glass. "Grace

Falls is a hundred and fifty this year, so they're having a celebration, and no I wasn't planning on going back."

"You know Alex will kick my ass if I don't at least try and persuade you." Maddie raised her eyebrow as she took a sip of her drink.

"Why don't we pretend you tried and save us all some time and that way we can talk about more pleasant things." Charlotte summoned a smile she didn't feel. In truth, she didn't want Maddie to try and persuade her. She knew seeing Erin's photo had made her vulnerable, and it wouldn't have taken a lot of convincing for her to agree. That thought in itself was unsettling enough. What worried Charlotte more was that even without Maddie's encouragement she was already thinking about returning home.

Chapter Ten

*I*n Erin's dream, she was in a comfortable bed. She didn't have to look to know the warm body pressed against her belonged to Charlotte. The bewildering spiral towards wakefulness confirmed that although some of the components of her dream were based in reality, the reality was vastly different from her dream.

Birds were much louder than she was accustomed to. However, those sounds were currently being drowned out by someone yelling loudly close to her ear. If she'd correctly identified the owner of the voice currently screeching 'Alex' at the top of her lungs, it would appear the warm body pressed against her belonged to Teddy.

At that thought, her eyes sprung open. She was outside. Wherever she was, it was outside. Which explained the birds, but not Teddy. Despite clearing her throat, her voice still sounded terrible when she mustered the words together to ask Teddy where they were.

"We're in Bear's tree," Teddy replied. "Mornin'."

Erin nodded. "Oh." She attempted to sit up only to find herself unable to move. "What the…" She looked down and realized both she and Teddy were bound to the wooden platform by what looked like an entire reel of duct tape.

"That was my thought entirely," Teddy drawled. "I don't want to alarm you further, but our predicament could get a whole lot worse soon."

Erin turned her head to look at her fellow captive.

"'Cause I really need to pee."

Spinning her head back to look towards the house, Erin ignored the thumping in her head as she yelled loudly for Alex.

It took another couple of minutes of combined yelling before the woman in question arrived and climbed the small ladder leading to the platform.

"Wow, you two are quite the dawn's chorus."

"Alex Milne, let me out of here now." Teddy twisted back and forth in an attempt to slacken the bindings, her movement made no difference to the taut tape, and she flopped back on the wooden platform with a grunt.

Alex smirked and waggled her finger. "Now, Claudia Roosevelt, is that any way to thank me for saving your life?"

The combination of the duct tape, Alex's quick reflexes, and Teddy's alcohol-slowed ones meant that when Teddy lunged, it only took Alex a split second to lean back out of the way. Erin, however, was at a disadvantage. Her reflexes were slow like Teddy's, and it was her inability to move out of the way that resulted in her face being pressed against the wood by Teddy's elbow.

"Teddy, what the hell? Will you quit!" she yelled, waving her own arms in an attempt to get Teddy off her.

Finally realizing her efforts were futile, Teddy calmed and settled back down.

"Thank you." Erin glared in her direction before looking at their captor turned savior. "I'm a little confused. Why are we here?"

"'Cause someone, and by someone, I'm looking at you, Teddy, thought it would be a good idea to climb up here last night."

"Why the hell didn't you just get us back down again?" Teddy thumped her palms against the platform.

"Good plan. Why didn't I think of that?" Alex tapped her forefinger against her lips. "Oh yeah, 'cause you both passed out before Matt got here and apparently it's hard enough getting a willing participant down, without it being two drunk comatose women," she yelled. A small satisfied smirk appeared when she saw both Erin and Teddy flinch at the noise.

"Anything could have happened to us. We could have rolled off," Teddy said in a somewhat more apologetic tone.

"What do you think the duct tape was for?" Alex grinned and pulled a pocket knife out of her back pocket and proceeded to cut the tape to free them.

Ignoring the agony from where the tape caught her skin, Teddy ripped the tape from her and crawled over Erin. "Outta my way. I need to pee."

Alex swung to the side, creating space on the ladder for Teddy to scramble down, which she did in record time. She then sprinted towards the house yelling 'freedom.'

Taking a more cautious approach to the tape removal, Erin sat up slowly. "Thank you for last night. Somewhere within my hazy memory, there is a recollection of you giving me some good advice."

Alex grinned and patted Erin's leg. "You're welcome. You are one of the nicest people I know, and you have to let her go."

"I will. Jesus, it's not like she had a hard time letting me go."

"Well she's an idiot, now come get some breakfast."

∞ ∞ ∞

60

Judging from the squealing Alex could hear, Sully had entered the coffee shop and was now accosting Lou. Their relationship meant a period of adjustment within the group of friends as long-established dynamics shifted to accommodate their new status. Alex was sure she still caught moments of 'how the hell did that happen?' in Ruth's eyes as she watched their friend with her little sister.

Wiping dough from her fingers, Alex stuck her head around the kitchen door into the coffee shop. "Matt, put her down and come in here."

She desperately wanted to tell someone about Maddie seeing Charlotte, but after the duct tape incident, Teddy was ignoring her and Ruth was off in St Anton. So, excluding Erin for obvious reasons, that only left Sully as her outlet of who would give a damn.

"Yes, ma'am." Sully saluted and stole another kiss before trotting around the counter. He entered the kitchen and took a handful of raisins from the open container on the work surface, ignoring the baleful look from Alex at his theft. "How was Teddy this morning?

"Madder than a wet hen." Alex grinned at the memory of Teddy's post pee rant.

"You tell her I was involved?"

Alex shook her head. "You're okay. I took one for the team. Just make sure she doesn't see those photos you took."

Sully gave her a lazy smile and tipped an imaginary hat. "So how's Maddie's trip home? Did he agree?"

Momentarily forgetting about Charlotte, Alex gave a tentative nod. As well as attending the conference in New York City, Maddie scheduled time to see her family in Brooklyn particularly her brother, so she could ask if he would be a donor for her and Alex to have a child together.

Sully grinned broadly. "I'm happy for you. But you know, if you need me to step up I'm willing to lend a hand again."

Alex ignored the rude gesture that accompanied his offer. "I'm sure you would and thank you, but this way our baby gets to have some Marinelli genes. However, if Maddie ever decides to carry then we may take you up on it."

"You okay about all this?"

Alex took a deep breath. "I'm a little worried we're doing this too soon. I mean we've only been together a year, and already we're talking babies."

Sully nodded carefully. "I get that, but you also have to face up to the fact you're not getting any younger. So if you want to do this, it should be soon."

Letting out a loud laugh, Alex smacked him in the chest with the back of her hand. "You're an ass you know that."

Rubbing his chest, Sully looked suitably chastised. "That didn't come out right. I just mean that none of us are spring chickens anymore, and we can't let opportunities pass us by." He looked furtively at the door of the kitchen before digging into the pocket of his jeans and pulling out a ring box.

"Oh. My. God." Alex snatched the box from Sully and looking at the ring inside. "You're...You're...Oh. My. God."

"Is that all you're gonna say?" Sully grabbed the box back and thrust it into the depths of his pocket.

"No. Yes. Oh my God." Alex flung her arms around her friend's neck. "I'm so happy for you and Lou...wait, it is for Lou?"

Sully huffed at Alex's joke. "Course it is!"

"Well, that's the second thing to leave me speechless," Alex said shaking her head.

"What was the first?"

Alex's face broke into an excited grin. "Maddie was at her conference thing last night, and you will never guess who she met there."

"Do you want me to actually guess or are you just gonna tell me?"

"Charlotte!"

"Charlotte?"

"Grace, Charlotte Grace!"

Sully let out a slow stream of breath. "You gonna tell Erin?"

Alex shook her head until it occurred to her there was more to Sully's query. She narrowed her eyes. "What do you know about Charlotte and Erin?"

As far as Alex was concerned what happened between Charlotte and Erin was one of the few secrets that Grace Falls managed to keep. She only knew because Erin confided in her during their ill-fated attempt to date.

"Probably knew before you did." Sully puffed his chest out and gave a self-satisfied nod, before smiling sadly. "You remember when I hauled her ass off you at Ruth's mama's that time."

"How could I forget." Alex grinned. She'd been sixteen when Sully stopped her impromptu making out session with Charlotte before they could get to the good stuff.

Sully gave her a sheepish look. "Yeah well, it was for the best. The reason I did it was 'cause the week before I was out fishing when I heard voices. Next minute Erin comes striding past faster than salts through a widow woman, followed by that damn mutt of hers. What was its name?"

"Daisy," Alex supplied, poking him in the side to carry on with his story.

He rubbed his hand across the stubble on his chin as he recounted the decades'-old incident. "Less than a minute later Charlotte comes out. She doesn't say a word. Just comes over to me and before I know what's happening she's kissing me. One minute I'm standing there minding my own business with my rod in my hand and the next—"

"If what you're about to say also includes the word rod, I will stab you," Alex warned.

Laughing Sully shook his head. "I can't say I'm proud of it, 'cause I know none of what happened that day was about me, but that's how I lost my virginity, and I didn't want you to lose it the same way. You deserved better."

Alex moved closer and snuggled into the side of her friend. "You know you just keep surprising me."

"What 'cause I'm an ol' romantic?"

"Nope, I honestly thought you were younger when you lost your virginity." Alex laughed, giving him a squeeze.

"That's it. I refuse to have any more children with you." Sully huffed, trying to disentangle Alex's arms from his waist.

Alex tightened her grip. "Matt"—she looked up into his blue eyes—"Lou is a very lucky lady."

Grinning, Sully planted a kiss on her forehead. "Aww you know luck has nothing to do with it. I'm serious, though, Erin doesn't need all that business getting plowed over again. Whatever happened, happened, and whatever Charlotte's doing now ain't gonna change the past for Erin."

"You're protective of Erin all of a sudden."

"I was at Auburn with her remember. I saw what got left behind. It's best to leave those ghosts in the past—"

He was interrupted as Lou flung the kitchen door open. "Are you two gonna hide in here all day, or is it possible that you could get your ass out here to help?"

Alex threw a look towards Sully. "You sure you wanna ask that question?" she whispered as she followed dutifully behind Lou.

It had taken a while, but Erin was feeling human again. The hearty breakfast from Alex helped take the worst off her hangover, and a hot shower and bucketful of coffee had taken care of the rest. Now she sat contemplating what they'd discussed. She laughed as she recalled the reason why Teddy had been so standoffish with her for decades. It made her consider how many things she'd potentially missed out on because of holding onto the past. It was time to let go, she knew that, but however much her head knew what she had to do, her heart was still reluctantly and stubbornly holding on.

She'd been fourteen when an awareness of being different from other girls at school had awakened. She was sixteen before she knew for sure what that was. She let her head fall back against the back of the sofa as she remembered the conversation with Charlotte. It was the summer of 1990, and Martina Navratilova had just won her ninth Wimbledon singles title. Erin often wondered whether the conversation would ever have happened if Zina Garrison had won the title instead.

"I didn't want her to win." Charlotte stared up at the patches of blue sky visible through the tree canopy while plucking at the grass stalk in her hand.

Erin rolled onto her stomach to look at her friend better. "Why not?" She reached out and absently stroked the head of Daisy laying behind her. The large brown dog quickly rolled onto its side hoping there might be the opportunity for a belly rub.

Charlotte shrugged, then tossed the stalk away, and sat up resting her chin on her knees. "They call me Martina at school," she mumbled, deliberately not turning to look at Erin. "And her winning is just going to make it worse when I go back."

"Well that's just 'cause you're a great tennis player and one day you're gonna win Wimbledon like her." Erin nudged against Charlotte with her shoulder.

"S'pose," Charlotte replied without conviction in her voice.

Scrambling onto her knees, Erin dusted off her T-shirt. "How come they picked her and not Steffi Graf?"

Charlotte bit her lip and wiped at a stray tear. "'Cause Steffi Graf isn't a lesbian."

Erin screwed her face up. "Well, what the hell has that got to do with anything?" A lump formed in her throat as she thought about her own situation. She was suddenly aware of the fragility of the most significant relationship in her life. If Charlotte was horrified by the prospect of being associated with a famous lesbian, how would she cope knowing about her best friend?

"Everything!" Charlotte stood up. "You don't understand." She gave Erin a sad smile before striding off.

Springing to her feet, Erin sped after her friend. "So help me understand. Why has someone winning a tournament on the other side of the world got you so bent out of shape?"

"They've picked on me from day one. First, it was my accent, so I lost that. Then it was how I looked"—Charlotte brushed the heel of her hand angrily across her eye furiously— "and then they started calling me Martina. I thought at first it was the tennis, and I was proud. I mean she's an awesome player, and yes I would have preferred Steffi Graf, but still, she's won everything. Then I hear a couple of the girls saying how they'd have to watch each other's backs in the changing rooms; what with me being a dyke with a girlfriend back home."

Erin sucked in a breath. "They think I'm your girlfriend?" Despite the situation, she couldn't help the butterflies that gathered in her stomach as she considered the possibility.

Charlotte nodded sadly and sniffed. "They'd been reading your letters, and I didn't know."

A deep blush covered Erin's face. "But there's nothing in my letters."

"I know that, and you know that." Charlotte puffed air out of the side of her mouth, causing her bangs to lift. "Erin, can you keep a secret?"

Nodding Erin crossed her forefinger across her chest. "Hope to die."

"What if I am what they say I am?" Charlotte's green eyes were wide open, her forehead wrinkled as she waited for Erin's response.

Erin pulled her top lip into her mouth and nibbled on it while she considered her reply. A small smile started to form as she stepped closer to Charlotte. She reached down to take Charlotte's hands in her own. Leaning forward she placed a gentle kiss on Charlotte's lips. There was a moment when Charlotte kissed her back, but then suddenly her lips were gone. When Erin opened her eyes, she saw Charlotte staring at her in shock. Erin's heart was beating so fast in her chest she was almost light headed. Before Charlotte could say a thing, Erin apologized and took off running with Daisy bounding to keep up with her. Leaving a bewildered Charlotte behind.

Erin groaned as the knocking on her door persisted, bringing her out of her reverie. She stood up and opened the door, recoiling in surprise at Teddy standing on her doorstep.

"You okay?" She poked her head out to see whether Teddy was alone.

Teddy nodded. "Can I come in?"

Moving out of the way, Erin swept her hand across to welcome Teddy into her home.

Teddy sat down on the edge of the sofa. "I wanted to make sure you were okay. From what I can remember, and my memory is patchy at best, we went over some stuff that could have upset you."

Erin sat down and considered what she'd just been thinking about. "You realize we've missed out on over twenty years of friendship because of something stupid when we were fourteen?"

"Totally." Teddy shrugged. "I'm an idiot. There's no reason why we can't make the next twenty count though, right?" She held out her hand.

Shaking it, Erin smiled. "No reason at all. Though it did get me thinking about what else I'm missing out on. So I have decided to stop being pitiful—"

"You're not pitiful," Teddy interrupted. "I will not have you speak about my friend like that."

"Okay not pitiful, but I'm not going to mope around and let life bypass me."

Sitting back and getting comfortable, Teddy clapped her hands. "Okay then, so what are we doing?"

"I'm going to put myself out there and meet people," Erin said with an emphatic nod. "Women. I'm going to meet women. There's a bar in Mobile that does a ladies night once a month. I'm going to go."

Teddy sucked air through her teeth. "That's damn near three hundred miles away!"

Erin shrugged. "I've been to others, but the one in Mobile was the best."

"Awww hell no." Teddy stood up. "You are not gonna drive three hundred miles to a bar. Jeez, girl, a round trip of six hundred miles just on the off chance some woman is willing to show you her tatas?"

"What option do I have?"

"If you're that desperate, I'll let you have at it on mine. Just don't expect me to touch anything back."

"You are such a great friend. I have no idea how I coped without you until now," Erin deadpanned.

Teddy's face was a picture of sincerity when she slapped Erin's forearm. "I know! I really am the best friend." Her seriousness lasted a full second before she broke into a wide grin. "C'mon we're going to Sully's. I have a plan that doesn't consist of you getting friendly with my bits."

Pulling her shoes on, Erin glanced up at Teddy. "You do realize I'm not attracted to you don't you?"

Teddy frowned. "Now why would you say that? Alex has been banging that same drum for years, and yet we all know I'm like lesbian catnip."

Erin chuckled as she followed Teddy out the door, wondering what was in store for her when they got to Sully's.

∞ ∞ ∞

"Matthew Sullivan." Teddy slapped her hand against the wooden bar top as she slipped onto a stool.

"Claudia Roosevelt." Sully mimicked Teddy's actions and slapping the bar.

Teddy pulled Erin in closer to the bar. "You are familiar with my friend here, Erin Hunter."

Sully frowned. "So we're staying with this weird ass formal thing?" Taking Teddy's closed eyes as an affirmative, he cleared his throat. "I do, and I would like the record to show that I have been friends with said, Erin Hunter, since I was a child and didn't take a twenty-odd-year time-out, before crazy stalking her and doing some strange BFF thing."

Teddy nodded solemnly. "So noted."

Sully jerked his head in surprise at Teddy's calm acceptance of his jibe. "What do you want, Teddy?"

66

"It has come to my attention that for my friend" — she stressed the word friend while glaring at Sully daring him to comment — "who is a lesbian, to meet women of similar inclinations, she will have to travel a godly distance."

Teddy sat forward, leaning her elbows on the bar conspiratorially. "Now it seems to me that we could save our mutual friend from this predicament. As to meet similarly inclined women she would go to a drinking establishment and it just so happens that you own said type of establishment."

Sully looked towards Erin. "You want me to host a lesbian night?"

Erin nodded hesitatingly.

"Okay." Sully shrugged as he stepped away from the bar to grab two sodas from the fridge.

"So I think it only fair that we host an event here at Sully's," Teddy concluded, carrying on with her list of reasons why Sully should do it. Ignoring the fact no one appeared to be listening to her and he'd already agreed.

Placing the two sodas in front of his friends Sully narrowed his eyes as he addressed Erin. "Did she hear me offer?"

Erin grinned as she picked up her soda. "Probably, but she has a whole speech prepared. I heard it on the way over here. Be grateful I talked her out of the PowerPoint."

"Do I need to be here for it, or can I go serve other customers, and pretend that I'm listening?"

"You're good. Thanks, Sully."

He gave her a wink. "No worries. We can do it once all the birthday stuff has calmed down. I'll put something in the papers here and in St Anton. If you know of any specific places, I should advertise let me know, and I'll get on it."

"So you see, Sully, as someone with a minor in business studies, you should be able to recognize the benefit of breaking into a diverse market." Teddy took a self-satisfied slug of her soda.

"You persuaded me, Teddy. I'm in," Sully said sardonically, before heading down the bar to other customers.

Teddy turned to Erin and nodded pleased with herself. "See, told you I could persuade him."

Erin rolled her eyes. "You had him at lesbian!"

"Go get it, Cooper." Erin tossed a stick then laughed as Cooper gave her his 'if you want the damn stick why throw it away' look before trotting off in the opposite direction. "Or don't, it's all good," she muttered, before taking in a deep breath.

It was going to be a good day.

She didn't know why, but having Teddy force her forwards rather than dwelling on the past, and Sully agreeing to host a lesbian night had her hopeful. They'd advertised the night and were now just waiting to see whether anyone turned up. She was still pondering her good fortune when she heard a loud splash and a string of colorful curses follow it.

"Goddammit, Cooper get out of the water," Sully yelled. "Erin, I know you're here somewhere. Come get this mutt of yours out of the creek before he scares all the damn fish away."

Rolling her eyes, Erin changed direction towards Sully's voice. "You yelling won't help none," she said, stepping through the brush to the water's edge.

Sully flashed a grin. "Don't suppose it will. Good thing I'm not set on catching anything today." He placed his rod onto a rock, sat down and held out a can of soda to Erin.

She settled down beside him and popped the can open. "You hiding?"

"Yup, I proposed to Lou last night."

"No! Really?" Erin held the back of her hand up to Sully's forehead. "You feeling alright, old man? Do we need to go get Maddie?"

Sully slapped her hand away. "You're a funny lady, you know that."

"Congratulations, Lou is a very lucky woman."

"I'm the lucky one." Sully sighed contentedly. "Anyways Ruth showed up on the doorstep at five a.m. with wedding planning stuff, so I hightailed it out of there."

Laughing, she held her soda can up in a toast. "Your secret's safe with me."

Sully lay back stretching out his long legs and squinting up towards the sun. "So what's happening in the life of Erin these days?"

Erin shrugged. "You probably know more than I do."

"No secrets in Grace Falls." Sully nudged her with his leg. "So what's the deal with Teddy being all up in your business?"

"It's funny how being duct taped to one another can bond a relationship."

Sully had the good grace to look embarrassed. "About that..."

"That secret is also safe. I knew Alex didn't come up with that on her own." Erin lay back, mirroring Sully's relaxed pose. "I think she's trying to save me."

"You're not broken! A little bashed around the edges maybe, but you're not broken. Don't let her make you feel that way." he sat up and looked intently at Erin.

"I think she sees similarities in our lives, I mean we both struggled to get over our first loves. She's okay." Seeing Sully's raised eyebrows, she reassured him. "Honestly, it's fine. The minute she does something I'm not comfortable with I'll tell her. In the meantime, it's good to have someone who knows about me and Charlotte, and who doesn't skirt around the topic."

Sully reached out and placed a hand on Erin's thigh. "I'm sorry. I should have done more."

Erin patted his hand. "You put me back on the...well, not straight, but definitely the narrow, and that stopped me from getting my ass thrown out of Auburn. You did more than enough. It's been long enough. I'm ready to move on."

"And on the topic of moving on, it looks like we'll have quite the crowd. I have been getting emails and phone calls already about the lesbian night."

"You think Grace Falls is ready for this?" Erin asked, swatting at flies.

Sully shrugged. "They're just gonna have to get ready."

Erin wanted to share his optimism, but couldn't help but think they were all being naïve in thinking their small town would accept, she paused wondering what the collective term for a group of lesbians would be, chuckling to herself when she settled on U-Haul.

"Don't worry yourself. It's gonna be just fine," Sully said with a wink. "I promise. Everything will work out."

Chapter Eleven

Charlotte was so thrilled. She was almost bouncing in her seat as the town car pulled to a stop in the parking lot of the private airfield in New Jersey.

"Just think. In a matter of six hours, we will be in Vegas." She slapped Molly's arm in her excitement. "We get to stroll the strip, eat crap, drink loads, and never sleep."

She thought her absolute joy of all things Vegas stemmed from growing up with a mother who was so 'stick up her ass' uptight about fun stuff. Charlotte loved it all; the sounds of slot machines in the airport to the funky aromas piped through the air conditioning to disguise the smell of smoke in the casinos. She tried to imagine her mother walking around with a plastic cocktail cup around her neck, and the image made her giggle.

"I love Vegas," she announced to a bemused Ellie and Joanne.

"My grandmother was based there during the war," Ellie said. "Pretty sure it was a lot different then."

Looking at her friend's faces as they climbed out of the car, Charlotte couldn't figure out why they weren't as excited as she was. It was meant to be Ellie and Joanne's bachelorette weekend. Yet they looked as though they were expecting a wet weekend in Maine as opposed to a four-day vacation in Sin City.

It had been a somewhat rushed arrangement in the end. As a perk of the job, Joanne had been given use of the private jet she usually flew bigwigs and celebrities in and Molly had taken it upon herself to arrange everything else. All Charlotte had to do was pack and show up at her door when the car arrived.

The trip was just what she needed. After meeting Maddie, memories from Grace Falls and Erin just kept springing up, often at the most inopportune moments. It was as if, after all this time of protecting herself and blocking the memories out, she had no defenses left. She could be standing in line at a deli, and she would hear Erin's laugh. It was so real she would turn around looking for her, sure she must be standing there. She knew Vegas would invade every sense she had, leaving no room for ghosts from the past.

As they followed Joanne towards the hangar, Charlotte tried to rouse her friends' energy levels a little. "You know you all could look happier. We're going to Vegas!"

Molly, dragging her carry-on case behind her, stretched and gave a loud, impressive yawn. "I'm sorry, I don't know about the others, but I'm just beat. It's been a long week." She glared at her sister and her fiancée.

"Yeah, completely," Ellie said, watching as Joanne slipped away to complete the paperwork for their flight.

Their excitement didn't increase during the flight. Even Charlotte's best efforts with her lip curling full-blown Elvis impression of Viva Las Vegas did nothing to improve their mood.

Finally, she'd had enough.

"What the hell is wrong with you all?"

The leather of the seat squeaked as she turned to get a better look at her friends. She saw Molly visibly gulp as Ellie shook her head and look pointedly at Molly.

Clearing her throat, Molly swallowed again and seemed to force herself to speak. "It's like this. We love you...very much."

Charlotte narrowed her eyes as her gaze flicked between Molly and Ellie.

"And it's because we love you that we're not going to Vegas." Molly looked like she wanted to vomit.

Unsure how not taking her to Vegas was proof of their love Charlotte responded cautiously. "Okaaaaaay."

"We're not going to Vegas and remember when I say this that we love you. We thought—"

"Oh for the love of Christ, Molly," Ellie interrupted, exasperated at Molly's rambling explanation. "Charlotte, this flight is taking us to Alabama. We will then pick up a car and drive to Grace Falls for their birthday celebrations." She scowled at Molly, who was sitting waiting for the inevitable shit storm to happen.

Charlotte's mouth opened and closed. Finally, her brain seemed to catch up with her jaw and words started to form. "So you're telling me instead of Vegas, where I can see women in bridal gowns riding a mechanical bull, I'm going to my hometown that I haven't been in for over twenty years. Where my mother is. The same mother who didn't bother to tell me of my father's death. We're going there so I can celebrate that town's birthday with people I haven't seen since I was seventeen?"

Molly bit her top lip as she nodded carefully.

Charlotte nodded as if processing the new information. Then yelled at the top of her voice. "Joanne Parsons, turn this goddamned plane around now!"

Joanne's voice came out the speakers. "I'm guessing from the noise back there, that you've finally told her. Charlotte, I'm sorry. I had nothing to do with this. Well, apart from the flying you there bit. The idea was theirs. I'm going to make a wild assumption you're asking me really nicely to turn around, but no can do I'm afraid."

Charlotte slumped back in her seat and glowered at her friends. "I am so not happy about this. Y'all are going to hell."

"See you're even talking all South now." Molly's half-smile slid from her face as Charlotte stared her down. "It'll be fun. You'll see."

Chapter Twelve

*E*rin pulled her overalls off and thrust them into the washer. She was grateful yet again she'd created a mudroom in her home that allowed her to strip off and dump her often foul-smelling clothing, particularly following a trip out to the Jackson holding.

What on paper was an easy check-up of their pigs, always resulted in a workout that no gym could provide, and Erin wearing as much of the pigs' pen as the pigs themselves. They were the orneriest creatures Erin had ever dealt with, as well as the most elusive. However, she was pleased her efforts had bagged them a hog for the roast tomorrow. The Jackson's were always happy to find alternatives to paying her with the green stuff.

Padding barefoot in her underwear into the kitchen, Erin smiled as the smell of fresh paint replaced the odor of swill and swine. That smell meant Sam had been around and started to paint the woodwork. Sure enough, there was a note on her kitchen table letting her know he'd completed downstairs and done the prep for upstairs but was now at Sully's. The rest would have to wait until after the weekend and the birthday celebrations were complete.

She admired his handiwork as she walked through the house, careful not to touch anything that had been painted. She planned to shower and clear off the last of the visit to the Jackson's and then go buy her little brother a deserved beer. She stripped off her underwear and threw the items into the hamper in her bedroom then entered the bathroom and kicked the door closed behind her.

A full ten minutes under the shower and her good humor with the world was restored. She stepped out of the shower, and roughly towel dried her hair then wrapped the small towel around her body. As she reached for the doorknob her brow furrowed. The large brass knob that was usually there was replaced by a hole.

"Oh no. Please no. Sam!" she yelled at the realization that her brother in his preparations had removed the door handles, and she was now stuck in her bathroom. "I will kill you." Her previous goodwill towards her brother was now replaced with a red-hot rage as she surveyed the room for anything she could use to aid her escape.

Ten minutes, and one broken toothbrush later, Erin sat down on the toilet in defeat. It was likely to be lunchtime the next day before Sam wondered where she was; if the thought occurred to him at all in amongst the celebrations. There was only one thing to do. If Erin wanted out, she had to do it herself.

Standing up, she secured the towel around her torso hoping it would be up to the challenge and opened the bathroom window. Peering out, she could see her bedroom window open. If only she could edge along to it, she would be home free. She looked down hesitatingly at the roof of the porch that encircled her property. While it was wide enough for her to edge along, she could only hope it was strong enough to take her weight.

She stood on the closed toilet lid, placed her hands on the window frame, and with a groan of effort climbed out of the window. Holding onto the frame, she slid her hand underneath a section of the wooden siding covering her home to check if there were any finger grips. Semi-satisfied there was at least something to hold onto, she carefully edged her way along the roof.

***

Teddy texted a quick *'I'm on my way'* to Alex as she walked along the sidewalk. Approaching Erin's house she saw the vet's truck in the drive. She quickly selected Alex's number from her contacts and called her.

"I was just texting back! You are so impatient," Alex grumbled when she answered the call.

"It's not that. I'm just passing Erin's. Is she at the bar?" She could hear the scraping of a chair on the floor as Alex no doubt stood up to get a better look across the bar.

"Nope."

"Okay, I'll go get her, you get the drinks."

"How 'bout you go get her and you get your own damned drinks."

"Duct tape," Teddy said quietly into her cell.

There was an audible huff before Alex responded with a reluctant 'okay.' It had been weeks, but Teddy was still finding mileage in Alex's guilt over taping her and Erin to the treehouse.

"Love you," Teddy chirped, hanging up the call and walking down Erin's drive. She was halfway down when a glimpse of movement at the side of the house caught her attention. She switched direction to investigate. Her mouth fell open as she realized the movement was Erin clinging to the side of her house. Teddy held her hand over her eyes to block out the hazy evening sun.

∞ ∞ ∞

74

"Hey, Peter Parker, you okay up there?"

The voice startled Erin, and her foot slipped slightly before she regained both her balance and composure.

"Sorry," Teddy called, "didn't mean to scare you. You lose something?"

Erin lifted her arm so she could look down at Teddy, instantly regretting the action as the ground seemed far away and solid, extremely solid.

"What the hell do you think I'd be looking for up here?"

"Your dignity?" Teddy laughed. "You want me to let myself in, and you can edge back to the window?"

Erin really, really, wanted Teddy to do that. Unfortunately, the house was locked up, and there was no way Teddy would be able to get in.

"Doors are locked."

Teddy pouted as she thought. Almost immediately her pout turned into a smile. "Okay just stay there. I've got an idea." She sprinted off back down Erin's drive.

"Where the hell am I meant to go?" Erin huffed.

It was five long minutes of holding onto the siding before Teddy's car appeared with a ladder sticking out of the open tailgate. Erin's calf muscles had long since started to protest as she stood with her weight on her toes, terrified of knocking roof tiles off her porch roof. Teddy pulled the ladder out of her car and trotted back towards Erin with a grin on her face.

"Where'd you get that from?" Erin asked as Teddy started to pull out the extensions and check the hooks were on safely before propping it against the porch.

"I appropriated it from the fire truck." She grinned as Erin's eyes widened in shock. "It's not like I'm not taking it back! Besides, it's a volunteer fire department so for twenty minutes I'm volunteering."

Erin's desire to get off the roof and onto firm ground far outweighed her concern at Teddy's light-fingers. She carefully made her way to the ladder, placed a hand on it, and swung her foot onto the closest rung. She ignored Teddy's 'God, I'm never going to un-see that' as she pulled herself onto the ladder and started her descent.

When she was finally on the ground, she pulled Teddy into a grateful hug. They repositioned the ladder under her bedroom window, and as she was about to climb back up, they heard a voice yell, 'Dr. Hunter, are you in?' The tone held just enough panic that Erin went to peek around her house.

Striding up her path with a large cat tucked under one arm was Mary-Beth Dean, and only a few paces behind was her neighbor, Felisha Dewar whose face looked like it was about to combust.

"Doc, you there?" Mary-Beth shouted, before stepping up onto Erin's porch and rapping the door loudly.

"Oh God." Erin groaned quietly. "I have a hunch I know what this is about."

Teddy's face sprung up beneath Erin's. "Felisha looks like she's about to crap out a raccoon. What's got her all het up?"

Felisha must have heard their voices because her head swiveled around towards the side of the house. Both Teddy and Erin sprung back and flattened themselves against the side of the house.

"Is that you Doc?" Felisha called, her voice getting louder as she walked closer. She clutched her chest in shock as Teddy suddenly appeared as if propelled around the corner. "Oh, Claudia Roosevelt, we're looking for Doc Hunter. Do you know where she is?"

Teddy later admitted she did consider telling Felisha that Erin was indisposed, but the thought was dismissed in seconds after she recalled the speed with which Erin flung her towards the two baying women. Women, who were well known for their generations-long feuds, which no one of sane mind got themselves involved in.

"Mrs. Dewar, good to see you. Mrs. Dean, you too," Teddy said, nodding good-naturedly towards the other woman, who now joined them. "You're in luck, the woman in question is here. Just ignore her attire, it's casual Friday." Teddy reached behind her and grabbed Erin's arm dragging her out.

Erin glared at her before turning her attention to the two women. "Ladies, how can I help?"

Mary-Beth pointed at Felisha. "You can tell her for a start that that cat there is my Foofoo."

Felisha rolled her eyes. "No matter how many times you say it; this cat is not your Foofoo. It's my Twinkle."

Blocking out the choking sound from Teddy, Erin checked the security of her towel before stepping forward. "Why don't we take it back a bit. Mrs. Dewar, I didn't realize you had a cat." Erin reached out one hand to stroke the head of the large ginger cat nestled in Mary-Beth's arms, her other hand gripped tightly to the towel covering what was left of her modesty.

"Well, there's no reason you should. I take it to the vet in St Anton," Felisha said defensively. "You tell her she can't just stride into a person's home and steal their cat." She poked her finger between Erin and Mary-Beth. "She's lucky I haven't called Harvey on her...yet."

Mary-Beth shook her head; her ample bosom went with the flow as well. Mary-Beth was one of those women who seemed not to have breasts, but instead one large bosom that on occasion could double as a shelving unit. "I can when it's my property in the first place, you thieving ol' witch."

Before the argument escalated into the inevitable name-calling and resulted in either Harvey Mack, the local Deputy Sheriff, being called, or the desire to turn the hose on the two women became too strong, Erin stepped between them. "Now, I'm sure we can sort this out amicably."

Teddy's eyebrows rose incredulously at the optimism of that statement. Erin scowled at her, warning her not to get involved. "Now it's been a couple weeks since Foofoo went missing. Am I right?"

Nodding, Mary-Beth hefted the cat up. "Yes, an' I've put flyers up all around the neighborhood, and not a peep of a sighting. Then tonight I go to put the trash out an' as I'm walking back in I look up, and I see Foofoo sitting in the window in her house." She tilted her head towards Felisha accusingly. "So I went an' got her back."

"Okay." Erin turned towards Felisha, "and you're saying this is your..."

"Twinkle," Felisha supplied, "yes she is."

"Well, it's all very easy to sort out. We put a microchip on Foofoo, so we can just take Foofoo...Twinkle," Erin quickly corrected, seeing the ire on Felisha's face. "We can take the cat down to the exam room, and I can scan for the chip."

Felisha moved quickly to snatch the cat from Mary-Beth's arms, surprising all of them with her speed. "I'm not putting my cat through unnecessary procedures."

"It's not a harmful—"

"I don't care," Felisha interrupted. "That's not gonna happen."

"Okay, then there's no way of proving whose cat this is." Erin turned to Mary-Beth and put a consoling hand on her shoulder. "I guess you can take small consolation you didn't see Foofoo get really sick. I got her blood work back finally today, and it would appear she was suffering from a rare condition called engaño. She would have started to exhibit the symptoms pretty soon. So I guess at least you're spared that and the cost of treatment, which would have been really high."

Mary-Beth looked momentarily confused, then seeing Erin's encouraging smile she placed her hand over her mouth to hide a burgeoning smile and nodded.

"What symptoms?" Felisha asked.

Erin turned her attention to the other woman. "Oh don't worry, it's genetic so no way Twinkle here will have got it."

"Yes, but what symptoms?" A hint of urgency entered her tone.

Erin looked up towards the sky. "Well let's see, it starts with hair loss. All of it. Then diarrhea starts and finally the vomiting. Projectile." Erin flashed her a grin. "But again Twinkle here should be fine."

She gave the cat a friendly pat on the head. "Now ladies if you don't mind?"

She looked over at Teddy, who was staring preoccupied towards the road.

"Teddy, are you okay to assist me?"

Teddy seemed to shake off whatever was bugging her and smiled towards the two older women. "No doubt I'll see you both tomorrow at the cookout." She followed dutifully behind Erin. When she was sure they were out of earshot she looked at her quizzically. "Engaño?"

"Spanish for deception," Erin said with a smile as she gripped the ladder ready to climb.

"So no disease then?" Teddy laughed as Erin shook her head. "So what do you think will happen?" She held onto the ladder, steadying it while Erin started to climb slowly up towards her bedroom window.

"Well first I need to place a call to the St Anton's vet and explain the disease. Then I imagine Foofoo will suddenly reappear on Mary-Beth's porch either tonight or tomorrow, and Twinkle will disappear."

Teddy grinned and looked up to continue the conversation, forgetting about Erin's attire. "Oh God, kinda hoping your twinkle disappears from my brain." She looked at the ground and shuddered as if trying to expel the image.

Chapter Thirteen

*M*olly put one foot out of their hired SUV. "When you said we were going to go to Hell, you weren't talking metaphorically. I think it's actually hotter than Hell here and it's evening. What's it going to be like tomorrow?"

"Hot, and you know if you get heat stroke I'm going to have no sympathy," Charlotte grumbled, pulling her bag out of the trunk of the car.

Unexpectedly, she was once again driving through familiar streets and had been unprepared for the numerous emotions that accompanied the drive. Nostalgia at seeing Ryries still on Main Street. Pride in her childhood friends as she passed Alex's coffee shop and Matt Sullivan's bar and sadness as they drove past the entrance for the lumberyard.

She'd managed to call Ruth while on the plane, after explaining to the others that Grace Falls was not the sort of place you could pull up to and find somewhere to stay. As she drove to the old Anderson house, all the previous feelings paled into insignificance. She was in no way prepared for her first sighting of Erin.

Erin was standing, in what was presumably her front yard, in only a bath towel remonstrating with Mrs. Dewar and Mrs. Dean. She'd slowed the car as much as she dared as they passed, only speeding back up when she spotted Teddy looking directly at her.

"I hope y'all will be comfy here," Ruth said as she unlocked the door and pushed it open so the visitors could enter her mother's home. "It should still look familiar, Charlotte."

When Charlotte stepped over the threshold, she was a child again. The décor had only changed slightly from her memory but over in the corner was the piano where for fifteen years she spent two hours every week learning to play, with Ruth's mama watching over her shoulder. She smiled as she walked towards it and pressed down on the keys. The sound was as familiar to her as her own breath.

"I was sorry to hear about your mama," she said turning to Ruth, who was staring at her as if she was an apparition.

"Thank you. You were always her favorite you know."

Charlotte laughed as she closed the lid. "I doubt that. She used to berate me something awful. Charlotte Grace, you have lazy fingers. Miss Grace, there are no shortcuts in life or in this piece of music. There is no excuse for not fingering correctly."

A small whispered 'Amen' from Joanne was followed by the sound of a slap.

Remembering there were others in the house, Charlotte and Ruth turned, and Ruth continued with her verbal tour of the property. "So the kitchen is through there. Upstairs are three bedrooms." She addressed the rest of the explanation to Charlotte. "Lou's old room has a single, mine has a double, and there's still a double in mama's room. I think you're familiar with that room at least."

Charlotte grinned at the comment. "I think I was in there for all of five minutes, but I should be able to find my way back there."

Ruth laughed. "I wasn't sure if y'all were up for the bar tonight. The celebrations are starting there but tomorrow is the bigger stuff. There's stalls and a cookout down at the playing fields from lunchtime. There're some supplies in the kitchen for tonight and breakfast. But if y'all don't feel like cooking in the morning then Ruby's is the place to go for breakfast. I'm sure Alex would love to see you, Charlotte."

Nodding, Charlotte gave a wry smile. "Can you do me a favor and keep my being here quiet for now?" She rolled her shoulders, trying to get rid of the tension that increased with each passing moment. "I think you and possibly Alex will be about all that's happy to see me."

Ruth rubbed her arm comfortingly. "There'll be others too, I'm sure of it. But I'll keep it low key." She clapped her hands. "So I should go let you get settled an' I'll see Y'all tomorrow."

Molly smiled warily at Charlotte. "See not so bad."

Charlotte didn't respond as she picked her bag up and climbed the stairs to claim a bedroom.

Charlotte didn't acknowledge the tentative knock at the bedroom door.

"I brought you some oatmeal. I thought you might be hungry and this is as good as my cooking gets."

Turning briefly at Joanne's voice, Charlotte barely acknowledged her before turning back to gaze out of the window.

"You draw the short straw?"

Placing the bowl down carefully on the nightstand, Joanne joined her at the window. "I'm the only one trained in self-defense." She watched closely as the corner of Charlotte's mouth rose up in amusement. "You doing okay?"

Charlotte let out a long breath and rubbed at her eye. "I guess, to be honest, I'm all over the place. I'm so angry with you all for tricking me."

"I'm sorry." Joanne shrugged. "I have no excuse other than sometimes it's easier to just go along with my sister than fight her and don't blame Ellie. She thought there was maybe some part of you needed this trip."

"The part of me that's not mad agrees with her." Charlotte sighed. "I've thought a lot lately about this place and the people I left here, and it was time to come home. I've spent the last half of my life running from the memories of the first half, and that's no way to live. I'm just drifting along; I have no idea what I want to do next. I don't share anything of myself with anyone. I have no girlfriend. I need to save myself from me!

"I want to make amends and apologize to those I hurt, confront my mother about the hurt she created and say goodbye properly to my daddy. Although I'll be honest with you, I really wish he was still alive so I could ask him what the hell he thought he was doing letting my mother ride roughshod over us all. Then just maybe I can find some peace."

"Well I'm no expert, but that sounds like a good plan." Joanne laid a comforting hand on Charlotte's shoulder. "You know when putting a plan into motion, it's better to have a full belly."

Charlotte left the window and collected the bowl. "Maybe I'll come downstairs and eat it."

Joanne smiled. "That'd be great."

∞ ∞ ∞

"Who do we know drives a red SUV?" Teddy plonked herself down beside Alex and Maddie and looked expectantly at them.

Both looked at each other before shaking their heads. "No one why?"

"No reason." Teddy shook her head as Erin walked back towards the table. "Erin, you've gotta tell them about the double D's."

"What they fighting 'bout now?" Alex asked around a mouthful of peanuts.

"A cat if you can believe it," Teddy said grinning. "I'm just going to go say hey to Ruth." She picked up her beer and walked towards her friend, who had just come into the bar.

"Teddy, how are you?" Ruth leaned on the bar as she accepted a beer from Sully.

Placing her bottle down carefully, Teddy nodded. "Good. Do you know someone with a red SUV?" She watched as Ruth's eyes widened momentarily as she took a drink from her beer.

She was saved from an answer when the door to the bar flew open, and Brett Ford strode in and slapped a newspaper clipping down onto the bar. "What in the hell do you think you are doing? What is this...this...abomination?" He ignored the fact that the music and all conversation had stopped.

Sully walked leisurely over towards where Ford stood and slowly turned the clipping around so he could read it. "That there is an advertisement, common practice in business. Something you should know."

"Don't you get smart with me. You damn well know what I'm talking about. What do you think you're doing advertising for this sort of thing? A good God-fearing town like Grace Falls doesn't need this kind of abomination."

Tossing a dishrag over his shoulder, Sully turned and held his arms out. "Seems we have a good proportion of the town in here tonight. So let's take a vote."

He jumped up onto the bar. "Folks, I have put an advertisement in newspapers for a ladies' night." He waved his hands to quiet down the few male whoops that accompanied his announcement. "I'm afraid guys, you're not why they'll be coming here. The ladies that are invited are lesbians." He grinned at Alex's sole whoop. "It's a Thursday night in a few weeks' time. Now anyone got any objections?"

He turned to look at Brett Ford when no one raised their hand.

A smug look on the lumberyard manager's face appeared when there was a cough and a clearing of a throat.

Sully turned back round to see who it came from. Ezra Jackson stood up and slicked down the few remaining strands of hair he had. "I gotta question, Sully," he said carefully. "Does that mean we can't come in for a drink that night?"

Sully quirked an eyebrow in Erin's direction, and when she gave a quick shake of her head, he took a deep breath. "Well no it doesn't, but if you do come in you will show respect to our guests. If anyone can't do that, then I'll toss you out of here so fast your teeth will shake, and it'll take you a while to get back in my good graces to return." He looked pointedly at Brett Ford.

Ol' man Jackson nodded slowly. "Won't be no trouble, jus' wondering was all. Ain't got no teeth to shake anyhow." He grinned a toothless grin towards the table with Maddie, Alex, and Erin. "Maybe we can get a good woman to court Erin finally."

The bar erupted into cheers as Erin slunk down in her chair with embarrassment and Sully jumped back down behind the bar.

"We don't care here if you're gay, straight or a withered ol' bigot. We'll serve you anyhow." He smiled towards Brett Ford. "Now do you want a drink?"

82

Ford scowled. "You should be ashamed!" He raised his voice to address the rest of the bar. "You all should."

Sully leaned closer to him. "If you don't want a drink, then take your out of date opinions with you and try not to let the door smack you on the ass on the way out." He turned back towards the bar and bellowed brightly, "Where'd all the music go?" A second later the volume was turned back up and normal service resumed.

Ford glanced around, realizing he'd no support he scowled and let out a small huff before turning and leaving the bar in the same fury as he'd entered.

"Well that was interesting." Teddy watched his departure then returned her attention to Ruth. "So red SUV?"

Ruth shook her head and started to make her escape towards where her husband was sitting with their son.

Stepping to block the way Teddy continued. "'Cause the damnedest thing happened earlier. I saw a red SUV drive into town and my eyesight ain't what it was 'cause I could have sworn it was Charlotte Grace driving it." She saw Ruth pale slightly. "Now since I don't know for sure what I saw, I'm not going to say anything to Erin, since there's no need to worry her unnecessarily 'cause we all know their friendship ended badly. But if I was a person who did know for sure something like that, I think I'd feel obliged to say something."

Teddy gave Ruth a final warning glance, then moved to let her past. She looked over towards where Alex and Maddie were sitting with Erin and hoped to God that her suspicions were wrong.

Chapter Fourteen

C harlotte lay in the dark staring at the shadows cast along the ceiling. The persistent memories of Grace Falls and Erin over the past few weeks had been nothing but a prelude to the state she was now in.

Being back in Ruth's old house and the scene of one of her mistakes, had Charlotte berating herself for her weakness in her youth. She wasn't proud of her actions after Erin kissed her. Confusion, at what it meant for them and for her, saw her make choices she would forever regret.

Her first was her immediate need to prove that it meant nothing, and she was straight. Poor unsuspecting Sully. She almost laughed recalling his shocked expression as she launched herself on him. The act, however, backfired in its purpose, as soon as their lips met she knew it felt wrong. She ignored the voice telling her it shouldn't be Sully. That it shouldn't be a boy, she was with. It should be Erin's lips and Erin's touch she should be feeling. His release was a relief, and her seduction of him ended as quickly as it began, and she had fled the scene in tears.

She'd avoided everyone in the week that followed. Up until Ruth's party. She'd gone in the hope of seeing Erin and talking about what had happened. When Erin didn't show, she tried to drown out her confusion with too many wine coolers. She could blame the alcohol, but in truth, it happened because she was young, confused, and horny. Everyone knew Alex liked girls. It had caused a stir the previous summer. Charlotte found herself gravitating towards the blonde, testing her flirting skills, wondering whether she could be as sure as Alex was of her sexuality or whether she was experiencing some strange sort of obsession with Erin.

She honestly couldn't remember who suggested going up the stairs, but she certainly remembered kissing Alex and pressing her down onto the bed. The feelings she experienced answered her questions in part. It definitely felt different than with Sully. It felt good. However, again she found herself wishing when she opened her eyes that the blue eyes looking back at her would be hazel. She felt part mortification part relief when Sully, of all people, dropped her on her ass. She'd looked at the two friends, one angry and the other equal parts confused and aroused, before deciding to get the hell out of that house. She again fled the scene. This time, however, her exit was marred by Erin standing at the bottom of the stairs.

"You okay?"

Charlotte didn't deserve the concern she saw in those hazel eyes. She nodded and pushed Erin out of her way. Running down the street and not once stopping or looking back.

She'd cried until it felt like she had no more tears. The hard rock providing no solace beneath her as she lay wrung out. This is not what she planned for her life. Although she didn't subscribe to the Virginia Grace three-point plan of her future; college-marriage-kids, she hadn't banked on being so fundamentally different from the norm she grew up around. She hadn't even known what the word lesbian was until the year before when she and Erin heard it attached to Alex and looked it up in the dictionary. Now only a year later she was coming to terms with the fact she was a lesbian and completely in love with her best friend.

"Is it true?"

The question and Erin's voice surprised her so much she fell from her perch on the stone. She'd been so deep in thought she hadn't heard her approach. She quickly got to her feet and focused on scuffing leaves with the toes of her sneakers.

"Charlotte, look at me!"

She raised her head and looked at Erin, whose face was ashen white.

"Is it true?" *Erin swallowed hard.* "Did you have sex with Sully and Alex?"

Charlotte sniffed and rubbed her gritty eyes. "I had sex with Sully, but not Alex. Sully stopped us."

The pain her words caused was apparent. Erin's eyes widened, and she stepped back as if she'd taken a punch to the chest.

"Why? Why would you do that?"

Angry and ashamed, Charlotte lashed out. "Why did you kiss me?"

Erin shrugged and took a step forward. "Because I love you."

Her answer seemed to suck all the fury from Charlotte's body. "Do you realize what you're saying? What that means for us? For you?"

"What do you think I've been thinking about all week?" *Erin shouted.* "I didn't ask for this. I wasn't even sure I wanted to feel this way. But I love you, and I wanted us to be together, and if you hadn't avoided me all week, we could have talked it through. I thought about it, Charlotte. I didn't go out and sleep with half the town to figure out what I feel."

Charlotte hung her head. "I'm so sorry. I'm not sure I can handle this. I mean, what will my parents say? I got sent to the other side of the country just for being friends with you." *The tears she thought had dried up fell again from her eyes. Firm hands gripped her wrists.*

"Do it," *Erin urged.* "Make the sign." *She pulled Charlotte's hands up between them.*

Slowly Charlotte looped her fingers into a chain.

"Remember, we're unbreakable. We'll figure it all out," *Erin said calmly, her fingers gently caressing Charlotte's wrists.* "Do you feel the same way about me?"

Charlotte raised her head and nodded. "God yes."

"Then we'll figure it out."

Erin smiled for the first time since arriving at their rock, and it was a glorious sight to Charlotte.

"Just stop sleeping with or trying to sleep with the rest of town and we'll be okay." Erin wiped the remaining tears from Charlotte's face before leaning in to kiss her gently.

Charlotte felt a tear slide down the side of her face towards her pillow as she remembered that night and what that kiss led to.

∞ ∞ ∞

Ruth was not looking forward to this conversation. Never usually one to balk at awkward conversations this could be the one that broke her. She paused briefly before pushing open the door to the vet's office and striding in.

"Hey, Cindy, she out back?" she asked breezily.

Cindy looked up from behind the reception desk. "Nuh-uh, she got called out at five this morning. One of the Chadwick's horses was foaling breech. Can I pass a message onto her?"

Instantly Ruth regretted waiting until morning before speaking to Charlotte and reluctantly getting her agreement to talk to Erin.

"Any idea when she'll be back?"

Cindy shook her head. "Nope sorry. She did say she hoped to be back for the cookout."

"Well, when she's back you tell her I need to speak with her urgently before she comes to the cookout."

Scrawling the message onto her pad, Cindy nodded. "Sure. See you later. It should be a good'un."

Ruth smiled apprehensively. "Yeah, it should."

∞ ∞ ∞

"How come you look so bright-eyed this morning?" Molly grumbled towards Charlotte, as she sat down beside her equally tired-looking sister and swiped her coffee.

Charlotte turned around from the stove where she was making scrambled eggs and waved the wooden spoon in her hand. "What do you mean?"

"Seriously? You managed to sleep through all that noise?" Molly asked incredulously. "I swear my apartment in Manhattan is quieter than this place."

Dishing out the eggs onto plates, Charlotte frowned. "You mean the sound of the crickets?"

Molly took a long, satisfying drink of her sister's coffee. "If that's what made that infernal noise all night, then yes."

"Y'all spend too much time in the city."

Charlotte ran water into the pot and started to clean it out. Today she would see Erin and hopefully not just from a distance. Despite thinking about it constantly during the night, she still had no idea what to say to her, other than how sorry she was at how things worked out.

She stopped scrubbing, held her hands still in the water and closed her eyes. Swallowing hard she imagined herself speaking to Erin. Yet every time her mouth opened no words would come. All she could think of was placing her hands on Erin's cheeks and kissing her. She was so absorbed by the thought she missed Molly's attempt to get her attention.

"Charlotte! What in the hell is that noise?"

Shaking her head to clear her thoughts, Charlotte turned towards the table and listened. She broke out into a grin as she picked up the noise. "That's the eldest Carter boy. God, he must be twenty-one by now. He was just a baby when I left." She spotted Molly's irritation at her rambling. "Ruth said we might hear him when she stopped round earlier. Apparently, he traced his family tree, and there's Scottish somewhere in there, so he's taking to—"

"Sacrificing a small animal?"

Charlotte laughed. "No! Learning the bagpipes."

Molly scrunched her face up. "Does he have to play them in town?"

"Oh, he's not in town," Charlotte said drying her hands. "He's a couple mile out but if the wind blows the wrong way it carries the sound apparently. Just be grateful they managed to get him to play later. Ruth said when he started he would play at five in the morning."

She tossed the towel in Molly's direction. "Just remember whose fault it is we're here. We could have been in Vegas in a casino wondering what time it was while we lost money. Instead, I'm facing a day where I will no doubt run into my mother."

"And Erin?" Ellie added softly.

Chewing on her lip as she thought about the prospect again, Charlotte blew out a long breath then smiled at Ellie. "And Erin. Right now I don't know which one terrifies me more." She moved towards the door.

"Fun starts at ten-thirty, so you have until then to become vaguely human again. A few words of advice on how to survive today. Do not engage in conversation with my mother. Ever. Ellie, do not publicize that you're a doctor or Emmett Day will have you checking something on him.

"If you are offered a drink by anyone male or female that has white blonde hair, demurely refuse. I don't care if you are dying of thirst, and it looks like the most innocent of iced tea. Chances are, the person offering is a member of the Jackson clan. They have the biggest pig farm around here and are also the biggest makers of moonshine. One drink and you're likely to lose your eyesight. Oh and if any of the Jackson men offer to show you their testicles"—she paused, then grinned—"aw hell, say yes, 'cause I promise you won't have seen the like before."

She nodded and left the room, leaving her friends open-mouthed.

Chapter Fifteen

E rin slammed the door of the vet's office and held her hands up in supplication to Cindy. "I know, I know. I'm late, but there wasn't anything I could do."

Cindy raised an unimpressed eyebrow at her boss's apologies. "What took you so long?" she huffed.

"It turned out more complicated. They waited too long to call."

Suddenly she was aware that Erin looked worn out. "You okay?"

Erin shook her head. "Lost both the foal and Rosie. Everything that could have gone wrong went wrong." She'd enough experience not to get upset when she lost a patient, but she'd delivered Rosie herself, and she was finding it tough to take. "I'm just going to go get cleaned up. We need to swing past the house to drop Cooper off, then we'll go. I promise."

Cindy waved her into her office forgetting all about the note on her pad.

***

"Will you stop checking your watch every five minutes." Molly nudged Charlotte with her elbow.

Charlotte managed another surreptitious glance before she reluctantly dropped her hand. It had been going too well. Her mother so far had yet to make an appearance. Unfortunately, the same could also be said of Erin.

The school's playing fields were awash with picnic blankets and parasols while families enjoyed the warm sun. Molly, on the other hand, was not enjoying the sun or the humidity and had doused herself with so much insect repellent that Charlotte was concerned about lighting a match anywhere near her.

"You three remember what I told you?" Charlotte asked as they walked towards the fire pit.

"Don't accept a drink from anyone with white blonde hair," the three chorused.

"Good, 'cause I don't fancy watching you having your stomach pumped."

She waved over to the various generations of Jacksons manning the fire pit and hog roast. Holding a hand to shield her eyes she saw her mother striding towards her and Charlotte swore her heart stopped.

∞ ∞ ∞

"Hey, Erin." Sully waved his hands, beckoning her over. "You two look like you could do with one of these." He held up a cup with iced liquid.

"These better be virgin 'cause she's on call," Cindy said, nodding towards the cups.

"Not a drop of fun juice went near it I promise." Sully dragged his fingers across his chest. "Just pure iced tea courtesy of Alex."

Without turning around, he jerked his head towards where Alex was standing talking to the local Reverend. He leaned in closer as he handed the drink over. "Tell me, is she still talking to Reverend Jones?"

Taking the cup, Erin nodded.

"Good. You can't go anywhere. Just stay here and pretend like we're talking," Sully begged, his blue eyes pleading with Erin.

"Why? What you done now?" Cindy asked.

"It's not me, it's Jess." Sully lowered his voice so only they could hear him. "You know how the two of them never really hit it off."

"What, you mean after she shouted out in church if it was God's house, where'd he keep his TV?" Erin crunched an ice cube between her teeth. "He can't still hold that against her, she was five!"

Sully nodded. "That was the start of it. The nativity plaything didn't help none either."

Erin laughed. "What? She was just showing good ol' southern hospitality by inviting Mary and Joseph into her inn, and offering her own bedroom."

Groaning at the memory, Sully rubbed a hand over his face. "If only it was that simple this time. Now it seems Jess is quizzing him on bible stuff, specifically on homosexuality in the bible. An' she's like a dog with a bone at him all the time." He risked a glance over his shoulder and saw Alex glaring at him. He smiled sheepishly at her and shrugged.

"You are a weak man, Matthew Sullivan." Erin laughed, slapping him on his shoulder.

"Or some may say wise. Anyways Alex is better at dealing with this sort of stuff than I am. Y'all heading over towards the games? They've got Teddy on the dunk tank. At least I think that's what they said." He stopped and screwed his face up. "Hell, with Teddy it coulda been the drunk tank."

Erin shrugged. She wasn't much in the mood after her morning. Even the prospect of soaking Teddy couldn't snap her out of it. "You best go rescue Alex, she wouldn't leave you on your own."

Sully clutched his chest. "Oooo guilt?! Low blow, Hunter." He waved them off and went to save Alex.

Erin made an effort to smile and chat with townsfolk as she walked through the various stalls. She was grateful for the plastic cup of iced tea Sully had thrust in her hand as, when she wasn't being sociable, she sipped merrily on the cold liquid.

"You want to play some games?" Cindy pointed over to where stalls had been set up with fairground games.

"You go on. I'm okay just wandering around." She saw the doubt on Cindy's face. "Honestly, go. I'm probably going to go find Sam and chew his ear off about my bathroom door." She pushed lightly on Cindy's shoulder. "Go. Win me something."

"Only if you're sure," Cindy said, already heading off towards the stalls and not waiting for a reply.

Erin smiled as she watched Cindy skip off. She took another sip of her iced tea then went in search of her brother.

Her route took her close to where the cookout was happening. She was pleased to see ol' man Jackson hadn't reneged on their deal, and the family were busy roasting a hog. It was then that she saw Virginia Grace striding across the grass. Erin snorted, wondering who Virginia had in her sights this time. Relieved it wasn't her, she twisted her head to see who it was she was bearing down on.

Until that moment Erin had never understood the phrase 'time stood still,' but she would swear blind for an instant that is what happened when her eyes locked with Charlotte's. Everything around her was a blur. The noise from the PA announcing the winners of the baking competition and the music from the high school marching band all faded into the background.

Suddenly, the moment was ripped apart by a loud blast. People were screaming and yelling while Erin stood rooted to the spot.

Charlotte's instinct to run the hell away from her mother powering towards her like a steam train fueled by Chanel was overpowering. She'd turned to look for an escape route when her eyes fell upon Erin. All at once she forgot about Virginia barreling in her direction and what had been a search for an escape route became a road to salvation.

She'd just stepped forward when an explosion from the fire pit blew her off her feet.

"Take these an' come with me."

Erin looked down in confusion at the pads being pressed against her chest. Her eyes followed the hands and arms shoving the medical supplies against her until she was looking down into Mack's brown eyes.

"You good?" the small nurse asked, shifting the pack she was carrying on her shoulder. "'Cause I need your help. Hold onto these dressings and put out your hand for me."

Doing what she was told, Erin looked down at the set of tweezers Mack had placed in her palm.

"I need you to come an' help."

Nodding, Erin tightened her grip around the tweezers. "But I'm not a doctor." She looked around and saw various people sitting with cuts, looking equally as stunned as she did.

"I got doctors coming out the wazoo," Mack said as she marched them towards the first aid tent. "There's a doc here from New York who's triaging folks, and Timothy and Maddie are taking the worst hit to the clinic, which seems to be mostly the Jackson clan and Virginia Grace. Though I think she was just hollering 'cause she ended up on her ass. I just need you to do first aid. Help clean cuts and the like. I'm not askin' you to operate." She squeezed Erin's arm. "You're a healer," she said as she swept open the canvas door of the tent.

"I'm a vet!"

Mack nodded. "I know that. Jus' don't stick your hand up anyone's ass." She ignored Erin's scowl as she held open the door and motioned for her to enter. "Not unless they ask you to anyhow."

"Erin?"

Ellie frowned as she cupped Charlotte's face gently. "It's Ellie, Charlotte. Did you hit your head at all when you fell?"

Charlotte shook her head. Apart from feeling a throb at her hairline, she felt okay. "I'm fine honest." She sat up abruptly. "Molly?"

Placing a calming hand on her friend's shoulder, Ellie gently stopped Charlotte from making any more sudden movements until she was sure she was okay. "She's fine. We're all okay," she reassured. "We were far enough back from whatever it was."

She gave Charlotte another quick inspection. "Okay, there's a first aid tent. Head over there, you're going to need that cut seen to. Take Molly with you, she's got some cuts too."

"Where are you going?"

"To see if I can help. Joanne's already in GI Jane mode and triaging."

Charlotte allowed her friend to help her to her feet. "Okay, come find me when you're done."

"Charlotte, you all right?" Molly asked, dabbing a tissue against a cut on her arm.

Nodding, Charlotte guided Molly towards the first aid tent. "I'm good. Let's go get cleaned up."

Thirty minutes passed, and they were still waiting. Much to Molly's chagrin, Charlotte kept allowing people to go in front of them. She knew Molly was starting to lose patience with her hesitation. Finally, Molly had enough. When Charlotte made a move to wave someone in front of them, she grabbed her arm.

"Oh no, no more. We are next."

Charlotte was about to respond when Mack emerged from the tent and gave them a cursory look. Her head recoiled at the sight of Charlotte.

"Well look what the cat dragged in. Welcome home, Charlotte."

A half-hour passed in a rush as Erin focused on cleaning wounds. Although the Jackson's seemed to have taken the brunt of whatever had happened, there were a large number of people who'd sustained wounds embedded with small pieces of glass. She was putting a dressing on the arm of a little girl when she heard Mack's voice.

"Okay, the vet is just finishing up, so you go to her, and I'll take you."

"Vet as in ex-military medic?" A voice she didn't recognize enquired.

She heard Mack snort. "Vet as in animals. If it bothers you, I'll take you. Erin, you got another head wound."

Erin nodded without looking up as she made sure the dressing was secure. "She should be okay. The cut wasn't deep, and I managed to get everything out," Erin said to the girl's mother. "You were very brave, Maisie." She smiled, lifting the girl down off the table.

Standing straight the smile slipped from her face as she found herself looking at Charlotte.

"You gonna help her or just gawk at her?"

Mack's voice snapped Erin back to the task at hand. She hoped she could remain professional enough to get Charlotte patched up and out of the tent so she could have a meltdown in peace. She yanked off her gloves and snatched another pair from the packet.

"Sit down." She indicated with her head as she pulled on the fresh gloves.

Charlotte sat down meekly not taking her eyes from Erin.

As soon as she sat, Erin could see dried blood along her hairline. Swallowing hard she reached out and touched Charlotte. As her fingertips gently brushed auburn hair aside, she hoped the lump in her throat would remain there and not come out in a sob.

"You have some glass in there. Are you going to be okay if I try and get it out?" Erin was thankful her voice was strong and clear, belying the raging torrent of emotions she was feeling.

Charlotte nodded. "I'm not very good with pain."

"I remember."

Using her fingers to hold back Charlotte's hair, Erin inspected the wound further before using the tweezers to remove the tiny fragment of glass. Feeling Charlotte tense up further beneath her, she exhaled softly and pushed aside her own torment to try and get Charlotte to relax as she worked.

"Remember that time when you thought you got bitten by a snake, and you were hopping around begging me to suck on your leg like Tarzan."

Scowling, Charlotte started to fidget in her seat until Erin's hand on her head stilled her.

"It coulda been a snake."

"It was a branch. I have never seen anyone make such a fuss. You were wailing an' hollering you were gonna die."

She snorted. "Yeah what about that time—"

"All done," Erin interrupted, stepping away and stripping her gloves off.

Tossing them into the waiting waste bin, she busied herself tidying dressings. She was determined to hold onto her emotions until Charlotte left the tent. She heard a quiet 'thank you' from Charlotte and the sound of her footsteps retreating from the tent.

Mack glanced up as Erin studiously stacked dressings. "So Charlotte's back."

Erin looked up and nodded. "Looks like it."

∞ ∞ ∞

Charlotte stepped out of the first aid tent. The pain from the cut was nowhere as painful as the ache she felt in her chest. She had tensed from the first contact. Erin's touch was so familiar to her that the emotional turmoil was almost too much to bear. After all these years and the first time, she would feel Erin's hands upon her would be under such clinical circumstances.

For a moment, the years drifted away. Charlotte could have sworn they were teenagers once more, playfully bickering all the while their eyes making promises that would be kept later when they were alone. Then that feeling was gone when Charlotte realized what Erin had been doing. The moment wasn't them slipping effortlessly back into the banter they'd shared before. Erin had merely been trying to distract her while she worked. She reached a hesitant hand up to her head and felt the small dressing covering the wound.

"You okay?"

She turned to see Molly's worried expression.

"I'm okay. Let's go find your sister and Ellie."

Chapter Sixteen

Teddy peeked her head around the edge of the tent. "Someone told me the vet was in here fixing folks so I thought I'd see if I can get vaccinated for foot 'n mouth." She grinned broadly stepping into the tent.

Erin stretched her neck out, wincing as it popped. "Are you the last?"

"Yup an' you'll be pleased to hear there's nothing wrong with me." She scowled at Erin's raised eyebrows. "At least nothing first aid will do for." She stepped aside as Mack entered the tent.

"Claudia Roosevelt, you're dripping all over the place. What in the hell happened to you?"

Teddy slicked her wet hair back and twisted it to rid it of excess water. "The whole damned school is what happened. Mack, you and Harvey ought to think about getting Lewis into Little League. The little shit has got an arm on him."

Mack chuckled. "He's been practicing since the minute he heard you'd be on the dunk tank."

"Good to know. I'll make sure he gets some more homework to take up some of that spare time," Teddy replied with a wicked look.

"You heard what caused it yet?" Erin asked.

"Ol' man Jackson hid bottles of moonshine inside the hog when he saw Harvey. Only the stupid old goat forgot to mention that to his kin. So they put it on the fire pit." Teddy shook her head. "Damned lucky no one was badly hurt. I saw Alex on the way over, and she told me to tell you from Maddie that no one needs to get kept in at the clinic."

Mack nodded and exhaled. "Well, in that case, I'm gonna go enjoy what is left of the celebrations. Erin, thank you for your help. You did good."

Erin nodded and smiled as Mack left. She turned to look at Teddy.

"Did you know?"

Immediately, Teddy knew what Erin was talking about. "I thought I saw her but wasn't sure. Ruth was meant to speak to you, so you weren't blindsided."

Laughing Erin shook her head. "Blindsided? I feel like someone just pulled the world out from under me."

"As someone who has spent the day literally having the seat being pulled out from under her, I don't envy you." Teddy put her arms around Erin for a hug.

Accepting the hug, Erin rested her chin on Teddy's shoulder. "You're wet."

"Aww honey, you have really got to work on your pick up lines." Teddy gripped harder as Erin started to squirm out of her hold.

"There is something wrong with you. You know that, right?" Erin began to giggle as she wrestled with Teddy.

Teddy gripped around her waist and hoisted Erin off the ground. "You only just figuring that out?" She dropped Erin back down and hooked their arms together. "C'mon there's still plenty of day left, and you have friends that want to celebrate with you."

"What about Charlotte?"

"What about her?" Teddy waved. "Let her spend time with her own damn friends."

Erin exhaled as she let Teddy lead her from the tent and back towards the main body of the celebrations. "Thank you."

"Don't mention it. Let's go get some fun juice from Sully. I reckon he owes me for telling everyone I was in the drunk tank." She tightened her hold on Erin's arm. "I don't mind when it's true, but that hasn't happened for weeks now!"

∞ ∞ ∞

"Honestly, what kind of place is this?" Molly shook her head as she dropped into an empty seat on the porch. "We get woken up by a man playing bagpipes, it's hotter than Hades, and then a pig explodes and almost kills us!"

She rested her head on the back of the Adirondack chair and listened to the sound of music from the evening festivities.

Joanne sucked on her straw. "Well, it ain't Vegas that's for sure"—She looked pointedly at her sister—"and whose fault is it that we're here?"

Ellie sighed. She was forever in the role of peacekeeper between the two siblings. "Technically it wasn't the pig that exploded, it was the moonshine. The pig was an innocent victim in all of this." She grinned as Joanne snorted with laughter. "Besides, we thought we were doing the right thing bringing her here."

Molly raised her eyebrows. "Yeah well if the pig didn't leave scorch marks on Charlotte, then the burn she got from the vet definitely did."

97

"Was it that bad?" Joanne asked.

Molly shrugged as she looked around to see whether Charlotte had returned to the house. "She not back yet?"

"Nope." Ellie snuggled closer into Joanne's side as they sat swaying on the porch swing.

Molly sat up and leaned closer. "You ever watch a film and have the hairs on your neck stand up 'cause you can almost see the sparks flying off a couple?"

Joanne nodded. "I sometimes get this tingle at the base of my spine when I see a couple I've rooted for finally kiss."

"Awww, you big softy," Ellie crooned, planting soft kisses against her fiancée's neck.

"Well if you'd seen them together your spine would have been tingling like...like a thing that tingles...a lot. I swear there was more fire between them than the exploding hog." Molly sat back. "I've never seen Charlotte like that before. She couldn't take her eyes off her. I could have bled out, and she would still have been giving the vet googly eyes. So where'd she go anyway?"

Ellie shrugged. "She just said she needed some air and was going for a walk."

Charlotte ignored the pain as the wire fence dug into her hands. She was grateful when she reached the top and was able to swing her leg over. There was a moment, when the fence wobbled that she considered this idea wasn't perhaps her best. Steeling herself, she twisted and brought her other leg over and started a steady descent until she reached a height she could jump down from. She landed and grimaced as pain shot through her knee. Limping she wound her way around the stacked logs and walked into the lumberyard.

The lingering smell of cut wood permeated the yard regardless of the time of day or year and brought back so many memories. She could literally feel her shoulders slump under the weight of them.

The sound of a shotgun cocking brought her rapidly out of the past.

"It's loaded so don't be planning on doing anything stupid." A voice said from behind her.

A slow smile spread across her face as she raised her hands in the air. "Chip Martin, you and I both know you're as likely to shoot yourself with that thing as shoot me."

She turned slowly. Despite the darkness, she could just make out the barrel of a twelve-gauge shotgun. "You'd struggle to hit a cow's ass with a banjo even if you were standing right behind it."

"Charlotte?" Chip asked, pointing the barrel of the gun to the ground and peering into the darkness. "Is that you?"

Charlotte lowered her hands. "In the flesh. Now put the safety back on that thing so I can come give you a hug." She could hear Chip chuckle as he stepped forward into what light the moon afforded them.

"Ain't loaded. Harvey Mack would have my ass in a sling if I was carrying a loaded gun." Chip grinned, displaying his haphazard teeth. "Well look at you all growed up."

Feeling like she was eight-years-old again, Charlotte ran and practically bowled the old man over in her exuberance.

"Well, that's what I call a welcome." Chip gripped Charlotte by the shoulders and held her at arm's-length. "Let me have a good look at you now."

He appraised her with narrowed eyes. "You could do with putting some weight on, but you've grown up into a fine young woman. Your daddy would have been proud of you."

At the mention of her father Charlotte bit her lip.

"Oh now, don't you start bawling, you'll have me blubbering with you." Chip pulled her into a hug. "I got some iced tea in the office. Why don't we go visit for a bit?"

As they walked through the yard, Charlotte noted some obvious changes had occurred since the last time she'd been there. New buildings had sprung up as the business expanded and larger modern units replaced the woodsheds she'd known as a child.

"Looks different huh?" Chip remarked as he stopped outside a log cabin. He fished a set of keys from his pocket. The chain that clipped them to his belt loop rattled as he selected the correct one and placed it into the lock.

"It does. Looks good." Charlotte took one last look around the yard before stepping into the cabin where the light would destroy her night vision.

"Looks can be deceiving."

Charlotte watched as Chip stored his gun back on a rack and busied himself with collecting cups and a jug of iced tea from the small fridge in the office. He was quiet as he poured two glasses and it afforded Charlotte the opportunity to study the man who, when she was a child, would happily take her around the yard explaining the machinery and processes when her father had work to do.

Chip had been the one who had guided her when she cut down her first tree, had taught her to drive the various vehicles used in the yard and more times than not wiped her tears after another run-in with her mother. Much to Charlotte's absolute delight, save for a few extra lines around his eyes and a few less teeth in his mouth, Chip looked the same as the day she left Grace Falls.

"So how come the yard foreman is out patrolling with a shotgun instead of enjoying the town's birthday party?"

Scrubbing at his neck, Chip shrugged. "Been a lot of petty thefts lately. Thought tonight might be too much of an opportunity for someone."

Charlotte frowned as she accepted the proffered glass. "That doesn't sound like the yard I remember. This is a new thing?"

Chip sat down and placed his feet on the desk. "Lot's changed around here."

"How's it been since Daddy's passing?"

She watched as Chip took a long sip of his drink.

"Been okay. Your mama hired a man in from Canada to run things."

His response didn't fool Charlotte for a second. She stood up and walked to the window. Placing a finger on the blinds, she created a gap she could see through. Despite the darkness, she was just able to make out stacks of timber across the yard.

"Seems he does things different than Daddy. Can't help but notice you're carrying a lot of stock in the yard."

Chip laughed. "You haven't changed one iota. Always the sharp one." He stood up and walked over to where Charlotte stood and whispered, "I shouldn't be telling you this. Men have been fired for less here lately." He ignored Charlotte's gasp and continued. "We got shipping problems. We're down to one rig at the moment."

"How many you normally got?"

"Four. Without them, we're struggling to get orders to customers on time."

"What's wrong with them?"

Raising his shoulders, Chip spun around and rested wearily against the wall of the office. It was evident making even this small an admission took its toll on him.

"They're with Peter Campbell. They failed inspection and need work done but he won't do it, and he's impounded them."

Charlotte's mouth fell open in surprise. "There has to be a reason. Unless he's changed, Peter Campbell is the easiest going guy."

"Still is." Chip looked like he was about to say more before he stopped himself. "Don't you worry none. I'm sure it'll all blow over like water over the falls."

Knowing the conversation was over Charlotte returned to her seat. "So how's Annie doing?"

Chip grinned at the mention of his wife. "Still my favorite pain in the ass."

∞ ∞ ∞

100

"Come on in. Door's open, Sam," Erin yelled in response to the knock at the door. Running one hand through her hair, she opened the fridge to claim a beer. As she popped the top off, she braced herself for her brother's inquisition. Bumping the kitchen door open with her backside, she spun into the room eager to lay the ground rules for the conversation she was about to have.

"I've had a really shitty day so I'd rather you didn't give me a hard time about..."

"Hi."

The last person she expected to see in her living room was currently kneeling down making friends with her traitorous dog. Cooper's disloyalty rose to a whole new level when he licked Charlotte's face in appreciation of her attention.

Charlotte stood up and pointed back towards the door. "I knocked."

Erin was frozen to the spot unable to move, speak, swallow or even breathe. Seeing Charlotte again so quickly and this time in her home had created an infinite loop within her head which she seemed unable to stop. Cooper flopped down onto his back at Charlotte's feet in an attempt to encourage further bonding. His continued betrayal snapped her out of her trance. "Cooper. Bed. Now. You are the worst guard dog in the world."

"Maybe he senses I'm not here to cause trouble."

Not willing to go down that route, Erin steered the conversation onto safer grounds. "How's the head?"

A tentative smile crossed Charlotte's lips as she placed her fingertips on the dressing covering her wound. "I'll live."

"How'd you know where I live?"

"I'm staying at Ruth's mama's place. I saw you out front when we drove by yesterday."

Erin's head lolled forward, she closed her eyes and nodded. "In the towel?" She could hear the smile in Charlotte's response.

"Yup, in the towel."

Still shaking her head, she sighed loudly. "And I thought today couldn't get any crappier."

Charlotte swallowed hard. "I'm sorry to just barge in. I thought maybe we should talk?"

"Erin, do you know your door is wide open?" Sam asked as he entered the room, stopping abruptly when he saw who his sister was with. "Awww hell no." He held open the door. "You don't get to come back as if nothing happened. Get out."

Throwing a pleading look in Erin's direction Charlotte barely managed to croak. "Erin?"

Chewing on her bottom lip, Erin shook her head quickly not raising her eyes from a spot on the floor. "I think you should go."

"I never..." Charlotte started and moved forward towards Erin. However, a movement from Sam stopped her from continuing. "I'm sorry for bothering you."

Erin watched her leave. The click of the door was louder than she ever remembered it being. She felt Sam gently take his beer from her grip and steer her towards her sofa.

"You okay?"

"Can we not talk?"

"Sure, we can do that." Sam sat down beside her and took her into his arms.

It was some time before Erin sat back up and using the heel of her hand rubbed her eyes. "Sam."

"Wha—?" Sitting up abruptly from his slouched position, Sam wiped his mouth.

"It's two a.m. I need to go to bed," Erin said stretching her arms above her head.

"I'm just gonna stay here." Sam pushed Erin off the sofa so he could lay down.

"Okay, see you later." Erin planted a kiss on her brother's forehead. "And maybe in the morning, you can tell me where the hell all my door handles are."

Snuggling down into the sofa Sam grumbled an inaudible reply.

Switching the lights off in the room, Erin looked over to where Charlotte had stood earlier. To her disgust, her mind was able to conjure up the image of Charlotte in her living room effortlessly. When she said 'goodnight' she wasn't sure whether she was speaking to the vision of Charlotte or her brother.

Chapter Seventeen

harlotte turned the heat down on the stove. She chewed on her lip, trying to rid herself of any lingering effects from the previous night. She wasn't convinced her trip to Grace Falls hadn't resulted in drowning her in new emotional issues rather than resolving old ones.

Before she'd left Erin's home, she'd allowed herself one final look. Erin's blonde hair was sticking up as if she'd just run a hand through it. Clad in only a tank-top and shorts, her limbs looked toned. It was a new memory to replace the one of Erin crying and begging her to be honest. However, Charlotte wasn't sure the new version would provide any comfort.

"Why are your bags in the hall?" Molly lumbered into the kitchen yawning.

"Because as soon as we've all had breakfast, we're leaving." Charlotte served eggs onto a plate and held it out to her friend.

As she took the plate, Molly gripped her friend's arm. "I'm sorry I made you come. I thought I was helping."

Charlotte smiled. "It's okay. It did help. It relieved me of any thoughts I might have been harboring that this is home." Seeing a look of dejection on Molly's face, Charlotte smiled. "That's a good thing. Honestly."

"Do you want to see your mom before we go?"

"Hell no."

"Hell no, what?" Joanne asked as she entered the room with Ellie.

"You saved me coming up to drag your asses down here." Charlotte grinned, holding out plates for them both. "Hell no, I'm not going to see my mother. What I want to do is have breakfast and get out of town."

Ellie took both plates and handed one to Joanne. "I met your mom yesterday when I was triaging. She asked whether I spoke English, despite the fact I was speaking it to her, and she also asked whether I was here legally."

Charlotte groaned. "I'm so sorry."

Waving her fork in the air, Ellie dismissed the apology. "Wasn't you who said it. Although I will admit, I was ready to drop her back on her ass."

"Well as quick as we can get squared away, we're out of here and going home."
Charlotte slapped eggs onto her own plate. "Can't happen quick enough."

∞ ∞ ∞

Erin woke up to the smell of fresh paint wafting into her bedroom. She stretched
lazily before grabbing a hoodie and going to investigate.

"You're up early?" She nudged her brother's ass with her toe as he sat painting
her baseboards.

Sam pulled the earbuds of his headphones from his ears, the tinny sound of what
sounded like the Spice Girls was still audible as he fumbled to stop it. "Thought I'd
get this finished for you. That way I can put the handles back on the doors, and you
don't have to go climbing naked and flashing your cooch to the whole town."

Erin cuffed the back of his head. "It was Teddy, not the whole town."

He carefully balanced the paintbrush on the tin and stretched his back, wincing
at the cracking sound. "You okay this morning?"

"Yeah, I'm fine. Was a weird ol' day but I survived. You eaten?"

Sam shook his head. "Nope. Was kinda hoping you'd offer to make something."

"Figures. Gimme ten minutes."

Restarting his music and placing his headphones back in, Sam started to whistle
off-key while he painted.

True to her word, ten minutes later the aroma of pancakes overshadowed the
smell of paint and Sam set his brush down. He grinned as he entered the kitchen as
Erin attempted to cook breakfast without tripping over Cooper, who was making a
nuisance of himself getting under her feet.

"Cooper, buddy. You're gonna want to get out of the way before she blows up at
you." Sam gripped the dog by the collar and dragged him out of harm's way.

"Thank you."

"No problem. Don't want my breakfast decorating the dog," Sam said as a stack
of pancakes were set down on the table. "These just mine, or for both of us?"

Erin sighed. "Both of us. So don't be eating them all before I've even sat on my
ass."

Sam slathered maple syrup over his share of the pancakes. "So you're sure you're
okay after last night? It's not every night Charlotte Grace shows up in your living
room. I can't believe you let her in the door."

"I didn't. I thought it was you and yelled 'come in' so she did." Erin snatched the
maple syrup from her brother before he used it up. "I'm fine. It was what it was. I

104

saw her yesterday at the cookout. She got hurt in the moonshine blast. I fixed her up and then she showed up here wanting to talk."

Finishing a mouthful, Sam took a slurp of orange juice. "Did you want to hear what she had to say?"

"No. Yes. Maybe...oh, I don't know." Erin sighed.

"Would it change how you felt or feel about her?"

"Not sure, but maybe it would change how I feel about myself."

∞ ∞ ∞

Charlotte knocked on the screen door of Ruth and Peter's home. She turned her back to the door and looked towards the rental car with her friends in it. When she heard the door open, she turned back and smiled at the sight of Ruth carrying her son Ben. "Oh, he is just gorgeous."

"Yeah, when he's asleep. Other times I swear he is the spawn of Satan. You wanna come in?" Ruth indicated with her head, stepping aside.

Giving another quick glance to the car, Charlotte held up five fingers and entered the house. "I wanted to return the keys to your mama's place."

"You going already?"

"Yeah. It's not exactly been the return of the prodigal daughter."

Ruth laughed. "Oh, I don't know. We beat them hands down. They only slaughtered cows. We blew up a hog for you."

Joining her laughter, Charlotte held out her hand to Ben, and her smile grew as he gripped her finger tightly. "Can't argue with that, can we, Ben." Her smile faded slightly as she returned her attention to Ruth. "Was anyone badly hurt?"

"Not that I've heard," Ruth said, leading her further into the house. "You want a coffee? We've just brewed some."

"No, I'm good. I should get going."

"You going already?" Peter asked as he entered the room, took his son from his wife and held him above his head. "You only just got here."

"Yeah well," Charlotte replied. "I got things to do back home." She hugged Ruth tightly then handed the keys over. "Thank you for everything."

"Don't be a stranger, Charlotte. There's still folks here that care 'bout you."

"I won't."

She was almost at the door when she spun back around. "Peter, how come you've got Grace trucks impounded?"

105

Peter glanced quickly at his wife, who shrugged in response. "They failed inspection. I got the parts, but until they pay me for the work I did last time, I'm not fixing them."

"How much do they owe you?"

Running a hand through his dark curls, Peter looked embarrassed. "Almost five thousand."

Charlotte whistled at the figure. "How the hell did they let that happen?"

Peter shrugged but was saved any response as Ruth stepped in. "Charlotte that's just the tip—"

"Ruth," Peter cautioned. He looked at Charlotte. "All I know is they owe me, and I'm not doing any more work until I'm paid."

Charlotte held up a finger. "Two seconds."

She opened the door, jumped down the steps leading up to the porch and sprinted to the car.

Ruth and Peter watched as she spoke with her friends and then went to the trunk. After a couple minutes of rummaging around, she closed the tailgate and ran back up the steps.

"Here." She held out a wad of cash. "There's two thousand there. I'll transfer the rest, and you can invoice me the cost of fixing those three trucks." She waved the money as Peter seemed reluctant to take it. "Whatever has happened between me and my folks, that business was my daddy's pride and joy. Plus, I don't want you out of pocket or them having to lay people off."

Peter placed a warning hand on his wife's shoulder to stop her speaking. "Thank you, Charlotte."

"Ruth has my contact details, so just let me know where to send the money."

"We will," Peter said, taking the cash.

Satisfied, Charlotte grinned. "Excellent. Thank you again for letting us use your mama's home. It was lovely to stay there and still feel her presence."

Ruth took her grumbling son back from her husband. "And that'll be the reason no one will buy the damn thing."

Charlotte reached out and ruffled Ben's soft hair. "Well I always liked your mama, but when it comes to mama's, maybe I'm not the best judge." She looked down towards the rental car; despite her initial haste, she was now reluctant to leave. "I should go. Take care."

∞ ∞ ∞

Ruth pulled the laundry out of her mother's ancient dryer. She was grateful that Charlotte and her friends had thoughtfully stripped the beds and placed them in the washer. She paused as she heard a thud.

"You know, Mama you really have to let go. Go fly. Be free. Go towards the light. You always liked Florida. Can't you haunt there or something? 'Cause I'd really like to sell this house." She balanced the laundry basket onto her hip and climbed up the ancient basement steps to return to the kitchen, continuing to berate her late mother the entire way. "An' people talking about feeling your presence here is not helping me sell."

She used her backside to open the stubborn door the kitchen. Entering the room, she screamed and dropped the laundry basket she was carrying.

Erin spun around, her screams mixing with Ruth's as they both stared at each other, frozen to the spot.

"What the hell, Erin!" Ruth yelled.

"You scared the crap out of me," Erin yelled in return.

"You scared the crap out of me!" Ruth shot back, bending over to recover the laundry. "What the hell are you doing sneaking around my mama's kitchen?"

Erin took a deep breath. "I wasn't sneaking. I was looking for Charlotte."

Ruth could see the apprehension almost cascade off Erin in waves. "She left early this morning."

"Of course she did."

Dumping the pile of bedding onto the table, Ruth fished out her phone. "I have an email address for—"

"No, it's okay. It wasn't important."

Ignoring her, Ruth copied Charlotte's email address onto a text message and sent it to Erin. "If it was important enough to drag your butt around here at the ass crack of dawn, it'll probably warrant an email."

Ruth pushed a chair out from the table, and as she took a seat, she started to talk quietly. "When Bear died it affected us all in different ways."

Erin sat down slowly.

"Alex cried a lot, which you'd expect since he was her brother." Ruth played absently with a loose thread on one of the sheets as she remembered the death of their friend. "Then just before the funeral, she stopped. She didn't cry at all during the service. Teddy didn't really speak for months, and every time we mentioned Bear's name she just looked so devastated we stopped talking about him. Sully, well he stopped having sex." She laughed at Erin's widened eyes. "I know!

"Peter just wouldn't talk about it at all. He flung himself into work. His dad was sick at the time, so it was easy for him to hide his face in engines all day, and then there was me." She exhaled a long breath. "I held my friends a little longer during hugs. I took a little longer to get pissed at them, and I damn well made sure they knew how much I loved them."

She sat back in the chair and tipped her head to the side. "I know you and Charlotte were real close when we were growing up, I don't know what happened to change that, but I do know losing a friend is just about the shittiest thing that can happen. If Bear walked into this room today, I would hold him and never let him go.

"So whatever happened between you two, maybe it's time to leave it in the past. I know it's possible. Jeez, Teddy and you barely spoke since your teens"—she held up a hand to stop Erin from interrupting—"and I know all of that was Teddy being an ass. She can be a pigheaded sonofa sometimes. But look at you two now. Plus, I don't think you'd be here if you didn't want to fix it."

Erin looked at her thoughtfully before finally sighing. "Thank you."

Patting her arm Ruth grinned. "No problem. Now can I ask you a question?"

Erin seemed to brace herself against whatever Ruth was about to ask, but whatever she was worried about didn't stop her from nodding in reply.

Ruth leaned forward and stared intently into Erin's eyes. "Can you feel my mama's presence in this house?"

Chapter Eighteen

Charlotte's feet pounded on the gravel track. The sun glistened off the reservoir as she did her third lap around the well-trodden path. She looked up as she ran, catching glimpses of the sun through the leaves. It had been four days since their abrupt exit from Grace Falls, and in those four days, Charlotte had yet to settle back into the city she'd called home for the majority of her adult life.

Suddenly there were too many people. The traffic was too noisy. The smells too overpowering. Only when she was in this man-made oasis within the city would Charlotte's heart stop aching. Surrounded by trees and nature, she found a semblance of peace.

The rhythmic beat of her stride provided a hypnotic cadence allowing her mind to wander from its current physical location back to Grace Falls.

Today's catalyst was an email from Peter. Her thoughts had returned to her hometown again. Yet were she, to be honest with herself she would acknowledge that the receipt for the truck repairs was only a convenient scapegoat. Her mind had never been far from the town, or Erin.

She stopped running and placed her hands on a tree to help her balance as she stretched out her calf muscle. Soon her stretching was forgotten as her hands caressed the bark of the tree. Its roughness against her fingertips comforted her. Spurred on by a thought she refused to acknowledge, she found herself running again. This time, instead of completing her lap, she was running through the park.

Dodging past tourists, she reached the exit on 59th Street. Making her way towards Midtown, her pace only slowed when she reached the crosswalks at the end of each block.

∞ ∞ ∞

Molly saved the document she was working on and took a sip of her coffee, wincing at the coldness of the liquid. Making her way towards the small kitchen that served her floor, she was stunned to see a sweaty Charlotte pleading with the receptionist.

"Charlotte?"

Charlotte spun around and grinned. "Ah, thank God. Do you have a minute?"

Ignoring the look of disgust on the receptionist's face, Molly motioned for Charlotte to follow her. "'Course, c'mon through. I was going for coffee. Can I get you anything? Water? Respirator?"

Shaking her head, Charlotte walked beside her. "Water for now. Respirator for later."

Molly dug a bottle of water out of the fridge and handed it to her friend, then poured herself a fresh cup of coffee. "Should I be worried that you've obviously run here?"

"I just needed to speak to you."

"You know there's this amazing thing called a phone you could have used." Seeing a scowl form on Charlotte's face, Molly let it drop. "Let's go back to my office, and we can talk."

"So what's so important that you needed to forgo modern technology?" Molly held the door of her office open for Charlotte to enter.

Before Charlotte got a chance to respond, or sit down, Molly gripped the waistband of her shorts.

"Hang on there, sweaty woman. I'm going to get something for you to sit on. Otherwise I'm going to be looking at your ass print all day." She opened a drawer and pulled out her under-utilized gym bag. Locating a fresh towel in it, she threw it to Charlotte. "Use that."

Scowling, Charlotte caught the towel and tossed it onto the seat before flopping down, immediately correcting her posture when she caught Molly glaring at her. She sat perched on the seat and waited for Molly to sit down before she spoke. "I have a business I want you to look into."

"For shits and giggles, or 'cause you wanna buy it?"

Charlotte opened her mouth to answer but stopped. She swallowed before responding. "You want the honest answer? I don't know."

Molly nodded thoughtfully. She picked up her pen and looked expectantly at Charlotte. "Okay, so what's the lucky company called?"

"Grace Timber."

With her pen poised in mid-air, Molly's mouth gaped open. "Grace Timber? You sure?"

Nodding Charlotte took a quick swig of water. "I think things are bad. I want to know how bad."

"Oookay, I'm going to ask you again. Are you thinking of buying?"

Charlotte sucked air through her teeth. "In the interests of the exercise let's presume yes. Do everything you would do if I wanted to buy it. I want to know every detail you can get."

"Is it even for sale?"

Laughing, Charlotte shook her head. "It's my mother's company now. I reckon the right offer would work. Provided she doesn't know it's from me."

Molly set her pen down. "I'll get right on it. Tell me what you know about it."

"What I know is twenty years out of date. I'm only interested in the five thousand acres of hardwood and pine. The other land owned by the family I don't care about."

"How much more than five thousand acres can they own?"

Charlotte shifted in her seat as if uncomfortable to answer the question. "The town. They own the land the town is built on and probably a good portion of the buildings too."

Molly let out a low whistle. "Okay, so what else?"

"We'll need the logging and mineral rights. The lumberyard and everything that goes with it; buildings, inventory, machinery, contracts. I'm not sure what their product base is these days. There were a whole lot of new buildings and machinery I'm not familiar with."

Quickly scribbling the list, Molly looked up when Charlotte paused. "That it?"

"The lodges. There're hunting lodges. I don't know how many now, but I want them and the hunting rights."

"You want?" Molly grinned at the look of determination on her friend's face.

Charlotte nodded once. "I want."

Charlotte was barely five blocks away when she felt her phone vibrate. She pulled it from the zipped pocket at the back of her shorts. Fully expecting it to be from Molly, she held her breath as she opened her email. The loud expulsion of air when she saw Erin's name in her inbox made other pedestrians turn to look in her direction. With trembling fingers, she selected the email. A broad smile took over her face as she read the two words in the email.

'I'm listening.'

Quickly dialing Molly's number, Charlotte felt her legs tremble beneath her. Her gait felt light as if gravity no longer applied to her and nothing was tethering her to the world. She growled as the call switched to Molly's voicemail.

"Moll, you're going to have to email or call my cell with that information when you get it. There's somewhere I need to be."

Hanging up the call and ignoring the incredulous looks of those around her, Charlotte skipped an entire block, before opting to run as fast as her legs would take her back to her apartment. She'd things to arrange and no time to waste.

Chapter Nineteen

"Why am I wearing these boots?" Erin winced as she inspected her feet, unsure whether her toes were even still alive.

Teddy huffed as she rifled through the assortment of clothing Erin had brought with her. "Because, as I've explained countless times, those boots have a one hundred percent record. They are a force of inexplicable power. The wearer of these boots never fails to score when wearing them, and since tonight the entire town is giving up the bar so you can get your gay on, you can't let them down by not at least getting a little action."

Erin stood up and started to walk up and down Teddy's bedroom. "They're chaffing my heels," she complained.

"Hang on, I've got blister pads somewhere."

Watching Teddy disappear, Erin continued to pace back and forth in an attempt to break in the boots, which were a size too small, and to burn off the excess energy that had had her on edge ever since she'd sent Charlotte an email that morning.

"Here." Teddy threw a pack in her direction before continuing her inspection of Erin's clothes.

Erin had just enough reaction time to catch them. "Thanks a..." She halted as she looked at the pack in more detail. "These are panty liners!"

Teddy looked up from her task. "I can't find the blister pads, so I improvised."

"Seriously! Teddy, you're killing me. If, and it's a really big if, I manage to meet someone I like and things get a little sexy, how quickly do you think it will take for the mood to disappear when she spots panty liners on my feet?" Erin shook the packet as she spoke.

Teddy held a top up and looked thoughtfully at Erin before shaking her head and returning it to the pile. "Let's be honest here. We both know you're not going to get to the boot removing stage with anyone tonight. You'll be fine."

"Never take up motivational speaking." Erin huffed as she sat down on the bed and attempted to remove the boots.

Teddy watched her struggle for a moment before sighing and getting up to help her. "I wasn't doubting your abilities. I'm just saying you're not that kind of girl."

Erin grimaced as Teddy gripped the boot and tried to wrestle it from her aching foot. "Hey, I've been a whore before." She stopped as Teddy snorted. "Okay, maybe that's not something to be proud about. I'm just saying how can I be confident when I know I've got a feminine hygiene product on my feet."

Staggering backward as the boot gave up its hold of Erin, Teddy blew out her cheeks. "Okay, you have a point. We'll nix the boots, but you can't wear anything you brought over. I'll loan you something."

Despite sensing she'd been played somehow, Erin reluctantly agreed. She regretted it almost instantly when Teddy clapped her hands together and set out to find something inappropriate for her to wear, leaving her to struggle with the remaining boot.

∞ ∞ ∞

Erin didn't know whether to be relieved or shocked that the bar was full. There was barely a seat to be had. Women were dancing to the music from the jukebox, the area around the pool table was crowded, and if Sully's shit-eating grin was any indication, the bar was doing well.

"So you were saying you were looking for a bit more adventure?"

Smiling at the woman that had been chatting with her, Erin took a long sip of the drink she'd been bought. "I guess I've been leading a quiet life for a time. Maybe it's time for a change."

The woman shot Erin a sultry look while she ran teasing fingertips up her arm. "Maybe that's something I can help with?"

Gulping, Erin took a moment to compose herself. "What did you have in mind?"

"Well, I like to entertain—"

"Alright, I've heard enough!"

Erin turned and glared at Teddy, who was sitting behind her at the bar. "What are you doing here?" she said through gritted teeth.

"Saving your ass," Teddy hissed back. Jerking her head at Erin's companion, she raised her voice so those around them could hear. "I'm guessing you're here trawling for some poor sucker to help you put on a show for your husband. Well, it ain't happening. So take your indecent proposal act somewhere else."

The woman scowled at Teddy, grabbed her purse and giving the bar one final scan, flounced out.

"You're welcome." Teddy reached over to swipe Erin's drink.

"The agreement was you chose the outfit. That was it. I don't need your help."

"Yeah? Well, your twenty-minute flirt with the tramp with the wedding ring mark says otherwise. You need a wingman."

"I don't need a wingman," Erin replied as she reclaimed her drink.

Teddy pouted as she waved towards Sully for a drink. "I was Alex's wingman for years."

"Yeah? And how many relationships did you help her with?" Erin looked over to where Alex sat with Maddie, both of them lost in each other.

Scratching her head, Teddy screwed up her face. "I prefer not to be performance orientated and would rather focus on the experiential aspect of my assistance."

"So none. Teddy, you need to butt the hell out."

"Hey, can I buy either of you gorgeous ladies a drink?"

Both Erin and Teddy turned towards the voice.

A young woman sat on a stool beside them with a cocky grin on her face. The sleeves of her Ramones T-shirt were rolled up with the outline of a cigarette pack visible beneath one.

"I'm gonna bet that T-shirt is at least twenty years older than you. Have you even gone through puberty?" Teddy asked.

"You're feisty, I like you." The woman was seemingly unperturbed by Teddy's remark. "So, can I buy you a drink?"

"I don't know? Are you legally allowed to be in a bar?" Teddy shot back.

Erin kicked out a leg, catching Teddy's shin. "Thank you, but we're both okay."

"Oh." The woman's head moved back and forth as she looked between the two friends. "I'm sorry I didn't realize you were a couple."

"We're not!" Erin's pitch went up a couple of notches as she replied.

"Hey." Teddy slapped her arm. "There is no need to sound so horrified. You would be lucky to be with me. You'd definitely be punching above your weight."

"I will punch—"

"So if you're not together..." The stranger interrupted Erin's threat to Teddy.

Turning back towards the younger woman Erin immediately realized her mistake. The persistent woman had a cocky grin on her face obviously thinking she still had a chance. Sensing that Teddy was about to speak, she turned to let her know her help wouldn't be required.

"So my name's Yolo. You know like 'You Only Live Once.'"

A false smile froze into place on Erin's face as she swiveled back to face Yolo. "Ooookay."

"I know you don't need a drink, but I was thinking maybe you'd agree to a dance, 'cause turning me down twice would just be plain mean."

Erin could almost hear the grin that she was sure was on Teddy's face. "One dance and then you'll go speak to someone else?"

Yolo's cocky smile dropped from her face to be replaced by a look of surprise. "You'll really dance with me?"

"One dance." Erin held up a finger. She stood up and bit back a sigh when Yolo slid off her stool. She realized their height difference meant Yolo's eye line was directly at the level of her breasts. She'd a feeling she was going to regret her decision.

As they approached the dance area the music slowed. The fast-paced beat was replaced by a slow one, and Erin's apprehension increased. She'd barely any time to relax before Yolo had a limpet-like grip around her waist and her head resting against her chest.

"So Yolo? Is that your real name?" Erin placed her arms on Yolo's shoulders and attempted to relax in the tight hold.

Yolo looked up reluctantly. "Yvonne Lowell."

Erin smiled genuinely at her dance partner. "My name is Erin. I'm gonna call you Yvonne from now on. Pleased to meet you, Yvonne."

Yolo sniffed and lowered her head.

"You know, Yvonne I'm going to give you some advice." Erin tried to lead their dancing so that it involved less pelvic movement. "I'm probably not your demographic."

"You're hot. That's my demographic." Yolo pulled away so she could look up at Erin and give her a cheeky wink.

"While that's kinda sweet... I guess. I'm not sure you really believe that." Erin stopped their uncoordinated swaying. "I'm getting the impression you're putting on a bit of an act here."

Yolo's eyes widened. "It's like you see the real me."

A panicked look passed across Erin's face as she feared her well-intentioned advice may have made matters worse. "I'm not the one for you, Yvonne. But I truly think when you meet the right woman, you won't feel like you have to put an act on"— Erin smiled sadly—"and when you do, make sure you don't let that woman go."

Yolo looked as though she was going to reply when a voice interrupted them.

"Mind if I cut in?"

A tingle started at the base of Erin's spine.

Yolo looked towards the interloper and nodded. "Sure, there's more than enough of me to go around."

Without turning around, Erin released Yolo. "I think she means me."

Yolo cocked an eyebrow in query. When she received a nod in response, she stepped away holding her hands up in surrender. "S'all cool."

116

Gulping, Erin finally turned around to face a smiling Charlotte. "You did mean me right?"

Charlotte's smile widened. "Yeah, I meant you."

She stepped forward and pulled Erin closer to her.

"You got my email then?" Erin queried, pulling back as a thought occurred to her. "Wait. Where were you when you got my email?"

"I was close."

Every ounce of tension left Erin's body as she pressed against Charlotte. It was as if time hadn't happened and she was seventeen again. They fitted snugly together just as they always had.

Her eyes closed and she bit hard on her lip to stop the sensation of being held by Charlotte from erasing everything still between them. She swallowed hard to summon up the courage to speak. Her voice was hoarse when she finally managed to get the words out. "So, I'm listening."

"I thought maybe we could discuss it somewhere a little less public?"

Erin looked around, registering the still full bar around them, she shook her head and exhaled softly. "Good plan." She could feel the warmth on her cheeks as she withdrew from Charlotte's embrace. "Tomorrow night, my place at seven? That is if you'll still be around?"

Charlotte nodded. "I'll still be around."

"Alright then." Erin moved to get around Charlotte. She paused when they were shoulder to shoulder. "Thank you for the dance."

She left before Charlotte could respond.

Maddie and Alex watched the exchange from their table. As Erin strode past them, Alex caught Teddy's eye at the bar. Maddie watched as Teddy grabbed her drink and came across to stand beside their table.

"You see that?" Teddy asked. "There was no *calmouflage* during that conversation."

"Don't do it!" Alex barely rushed the words out before Maddie spoke.

"Did you say camouflage?"

With a triumphant grin on her face, Teddy scrunched her nose in Alex's direction, before turning to Maddie to explain. "Not like hunters wear. *Calmouflage* is when you give off that calm, chilled vibe when really the world is turning to crap

117

around you, or you want to rip someone's face off Hannibal Lecter style. I invented it."

Maddie looked towards her girlfriend. "You're right. I shouldn't have asked. Anyway, it looks like they've got a lot of stuff to work out." Maddie glanced over to where Charlotte was making her way off the dance floor. She turned in time to see the look exchanged between Alex and Teddy. "Oh no! You two are not getting involved."

"Of course not." Alex placed a kiss on Maddie's cheek, before standing up and hooking her arm through Teddy's. Ignoring Maddie's complaints, she directed Teddy towards the bar and out of Maddie's earshot.

"I'm serious!" Maddie frowned as Alex responded with a backward wave. "Might as well be talking to myself." She closed her eyes and shook her head. She opened her eyes just as a young woman in a Ramones T-shirt spun one of the seats from their table around and started to sit down beside her.

"Hell no." Maddie shook her head and waved her hand. "I have underwear older than you."

∞ ∞ ∞

"One skinny Americano with an extra shot." Alex placed a silver travel mug down in front of her girlfriend.

Maddie reached out and wrapped her fingers gently around Alex's wrist. "I think you'll find I'm in the exclusive customer program that gets me extras."

Alex grinned as Maddie pulled her closer. "Really? And what extras does the program entitle you to?"

"Oh, you know just the usual, free coffee, discount on food, and sex. Yeah, the sex bit is where your customer satisfaction scores are really showing a spike." She placed her hand behind Alex's neck and pulled her towards her until they were millimeters apart. Her pulse sped up. It had been just over a year since they got together, yet even the anticipation of kissing Alex was enough to set Maddie's heart racing.

"Yeah, well you're just gonna have to park that request since we both have work to do, but I'll make good on it tonight." Alex kissed Maddie soundly before groaning as the bell above the door signaled a new customer. As she straightened up, she saw a blushing Charlotte hovering beside the door. "C'mon in, don't let the cool out."

Charlotte hesitated before coming in and closing the door. "I was just looking for some breakfast."

"Well, then you've come to the right place." Alex pulled out a chair at Maddie's table and gesturing for her to sit. "And that's mine. You better not have written in any answers, Madeleine Marinelli." She lifted the newspaper, which was open at the crossword, off the table and rolled it up possessively.

Maddie grinned as Alex made a show of swatting her with the paper before trotting off to get Charlotte a menu. "I wouldn't dream of it," she called after her retreating girlfriend. "Although seven down is Florence."

The dishcloth never had a hope of reaching her, but the intent was clear as Alex scowled in her direction. Turning her attention from any further possible assault, Maddie regarded Charlotte as she took a careful sip of her coffee. "So I thought you left?"

Charlotte leaned over the back of the seat to scoop up the dishcloth sitting innocently on the floor. She placed it on the table and settled further into her chair. "That makes two of us. What was it you said about this place sucking you back in?"

Laughing, Maddie toyed with the dishcloth. "They ought to put a warning on the town sign alongside the population count."

Charlotte sat forward. Her face pulled into a frown. "Have you ever been so terrified to speak that you're not sure whether the words will get past the lump in your throat?"

Maddie didn't need to consider her reply. She sat forward and mirrored Charlotte's pose. "I resigned from my job. Packed my life back up into my ancient car to hightail it back here to persuade a woman, who I'd known for all of about a week and who at that point probably wanted to punch me, that she should spend the rest of her life with me." She smiled at the memory. "So yeah, I know a little about pressure."

"I'm getting the chance to speak to Erin tonight, to tell her my side of what happened when we were teenagers." Charlotte blew out a breath. "And I'm scared that if I don't get this right, I could lose any chance I might have of keeping her in my life."

"Tell the truth and speak from the heart," Maddie said, patting Charlotte's arm. "I usually find that's the way to go."

The sound of the bell above the door, followed by a crash from the door banging against the wall halted their conversation. A puffing Cindy stood gripping the doorframe.

"Doc, you're needed at the clinic. It's Erin. They're bringing her in."

Chapter Twenty

"What happened?" Charlotte asked as they ran towards the town's clinic. Despite wanting to run at full pace, she kept beside Maddie and Cindy. It would be useless to arrive at the clinic before the town's doctor.

"Foster's ranch. Horse kick. Erin hurt." Getting even the briefest of words out took its toll on Cindy, and she lost step with them for a moment.

The three women arrived at the clinic in various states of breathlessness. The sense of panic that had fueled their run was now absent as whoever was bringing Erin in hadn't yet arrived.

Mack appeared from Maddie's office looking between Cindy's puce face, Maddie's game face, and finally Charlotte's worried expression. "What the hell happened?" she asked as Cindy flopped down into a chair in the waiting area, and Maddie brushed past her into one of the exam rooms.

"Erin got a call out to the Foster's ranch this morning. Next thing I get a call from Carl Foster saying she got kicked by one of their studs and to go get the doc as they're bringing her straight here." Cindy managed to huff out between breaths.

Without saying anything further, Mack disappeared into the exam room where Maddie was and reappeared a minute later pushing a gurney with an orange backboard balanced on it.

"Don't just stand there," she said to Charlotte, who obediently followed her out of the clinic to wait on the sidewalk.

Charlotte paced back and forth impatiently.

"You know there isn't but a month goes by before she's getting bitten or scratched or trod on," Mack said neutrally. "If our patients hurt us half as much as those animals do her, I'd have found a new occupation."

Turning, Charlotte smiled. "Thanks, but I saw your face when you heard what happened, and I reckon this isn't one of your usual incidents."

Mack returned the smile. "Dammit, an' I thought my poker face was better than that."

The noise of a loud engine halted their conversation and broke the relative quiet of the morning. They watched a blue truck approach at an alarming speed. The sound of the engine was accompanied by a regular blast from the horn as the driver screeched to a halt beside them. The driver flung open the door and jumped down, waving to Mack as he ran around to the rear of the truck. "She's in the back."

Charlotte held her breath as she stepped forward. She was unable to see anything in the flatbed of the truck other than bales of hay, and a worried-looking young man running his fingers through his hair.

"Chuck Foster, I had better be dead, 'cause there's no other reason for you to be driving like a maniac through town."

At the sound of Erin's voice, the breath Charlotte had been holding left her in a rush. She stepped around to see Erin laying in the rear of the truck, surrounded by bales of hay buffering her movement.

Mack allowed a sheepish-looking Chuck Foster to help her up onto the truck. "How you doing Erin?" she asked, attempting to recover from her ungainly entrance, which involved Chuck Foster laying hands on places only her husband was familiar with.

"Well I've been better," Erin replied, her smile turning into a wince.

"What happened?" Mack glared at Chuck, who instinctively took a step back.

Erin gripped her arm around her side. "I took a kick from one of Chuck's stallions. It caught me in the ribs."

The young man who was sitting in the truck beside Erin shook his head. "I'm sorry, Doctor Hunter, I thought I had him."

Grimacing with pain, Erin shook her head. "It's okay, Carl. I've been around animals long enough to know the biting, scratching, and kicking ends. Today I just wasn't fast enough to get out of the way. It's no one's fault."

"Did you lose consciousness at all?" Mack pushed hay bales out of the way to get closer to her.

"Unfortunately not, was awake and felt the whole damn thing, including the warp speed drive here. It's just my ribs. Nothing else got damaged."

Chuck's cheeks reddened at the comment.

Mack laughed as she crouched down beside Erin's head and carefully placed a cervical collar on her. "Let's not take any chances. You think you can roll over so I can slide the backboard in?"

Erin looked up at Mack and winced. "Probably, but only with a whole lot of pain, and a load more cussing. I think one might be broken."

"I think my delicate ears can cope with the odd cuss word." Maddie pulled herself onto the truck and collected the backboard from a willing Chuck. She positioned herself so she could help Erin move. "Hey, Erin. Bad day at the office?"

"Something like that."

"Well let's get you in and get drugs into you. After three?"

On the count of three, Erin let out a loud yell followed by a volley of expletives as she was returned to her prone position.

Mack waited for a moment for Erin to compose herself. "You still okay?"

"Yup, just working out my next round of swear words for when you try and get me down out of this thing."

Maddie stopped securing Erin onto the backboard for a second and leaned over so she could see her face. "My personal favorite was monkey shit fucker."

Erin smiled weakly. "Why thank you, I worked hard on that one."

"Okay, we're good to go." Maddie jumped down from the truck and gripped the backboard's handles near Erin's feet. "I'm going to need you all to help move her off."

Chuck and his son Carl immediately moved to help. Charlotte hesitated, unsure her presence would be welcome but stepped forward to help when Mack jumped down off the truck. She gripped the handles of the board nearest to Erin's head.

If Erin was surprised to see Charlotte beside her, it didn't register on her face. "Hey."

"Hey, you." Charlotte lifted the backboard along with the others, moving carefully so as not to jostle Erin. "You really okay? Or are you pretending to be tough like when you broke your big toe?"

"Totally pretending."

"Let's get her in," Maddie said, once they'd placed Erin on the gurney.

Charlotte paced back and forth in the waiting room. She was conscious her movement was being watched by the seated inhabitants. They were no doubt puzzled enough to see Charlotte Grace back in Grace Falls, never mind seeing her wearing a hole in the floor of the clinic. It had been a half hour since Maddie and Mack wheeled Erin through to the exam room and neither had reappeared. The absence of news started to wear Charlotte's already frayed nerves further.

A flurry of movement at the entrance caught her attention. The door flew open, and Sam strode into the clinic. His head moved wildly as he looked for either Mack or Maddie. Spotting neither, his eyes landed on Charlotte.

"What the hell are you doing here?"

Neither the full waiting room of local residents nor the knowledge that Sam was lashing out due to fear stopped Charlotte from responding to his tone.

"I was with Maddie when she got the call. Nice of you to show up."

Anger flashed across Sam's face as he reached her in two strides, so they were almost nose to nose. "You are not wanted nor needed here."

"Erin should be the one to decide that. Not you."

"When it comes to you, Erin loses the sense she was born with. You almost destroyed her and yet you come back like nothing happened and stir it all up again."

Frustration fizzed off Charlotte. Yet again she was painted as a villain in what happened. The tenuous hold she had of her self-control withered with the renewed accusation.

"I destroyed me too, Sam," she yelled.

"Yeah, well at least it was your choice," Sam shouted back in return. "You are nothing but a chicken shit, Charlotte Grace. You denied everything Erin was to you just so you could go on being a Grace. You chose being a Grace over Erin, and you can't just swoop back in, and expect her to forgive you."

Charlotte inched closer. Her teeth gritted as she stared intently into Sam's eyes. "You have no idea. You have no clue what happened back then and what I chose. So don't preach at me, Sam."

"Yeah?" Sam tilted his head. "So tell me I'm wrong."

"You're wrong." Charlotte could feel the anger pulsing through her body, then realizing for the first time she had a chance to set the record straight, she relaxed. "Almost every memory I have of Erin there's an animal involved."

"What the hell's that got to do with anything?" Sam shook his head.

"All she ever wanted to do was work with animals, and the Grace Falls Foundation sponsorship was going to make that happen."

Sam looked at Charlotte in confusion.

"My mother found out about us and threatened that if I didn't end it, the foundation would pull the sponsorship. So everything you think you know about what I chose is wrong. I chose her. I chose to give her the future she deserved, and I chose to break both our hearts to make it happen."

Charlotte's shoulders slumped with relief. Finally, someone in Grace Falls knew the truth of what happened. She turned and took in the numerous faces sitting in rapt attention. Apparently now more than one person knew and unfortunately none of them was the person who deserved the explanation.

"Are you two finished putting on a show for the whole town?"

Both Sam and Charlotte spun around at the sound of Erin's voice. She stood clutching her ribs wearing a hospital gown. Her face was pale, but neither could ignore the furious expression on it. They both started to speak and walk towards her, but she held out a hand to stop them.

"Imagine you are sitting in unimaginable pain, waiting on painkillers to kick in and take away the agony in your ribs. Now imagine hearing two people yelling at each other and airing your dirty laundry for all and sundry. If you can imagine that you can then surely understand why both of you are the last people I want around me right now.

"So if you don't mind, go make yourselves useful and collect Cooper and my truck from the Foster's Ranch, while I go back to being cared for...and be thankful it was me that came out here and not Mack."

Sam and Charlotte had the grace to look sheepish while Erin tore a strip off them both.

"Sorry," they both muttered.

"Don't be sorry. Be gone." Erin tramped off attempting to keep as much of her ass as possible covered as she walked.

Sam blew out a long breath then turned to Charlotte. "My truck's outside."

Charlotte nodded and silently followed him as he led the way.

∞ ∞ ∞

They rode in silence. Both took more interest in the road than was strictly necessary seeing as they were the only vehicle on it. Finally, Sam made a small coughing sound that was almost a growl.

"Was that what really happened?"

Charlotte let out a long breath and ran her hand through her hair. "It was the abridged version. In reality, there was a lot more shouting and tears from me and a whole load more threats from my mother."

"Why didn't you ever tell Erin the truth?"

Shrugging, Charlotte turned in her seat. "I almost did about a thousand times, but I was told not to contact her. If I had it would have put her sponsorship at risk."

Sam sucked his bottom lip into his mouth as he contemplated Charlotte's explanation. Finally, he nodded and glanced in her direction. "You know she wasn't the only one you hurt."

The rawness of his words hit Charlotte straight in the chest. She'd anticipated anger from Sam, he'd always been protective of his big sister. What surprised her was that her departure and the manner in which it happened had hurt anyone other than her family and Erin.

"Sam, I'm sorry—"

"I don't need you to apologize. I just needed you to know. You doing what you did meant I lost my big sister in a different way than her jus' going off to college an' I sorta thought of you as my big sister too...only you weren't as mean to me as Erin."

Charlotte let out a laugh. "She was pretty horrible to you. Remember when you wouldn't leave us be and she pretended to call Santa, and cancel all your presents."

"A line of trust was broken that day." Sam grinned at the memory.

"I am so very sorry. I thought I was doing the right thing for everyone at the time. If it's any consolation, while I'm not sorry my decision meant Erin got to be a vet, I have regretted every day since then that I hurt her."

He nodded, and Charlotte sat back in her seat. The entrance to the Foster's farm became visible in the distance as the thick atmosphere between them felt as though it had lifted somewhat. It wasn't entirely relaxed, but it was a start.

"So, I'm training for the Winter Olympics," Sam said nonchalantly.

"Seriously? I thought Ruth was just joking when she told me."

Sam frowned, a familiar wounded puppy look that Charlotte had seen countless times during their childhood when Erin told him to leave them alone. She had to resist the temptation to ruffle his hair as she had in the past.

"Why does everyone have that reaction?" he sighed.

Chapter Twenty-One

"So you know the drill, ice packs for twenty minutes every hour. Painkillers regularly and don't try to be a hero and not take them. It's not big, and it's not clever. Deep breaths and coughing exercises every two hours." Maddie signed off her notes then looked up at Erin to make sure she'd taken the instructions in.

"When can I get back to work?"

"Take a couple of days. Office work should be okay. Then light duties in four weeks, and we'll see about anything else after six weeks."

"Six weeks!"

Maddie shrugged. "Just be thankful you were wrong about that break, and you've only bruised your ribs. Had it been broken we'd have been talking six minimum."

Erin part growled, and part groaned as she slipped off of the bed. "What you got that will relieve the symptoms of the whole of town knowing your business, and a good portion of them having seen your ass?"

Laughing, Maddie opened the door. "Time will heal that as well. Although it may take longer than six weeks. Particularly the ass bit."

Erin gave her the side-eye as they stepped out into the hallway.

"Your ride is here," Mack said with a mischievous look on her face.

Coming into the reception area, Erin was greeted with her brother bearing a look somewhere between remorse and relief.

"You okay?" he asked quietly.

"Peachy." She held out the paper bag with her painkillers in it.

"Okay then." He took the bag and nodded his head in greeting towards Maddie. "Thanks for taking care of her."

Maddie waved her hand in the air. "No worries. You make sure she takes those." She pointed at the bag in Sam's hand.

"Will do."

He rushed around Erin to open the door for her and nodded again to Maddie and Mack as his sister left the clinic.

∞ ∞ ∞

"What you got that weird look on your face for?" Maddie asked, seeing the wide grin on Mack's face.

"Wait two seconds."

They didn't have to wait that long when a loud 'Hell no, Sam Hunter, I am not riding in that golf cart again' rang through the building.

"That." Mack chuckled, then turned and waddled off to the waiting room. "Right, who's next?"

∞ ∞ ∞

"Jesus that's cold," Erin whined as Sam dropped another ice pack gently onto her ribs.

"That's kinda the point." He slumped into a chair and took a slug from his soda bottle, ignoring his sister's pointed glare. "You still in a huff with me about the golf cart?" Sam sat up straight and pointed the neck of his bottle in her direction. "You went straight to seeing the bad. Thinking I was just trying to pull some stupid prank, when alls I was doing was getting a vehicle I thought you could get in and out of easily without hurting your ribs none."

"I apologized already, Sam."

"Well, I'm just sayin' that my feelings got hurt."

Erin was about to expound upon her own feelings and how they might have been trampled on when he chose to go ten rounds with Charlotte in front of half the town. But she knew from his contrite behavior since he collected her at the clinic, that he was sorry. Making him feel worse wouldn't do either of them any good. Instead, she decided to focus on the other half of the debate team.

"So did you and Charlotte speak when you picked up my truck?"

Sam toyed with his bottle. "A little."

"Don't make me come over there and kick your ass little brother."

"Yeah we talked, and you should probably talk to her too."

"It didn't take her long to get you singing a different tune," Erin scoffed, surprised by the change in her brother's opinion.

Huffing, Sam shrugged. "You should still speak to her."

"I think I heard all I needed to hear along with the rest of the town," Erin snapped, wincing as she jerked her body in her anger.

"Alls I'm saying is you said you'd give her a chance to explain. Hearing her and me going at it in the clinic doesn't sound much like you giving her a chance."

Erin stared into the fireplace. She knew her brother. He was stubborn, and he could hold a grudge. Hell, she only had to mention the Third Saturday in October, and he would be all up in arms about the Tennessee Volunteers. His vitriol could last days.

For him to change his mind so radically about Charlotte, meant he'd heard something sufficient to do almost the unthinkable. She hadn't heard the entire argument, only the tone of the raised voices as opposed to the content being yelled. But what she did hear was Charlotte admitting she'd broken both their hearts and she'd taken a small amount of comfort from that.

"Will you drive me over to the Anderson place?"

$$\infty \quad \infty \quad \infty$$

The golf cart pulled up noiselessly on the street outside the Old Anderson House. Erin sat for a moment staring towards the house, remembering the hours she'd waited outside the property as a child for Charlotte to complete her piano lessons.

"You goin' in?" Sam asked.

She turned and gave her brother a half-smile and nodded. Despite her earlier complaints, she was grateful Sam had brought the golf cart as it was indeed easier than climbing in and out of his truck. Still, the action to raise herself off the seat caused her to catch her breath in pain. As she walked up the path towards the house the whirring of the golf cart's motor told her, without looking, that Sam had left her there.

Taking a deep breath, she climbed the steps leading up to the veranda. Pulling the screen door open she knocked on the door and waited.

$$\infty \quad \infty \quad \infty$$

Charlotte had deliberately avoided going to Erin's Rock on her previous visit. The place where she first met Erin and where they'd spent so much of their childhood and teenage years, would have been too much for her to handle. However, this time, she felt stronger.

She'd started to make some amends, with Sam at least. Her original plan of apologizing to Erin and finally confronting her mother was back in play. The one fly in the ointment was, she had no idea of how Erin might react following her argument with Sam. She was bound to have heard at least part of what was said.

She caressed the stone. Its rough texture was so familiar to her she felt as though she'd passed through a portal in time. She hoisted herself onto the rock and lay down. She felt a veil on her memories slip, allowing the memory of when things started to go wrong to appear.

Charlotte heard the noise of clothes being discarded followed by the sound of someone entering the water. She turned. All she could see was Erin's bright smile and her hair fanning out around her on the water. The water rippled with the movement of her arms and legs under the surface as she treaded water.

"What happens if we get caught?" Erin asked, bobbing up and down.

"We're not gonna get caught." Charlotte slipped into the pool and slowly swam towards her girlfriend.

Erin cast a glance up towards the large colonial-style property that was the Grace Family home. "You're sure?"

"Positive," Charlotte replied, as she reached Erin and started to float beside her. "Daddy is in St Anton, and Virginia takes a sleeping pill at night. She won't hear a thing."

"Well in that case." Erin's smile grew wider as she reached out and grabbed Charlotte around the waist and pulled her closer. Their lips met in a slow, languid kiss. They felt unhurried despite knowing their time together would soon be limited.

Erin had been accepted at Auburn on their Pre-Veterinary Medicine course. Along with Ruth, she had received the Grace Falls Foundation's education scholarship, which would allow her career aspirations to become a reality.

Their long-distance relationship was going to have to continue for longer following Charlotte's acceptance to Cornell. Knowing they were on borrowed time, they cherished every moment they had together, and the midnight skinny dip in the Grace pool had been Charlotte's idea.

Charlotte pulled away and circled her arms around Erin's neck. "What happens if you meet some amazing girl at college?"

Erin shook her head, small drops of water shimmered in the moonlight as they fell from the tips of her hair. "Not gonna happen."

"How can you know for sure?"

"'Cause you're the only girl for me. Remember, we're unbreakable. Besides, there won't be anyone at Auburn who's as hot as my girlfriend."

Charlotte grinned as Erin pulled her tighter against her body. She brought her legs up and wound them around Erin's waist, letting Erin take the strain of keeping them afloat. "Well, when you put it like that."

They spent an hour in the pool lazily swimming around and playing an elaborate game of catch. Neither girl knew the rules nor cared, as getting caught resulted in long kisses and caresses.

Reluctantly Charlotte swam to the side and pulled herself effortlessly out of the pool to sit on the side. Her legs dangled in the pool, creating patterns on the surface of the water.

"Where do you think we'll be in twenty years?"

Erin frowned. "God, we'll be thirty-seven. That sounds so old." She grinned as she swam up to Charlotte and rested her arms on her thighs. "We'll be here. I'll be the local vet, and you'll have taken over the lumberyard."

"You think?"

"Or we'll be rich and famous living a glamorous life in LA. Either one is good."

Charlotte laughed. "Somehow I can't see us in LA but here would be just fine." She held onto Erin's arms to keep her in place as she bent down to kiss her. "Just fine," she murmured against Erin's lips.

With a practiced movement, she swung her leg over the window ledge and pulled herself into her room. Dropping onto the floor, she pushed down the wooden sash and case window as slowly and as quietly as she could. It was only when she turned, her smile still evident on her face, that she saw her mother sitting in the old wicker chair that had been handed down by her grandmother.

"Mama!"

"Charlotte."

"You damn near scared the hell out of me."

"Then we're even because I can assure you I almost had a stroke a few moments ago when I looked out of the back room window towards the pool and saw you cavorting with that girl."

Charlotte's heart rose to her throat so much she felt it would block her ability to swallow. "Her name is Erin." She winced, annoyed with herself that there was an evident shake in her voice. "You know her name is Erin."

Standing, Virginia took in a deep breath. "We will talk about this more tomorrow in the light of day. No good comes from discussing emotional matters before slumber."

For the briefest of moments, her mother had a deep frown on her face before the cold and self-possessed mask Virginia Grace wore so easily slipped back into place. "Sleep well."

There had been no sleep that night for Charlotte. She'd sat fretting about what her mother would say the next day and more importantly what her father would think of her. She dressed carefully, shirking her usual pastime of dressing to annoy her mother. Today she wore clothes she knew Virginia Grace would approve of, as if her choice of dress would somehow influence her mother.

When she stepped into the dining room, she was surprised to see only her mother sitting there. She looked around in the room for her father but stopped when her mother spoke.

"Your father and I have decided I should be the one to handle this matter. Becoming aware of your only daughter's dalliance with the same-sex is not palatable for a man of your father's upbringing."

Charlotte blinked back tears and nodded, hoping she could at least open the dialogue she took a hesitant step towards the table. "I'm sorry you found out the way you did. I know—"

Virginia slammed her hand down on the table stopping her from continuing.

"Do not presume to tell me what I do and do not know, Charlotte. I can tell you what I thought that I knew. Up until last night, I thought I had a perfectly normal daughter. A daughter that I could be proud of. One that lived up to the great tradition of our family."

"I'm still those things, Mama."

Virginia pressed her palms onto the table and leaned forward. "No, you're not. You're a travesty. A disgrace to this name and I will not allow your deviance to continue."

The rage started somewhere at the soles of her feet, gathering pace as it traveled through her body. It coursed through her like molten lava until all her hurt and frustration poured out of her mouth. "You talk about this family name like it's something you have to preserve. We're not royalty! We're a generation of a family that through some awful dealings, ended up owning a town. You're not even a Grace, you're a Watson. You put on all these airs and graces like you're Scarlet O'Hara.

"You have been a pretty terrible mother up until now. God gave you this opportunity to redeem all of that by saying that you love me and that you don't care who I love. Instead, you resort to name calling and —"

The slap shocked both of them. Virginia stood looking at her hand as if it had secured a mind of its own, while Charlotte gasped and held her cheek. Her eyes were wide as she watched her mother.

"How dare you say this family is nothing," Virginia rasped. "It's what has put a roof over your head, meals in your stomach and paid for your education." A victorious look flashed over her mother's features. "There are still things that we control."

Still holding her throbbing cheek, Charlotte began to open her mouth. Her mother raised a hand to stop her, and she shrank back in expectation of another blow.

Her movement seemed to surprise Virginia, who looked at her hand then dropped it slowly. "I discussed this with your father this morning. We've agreed that whatever it is you have with the Hunter girl, it stops now."

"I love her."

Virginia ignored her daughter and continued to lay out their solution. "This is just a phase. There is no need to make this bigger than it is. You can redeem yourself. You will go to college as planned and we will look for a suitor for you."

"You can't just marry me off. I love her."

"You're seventeen. What do you know about love?" Virginia scoffed. "In this family, duty comes first."

"I won't end it." Charlotte raised herself up defiantly.

"If you do not agree to these terms, the sponsorship currently offered to pay for fees and tuition for the Hunter girl will be withdrawn immediately."

Charlotte let out a gasp. She'd ignored the plans they had for her. The details weren't anything she hadn't heard from her mother before, but she knew the money from the foundation was everything Erin depended on for her dream of becoming a vet.

"You can't do that."

"We can and we will. Furthermore, if I find you have been in contact with her when you are at college, we will withdraw her payments. You will end this nonsense today."

"When she finds out you're holding her education to ransom over our relationship, she'll choose our relationship."

Virginia sighed. "If you're both willing to sacrifice her future for some teenage romance then you're more foolish than I thought. I know she worked hard to get the grades to qualify for the foundation's money. It would be a shame to see that work wasted."

Charlotte closed her eyes, she couldn't let her mother ruin Erin's future. From the moment they'd met Erin's love of animals was apparent. From the age of eight, she'd hung around the town's vet practice doing anything and everything she could. She'd made herself so invaluable they eventually hired her part-time when she turned sixteen. She was destined to be a veterinary surgeon.

Charlotte opened her eyes and stared her mother down. "She won't believe my feelings have changed," she said, her voice quivering.

"Then you should think hard on how best you can convince her. Because if you don't, she'll be left working part-time in the vets for the rest of her life. This ends today, Charlotte, one way or the other."

"Hey."

The voice surprised Charlotte so much that she sat up too quickly and lost her balance. Her arms and legs flailed in vain as she tried to catch herself before she fell from the rock. She felt herself fall backward and braced herself for the inevitable landing when two arms surrounded her, halting her descent.

"Sorry, I didn't mean to startle you."

Charlotte's stomach leaped, not at the fall but at Erin's breath against her ear. "You should have let me fall. You could have hurt yourself more," Charlotte admonished, reluctantly extracting herself from Erin's hold and hopping down off the rock.

"I'm okay."

Looking at Erin's pallor, Charlotte wound her arm around Erin's waist. "You're about to faint, you should sit down." She carefully helped Erin to the ground, mindful of the small yelps coming from her.

Erin gazed woozily up at Charlotte. "Fancy running into you here."

Letting out a relieved laugh, Charlotte sat down beside her. "Yeah, well, whenever I had a problem I always seemed to wind up here."

"I figured that. I went to the Anderson house first." Erin rested her head back against the stone, closed her eyes, and took a moment to recover.

Charlotte watched her carefully, struck by how beautiful she still was. Small lines at the edge of her eyes were the only visible difference between the teenage version of Erin that remained in Charlotte's memory. "You cut your hair."

Erin popped one eye open and rolled her head so she was looking at Charlotte. "It's been a long time. If I hadn't cut it, I'd look like Cousin Itt by now."

Wiping her hand over her face in an attempt to clear her brain, Charlotte exhaled. "I'm sorry. That wasn't meant to come out of my mouth. I was just looking at you and thinking how you haven't changed. You're still beautiful."

Charlotte could have sworn she saw tiny walls appear in Erin's eyes. The softness in her eyes changed visibly enough that Charlotte almost recoiled. "I'm sorry," she murmured, trying to recover ground. "When I see you, it's like my brain goes on standby. I didn't mean to upset you."

Erin huffed out air and scrubbed both hands over her face. "You said you wanted to explain what happened?"

"I do." She reached out to place her hand on Erin's forearm, hesitating at the last second, unsure of how her touch would be received. "I also want to apologize for earlier. I shouldn't have said those things to Sam."

"No, you shouldn't have." Erin spun her head around to glare at Charlotte. "I don't like having my private business become the fodder for town gossip. Between you and my pig-headed brother you've given them enough to be going on with 'til Christmas."

Charlotte felt her cheeks flame in embarrassment. "I am sorry." She scrunched her face up in attrition. "If you want I can go moon Harvey Mack and get myself arrested. That should take the heat off you for a bit?"

Relief blossomed in Charlotte's chest when Erin laughed.

"I may take you up on that."

Erin relaxed back against the rock. Sensing a slight thaw in her demeanor, Charlotte decided to take the bull by the horns.

"She saw us in the pool that night. She was waiting for me when I got in. She said she would speak to Daddy, and we would discuss it in the morning. I swear that night I thought a hundred times about just packing my bags, climbing out of the window, and coming to you. There's still a bit of me wonders what would have happened if I'd done that."

She swallowed hard, trying to shift the lump that had taken up residence in her throat. Sounds of leaves rustling and birds chirping faded into the background. All she was aware of was her heart beating steadily in her chest and the soft breathing of Erin next to her.

"The next morning, it was just her. Daddy was so disappointed in me that he couldn't even face me." She tried desperately not to cry. "I never saw him again. I can't even remember the last conversation I ever had with him."

Wordlessly Erin pulled Charlotte into her arms.

Charlotte allowed the comfort for a few moments before shaking her head and pulling back. She wiped uselessly at her face in an attempt to remove the evidence of her grief. "I'm sorry. I'm meant to be explaining. This is supposed to be about you, not me."

Erin reached and placed a lock of hair behind Charlotte's ear. "It's about both of us."

Nodding, Charlotte took a few breaths to compose herself before she continued with her story. "I got the 'you're a disgrace to the family' speech and how while I was away at college they would 'find me a nice boy to marry.'" She heard Erin's hollow laugh. "I know. It was a variation on the same theme I'd been hearing since I was thirteen but this time I got angry. I said some stuff I probably shouldn't have, and she hit me."

Charlotte raised her hand to her cheek as if still able to feel the heat caused by her mother's blow after all this time. "And that's when my parents showed how creative they could be at manipulating me. I was told I was to end our relationship and have no further contact with you, or your sponsorship would be pulled. All your dreams, all your desires would just vanish."

"I can't believe they did that," Erin whispered.

They sat in silence both absorbing her account of events. Charlotte toyed with the hem of her T-shirt waiting on Erin's saying something, anything.

Erin scrambled to her feet, wincing at the effort. "And I can't believe you let them." She looked down at Charlotte. "We could have worked something out, done something. Instead, you let them break us apart."

Charlotte thought her heart would shatter again at the hurt in Erin's voice.

"You broke my heart, Charlie. I loved you completely, and you broke my heart."

134

"I didn't think I had a choice." Charlotte could barely breathe as she heard Erin use her nickname for the first time since her return.

"Of course you had a choice," Erin shouted. "I heard you say to Sam that you chose me. You chose my future? How gracious of you. What about us? You should have chosen us. All this time you let me think—"

Charlotte interrupted Erin as her own anger ignited and she leaped to her feet. "I have a lot of regrets. I hate that I broke your heart. I hate even more that it's taken this long for me to see you again. But I am not sorry you got the education you deserved. We were seventeen, we were kids. There were no guarantees you wouldn't turn around and resent what you lost. College without any financial support is tough, the loans, and then working while studying."

"You took everything we had, everything we shared, and you ripped it up in front of me. You think that wasn't tough?" Erin countered. "You think I don't resent you now? You didn't even try to fight it, Charlotte. That's what hurts the most. You were what I wanted. You were what I desired, and you didn't even let me choose. I thought you could do anything, that you were strong. If someone told me you'd hung the moon, I'd have believed them, and yet at the first sign of trouble, you bailed. You didn't even believe in us to give us a chance."

Charlotte knew her tears were renewed and flowing freely down her face. "I tried—"

"Obviously not hard enough. I've got to go; I have painkillers to take."

With her back pressed against their rock, Charlotte's knees buckled underneath her, and she slid down the hard surface. She sat back down on the fresh earth and sobbed as hard as she had all those years ago.

∞   ∞   ∞

Erin knew she only had a few minutes before she would be crying like Charlotte and for the first time ever she didn't feel comfortable being vulnerable in front of her.

She left the clearing and walked briskly back towards town. Thankfully the sound of Charlotte's sobs faded with every resolute step she took. When she was sure she was out of earshot, Erin doubled over and vomited. The pain in her ribs at the effort only slightly overshadowed the pain in her heart.

Chapter Twenty-Two

*I*t was unusual for Charlotte to call and ask her to come up to the house during the day. Virginia's almost constant presence meant most of their time together was spent out in the woods that surrounded the town. Erin's heart beat faster as she almost ran towards the Grace house.

It had been less than twenty-four hours since she left Charlotte at the poolside and she could hardly wait to see her again. Perhaps if the coast was clear for once, they could actually make love in a bed. Not that she minded their out of doors activities. She definitely had no complaints about what happened at the pool, but a bed would be a welcome change. Her footsteps increased in speed with the thought, and she was almost at a full sprint when she reached the driveway.

Her speed faltered when she spotted Virginia Grace's car parked to the side of the house. However, seeing the front door open and Charlotte waiting for her had her speeding up the drive towards the house.

As she got closer, she could see tell-tale traces of tears on Charlotte's face. Her eyes were red and puffy while her whole face was paler than normal.

"You okay?" she asked as she walked through the door Charlotte held open for her.

Before Charlotte could respond Virginia Grace's voice rang out in the hallway.

"Thank you for coming, Miss Hunter. My daughter has something she would like to say to you."

Baffled at what was happening Erin stood switching her gaze between her girlfriend and her mother. Charlotte seemed unable or unwilling to meet her eyes and the longer they stood there in silence her feelings grew more ominous.

"Charlie?"

Finally, Charlotte raised her head and looked towards Erin. Her tongue darted out to lick her dry lips, an action Erin had seen countless times in prelude to a kiss. However, this time, the flip of her stomach was not caused by arousal but by fear.

"I've been playing with your feelings, and I'm sorry."

Erin shook her head at the barely croaked out words. "What do you mean?"

"What happened between us was a stupid teenage experiment that went on for too long. I took it too far."

"I don't believe you."

"I know I shouldn't have encouraged you, especially since I don't feel the same way. I got distracted by having someone be in love with me."

"Why are you saying this?" Erin looked accusingly over towards Virginia. "What has she threatened you with?"

Charlotte took a breath, gazed at Virginia, and straightened her spine. She stood stock still and met Erin's eyes for the first time since her arrival. "My college fund. It's my future. I'm not willing to risk that for you. What we have isn't worth that."

Erin stumbled back as if hit in the chest. "You can't be serious."

"I am. I've worked hard to get into Cornell. I'm not going to give it up for you." Charlotte lowered her eyes as she delivered the fatal blow. "You're not worth it."

An ache settled deep in Erin's chest as she felt each word spoken by Charlotte cleave pieces from her heart. She glanced at Virginia and had to fight the urge to punch the older woman.

Looking at Charlotte one last time Erin shook her head and blinked back the tears that were falling.

"Congratulations, Charlotte, you've managed to become the one thing you always said you didn't want to be."

Turning to leave, her eyes caught sight of Charlotte's hands moving.

Erin sat up abruptly in bed and yelped at the pain in her side. Once her breathing had returned to normal, she swung her legs out of bed and stood shakily. It wasn't uncommon for her dreams to return to that day, and she was used to her brain repeating what was easily one of the worst days of her life. However, as she trod down the stairs to get a glass of water, she couldn't shake the feeling that this time it was different.

She turned the faucet on and stared out into the darkness. She held her glass under the stream of water as she replayed the dream. She mentally ticked off the components; Virginia Grace and her annoying pompous face, Charlotte and her vicious words, and then a vague memory of Charlotte inserted itself into her checklist, most specifically Charlotte's hands.

She frowned wondering whether the memory had always been there or was it something she'd created recently. She struggled to try to recall what it was about Charlotte's hands that bothered her.

When her brain finally supplied the answer, she turned off the water, placed her glass into the sink, and left the kitchen. Ignoring her attire and lack of footwear, she opened her front door and set off towards the Anderson house.

∞ ∞ ∞

The loud thumping woke Charlotte. She groggily made her way down the stairs to the front door, ready to shout at whoever thought it appropriate to bang on her door at three in the morning. She opened the door forcefully and was ready to let rip when Erin barged past her.

"What the—?"

Erin spun around with a wild expression on her face. "How did you try?"

Charlotte looked at the woman standing in the hallway. With her sleep-disheveled hair, tight tank top, and striped shorts she wondered whether Erin had over medicated and considered calling Maddie.

"What do you mean?"

"Earlier. You said you tried. How?"

Finally realizing what Erin was asking, Charlotte slowly moved her hands and with her fingers, formed interlocking circles.

Erin's face crumpled. "I didn't —"

"No, I should have tried harder. I've been thinking about what you said earlier and—"

Whatever Charlotte was about to say was lost as Erin stepped forward and pulled her towards her. In an instant, Charlotte was both off balance and strangely centered when Erin's lips touched hers.

She'd barely recovered from the shock enough to respond, when the kiss, as quickly as it was initiated, ended. She raised her hands to touch Erin only to find them reaching into empty air.

Erin stood touching her lips, her eyes were wide with astonishment as if her actions were as much of a surprise to her as they had been to Charlotte.

"I'm sorry, I..." Erin frowned. "It's the drugs. I should go."

Before Charlotte's brain was able to engage fully with her body to enable her to move or speak, Erin opened the door and was halfway down the path. She reached the door at the same time Erin reached the gate at the end of the path. Her voice came out almost like a breath.

"Erin."

Whether she heard her or not Charlotte didn't know, but Erin stopped as she closed the gate and looked up towards the porch where Charlotte stood. Charlotte's breath caught in her throat as a smile appeared on Erin's face before she turned and ran off down the sidewalk.

Charlotte lifted her fingers to touch her still tingling lips and smiled. In that briefest of kiss, she had felt more alive, more grounded and more aroused than she had in over twenty years.

$$\infty \quad \infty \quad \infty$$

Erin made it barely twenty paces down the sidewalk before the adrenaline wore off and she remembered her bruised ribs.

"Holy crap." She bent over and held her side, trying not to breathe deeply. Suddenly she was aware of every feeling in her body. She snorted at the absurd thought that the kiss had awakened her like Sleeping Beauty. "More like the drugs have worn off."

She straightened up and stepped carefully on the sidewalk while shaking her head at her own impulsiveness. Impulsiveness which now had her walking the streets of Grace Falls in her nightwear and bare feet.

She stopped as the memory of the kiss hit her. What was she thinking? She closed her eyes as she slapped her palm against her forehead.

"Hey, Erin."

Erin leaped in the air. Her squeal, a mix of pain and terror, managed to set off several neighborhood dogs barking. She turned to see a smiling Peter Campbell in his pajamas standing with a stroller.

"You can't sleep either?" Peter grinned sleepily nodding towards the stroller. Seemingly oblivious to Erin's discomfort or attire.

Pressing her hand onto her ribs, Erin finally composed herself enough to speak. "Something like that."

"Walk with you?"

Ignoring the absurdness of the situation Erin fell into step with Peter. "So is this a common thing for you?"

Peter nodded wearily. "Nighthawk here doesn't seem to like to keep regular hours. He usually quiets down after a couple of minutes out walking. Thankfully tonight he's been quiet since we left the house. It's good for Ruth to get a break. Oh hey, I heard you're coming for lunch on Sunday. Could you bring your mud pie? I haven't had it in ages."

Erin looked at him puzzled. "I am?"

Her confused look was swiftly joined by a similar one on Peter's face.

"I'm sure I heard you were coming. Teddy was talking to Ruth about it. Maybe I got it wrong. Dammit, I really wanted that mud pie." They stopped as they reached Peter and Ruth's home.

"Well, I'll see what I can do."

Erin smiled. She leaned down to look into the stroller to say a quiet goodnight to Ben. "Ummm, Peter. I don't want to alarm you, but Ben's not in the stroller."

Peter's sleep-deprived brain struggled to comprehend her words, and it took him a moment before he joined her to look into the stroller. Sitting where his slumbering son should have been was the large soft toy that, when its stomach was pressed had Teddy and Alex singing an entirely off-key version of the song 'Ben.'

"What the—?"

"You lost something?"

Both Peter and Erin turned towards the voice. Standing on the porch was Ruth with a bemused smirk on her face and a sleeping Ben in her arms.

"Crap, I did it again didn't I?" Peter's shoulders slumped, and his head fell forward dejectedly.

"Yeah you did," Ruth replied smiling. "Hey Erin, looking forward to seeing you on Sunday."

Erin nodded, still somewhat confused she knew nothing about the invite but suspecting Teddy was involved in about a hundred different ways.

"Yeah thanks, I'm going to bring mud pie."

Peter shot her a grateful look as he opened their gate and trod up the pathway pushing the stroller.

With a wave, Erin was back walking on her own. Deliberately attempting to ignore the fact she'd just kissed Charlotte Grace.

What's more, she wanted to again.

Chapter Twenty-Three

With each step, Charlotte's nervousness amplified. She'd barely slept as her mind turned over whether she should go to see Erin or wait and let Erin come to her. In the end, it came down to one simple thing. Charlotte needed to see Erin's face. She needed to look into her eyes and see whether there was regret there or if the tiniest spark of what they once had could be nurtured back to something more.

Her legs felt heavy as she stepped up towards Erin's front door. Music blared inside the house, and she had to repeat her knock with a heavier hand after a weak first attempt. The music was turned down, and heavy footsteps sounded through the house.

"Goddammit, Teddy, I already told you..."

The door flew open, and Charlotte was faced with a frazzled looking Sam.

"You're not Teddy." He frowned and looked beyond Charlotte as if convinced that she was sheltering Teddy behind her.

"And you're not wearing any clothes," Charlotte replied, noting Sam's appearance.

"Ah relax, I've got my tighty whitey's on." Sam grinned, holding the door open for Charlotte to enter.

She walked into Erin's house, only slightly more relaxed than she'd been on her previous visit. "Is there a reason for the lack of any other clothes?"

Sam shrugged and closed the door. "I'm painting," he said as if this was a more than adequate explanation for his lack of attire. "You looking for Erin?"

"She here?" Charlotte craned her neck for any indication Erin was in the house.

"Nope." Sam sighed. "I guess you two spoke some last night."

Charlotte opened her mouth to reply then closed it again and scowled. "Could you put some clothes on?"

Sam raised an eyebrow and placed the tips of his fingers onto his nipples. "Gimme a minute, and I'll make myself presentable."

While she waited for Sam to dress, Charlotte wandered around Erin's living room trying unsuccessfully not to snoop at the photos and books on display in her bookcase. Her breath caught as she saw a familiar book.

"So, I'm guessing my sister doing her Houdini act this morning means things didn't go too well?"

Charlotte let her fingers linger on the copy of Doctor Dolittle she'd given Erin on her seventeenth birthday before she turned towards Sam and shrugged. "I'm not totally sure how things are between us. That's why I'm here. I thought we should talk some more."

"Well, it seems Erin doesn't want to talk to anyone. When I got here at eight, she was gone, along with Cooper and her truck. You want water?" Sam asked, heading into the kitchen.

Charlotte followed him, curious to see the rest of Erin's home. "Thanks." She took the proffered bottle of water. "Should we be worried? I mean with her injury and all, maybe—"

"She's tougher than she looks." Sam shook his head. "She sometimes takes off like this when she's got a lot on her mind." He took a long drink of water and let out a satisfied sigh. "When our dad died she was gone almost three days."

Charlotte paused mid-sip. "I didn't know."

"Yeah, well, you missed a whole bunch of stuff."

She looked at Sam to see whether there was any hint of accusation on his face. However, he just smiled sadly at her.

He shrugged a shoulder. "Can't be helped now. No point whining over yesterday's sorrows."

Charlotte was almost hesitant to ask about the rest of their family. Somehow sensing her reluctance, Sam plowed on between swigs of water.

"Our momma never did like living here away from her family in St Anton. So pop was barely in the ground when she'd up'd and moved in with her sister."

Charlotte nodded. "You think that's where Erin's gone?"

Sam chuckled and shook his head. "I'd bet you my next three paychecks Erin is nowhere near mama and Aunt Sadie."

"Why's that?"

He cocked his head to the side. "Momma never really got on board with Erin being gay. Don't get me wrong she's not as bad as your mama, but she and Erin don't connect much nowadays. So I can't see Erin running off to St Anton. But I will bet that wherever she is, she'll be fine."

He threw his empty bottle in the trash and wiped his hands on his pants. "If you don't mind, I'm gonna get back to work." He paused, a grin appeared on his face that for a moment reminded Charlotte of Erin so much so that her breath caught in her throat. "Of course, if you've nothing better on, you could always help?"

A frown appeared on Charlotte's face. "Do I have to take my clothes off?"

Sam let out a full-bellied laugh as he left the kitchen. "Clothing is optional."

Charlotte threw her bottle in the trash, and mirroring Sam's actions she wiped her hands on her jeans. "Yeah well, I'm opting that we both keep our clothes on."

Sighing, Sam handed her a paintbrush. "Just don't come moaning to me when you get them fancy jeans covered in paint."

She gripped the paintbrush and followed Sam. "Duly noted."

∞ ∞ ∞

Alex groaned inwardly as the bell chime signaled another customer. She was hiding in the kitchen taking a few minutes to stretch her back and catch her breath during what was the usual Saturday lunchtime rush. She slapped the door with the palm of her hand and plastered a smile on her face. The fake cheerfulness quickly dissolved into actual happiness when she saw Charlotte standing at the counter.

"Hey you, I was hoping I'd get a chance to speak to you," Alex said, moving out of the way of a harassed Lou.

"Well, here I am." Charlotte smiled. "Can I have two coffees and two of those cookies to go?" She pointed at the plate of cookies in the display.

Alex smiled as she grabbed a couple of cups. The 'to go' option had only been introduced as a result of Maddie's arrival in Grace Falls. Anytime someone asked for their coffee to go, she always pictured Maddie's incredulous face when Lou handed her coffee over that first time in a sippy cup. Thankfully they now had cups that allowed them to offer the service properly.

As the coffee dripped into the cups, she quickly gathered a bag and the tongs for Charlotte's cookies.

"So I was going to ask how things are going since your return, but since you've been at Erin's all morning, I'm going to assume things have gone well." Alex smiled as she handed over the bag of cookies.

"How'd you...?" Charlotte narrowed her eyes and frowned. "Never mind I keep forgetting everyone knows everything here."

Alex grinned as she collected the cups of coffee and placed them on the counter. "Well you know this town, but in this case, you've got paint on your forehead which is Erin's choice for her spare room."

Charlotte's hand went immediately to her forehead to touch the incriminating dollop of paint. "You're like a regular Sherlock Holmes."

Laughing, Alex tossed a couple of lids down on the counter. "Nah, I'm a mama. We don't miss much. So you and Erin..."

Sensing her hesitance in answering Alex leaned over and put the lids on the coffee and lifted them off the counter. "How bout I give you the guided tour of the kitchen?" With a coffee in each hand, she cocked her head towards the kitchen door. She turned and whispered to a wide-eyed Lou, "Five minutes I promise, and I'll clean out the juicer tonight." Any complaint about to leave Lou's lips promptly halted at the offer. Alex bumped the kitchen door open with her backside and held it open until Charlotte made her way around the counter and into the kitchen.

"So?" Alex let the door go, walked into the kitchen, and placed the cups of coffee down on the work surface.

"Where do I begin?"

"To tell the story of how grateful love can be." Alex sang. Her off-key warbling garnered a confused look from Charlotte. "Not an Andy William's fan then."

"Sorry I am so far out of my comfort zone right now; I don't know who I am."

Alex cast a glance over towards the door, knowing her promise of five minutes was optimistic at best. She walked to the fridge and pulled the door open. "Milk?"

"Sorry?"

"For your coffee. Do you want milk or creamer?"

"Milk's good."

Alex nodded, and with a milk carton in hand, she returned. Within a couple of seconds, lids were removed and milk added to both cups. She gave Charlotte a cup and lifted the other to her lips. As she drank, she raised her eyebrows, encouraging Charlotte to speak.

Charlotte relaxed against the counter and picked idly at the seam of the cup. "She kissed me."

A gurgling noise came from Alex's throat as the mouthful of coffee she'd just taken took a different route than planned. With a cough, she managed to clear her throat enough to rasp a response. "Erin kissed you?"

"No Mack did," Charlotte quipped. "Of course Erin."

"Sorry, I just wasn't expecting that."

"You and me both."

"When? Where? Wha—"

"Last night. We spoke some yesterday and cleared up some stuff from our past. She appeared at my door in the middle of the night and kissed me."

"And how's things been this morning?"

"That's just it." Charlotte sighed, placing her coffee cup down and running a hand through her hair. "I went round to speak to her, and she'd gone. Sam was there painting, so I've been helping him."

"Was he wearing clothes?"

Charlotte let out a bark of laughter at Alex's question. "Just his underpants."

"Oh, sweet lord! You count yourself fortunate. He volunteered to paint the clinic for Maddie, and it took weeks for her to be able to look at him in the face without blushing. She walked in as he was taking a dance break and apparently everything was swinging." Alex chuckled at the memory.

"Did you know he's serious about the Olympic thing? He's been offered a training place in Finland."

"Yeah, I know he's serious about it. Well, as serious as he gets about anything, but no I definitely didn't know about the training offer."

"I think he's scared to take it and leave Erin."

"Well, that's just plain foolish. Erin will be alright."

"You think?"

Immediately Alex knew Charlotte wasn't asking about Erin's ability to cope with her brother's absence.

"She takes off sometimes to get her head clear. You coming back. Her finding out about why you left." Alex waved a hand before Charlotte started to rant about the town knowing her business. "You can't have a stand-up fight and air your laundry in public then complain 'cause someone's seen your Spanx, Charlotte." Softening her tone Alex continued, "Then there's the fact she kissed you. All in, Erin has a lot going around that pretty head of hers."

"I know." Charlotte's head dropped until her chin touched her chest. When she looked up again, her eyes were moist. "I just want to see her."

"Well I have it on good authority she'll be at Ruth's for dinner tomorrow, so how 'bout you come along too?"

"How do you know she'll show?"

Alex grinned. "'Cause Ruth'll kill her if she don't."

Charlotte's face brightened as she nodded towards Alex's hand. "You owe Sam a coffee."

Erin brought her hand down from the bell and gripped the packaging tightly before she realized she was probably squeezing the life out of the cake inside. She hoped Peter would forgive her for buying a mud pie instead of making one, but by the time she'd arrived back in Grace Falls, it was too late.

She'd driven for almost seven hours straight, save for comfort breaks and gas stops, without any clear idea of a destination. It wasn't until the warm air from the

Gulf of Mexico was gently ruffling her hair that she realized she was on the same stretch of sand as she'd escaped to following her father's death.

The drive and her time at the beach gave her plenty of time to reflect on her feelings about Charlotte's revelation. She'd reassessed what Charlotte's abandonment had created in her, the self-doubt, the lack of trust, and she reviewed the decisions she'd made as a result.

The whole exercise had left her feeling aggrieved. She was annoyed she'd allowed that one incident as an adolescent to impact her life right up into almost her forties. She'd also contemplated the opportunities she'd missed out on and the relationships she'd failed to allow to grow, all because of her fear.

She started to regret not smacking Charlotte instead of kissing her...almost. The kiss played on her mind for a good portion of her trip; how the simple touch of Charlotte's lips on hers ignited something that had lain dormant for a long time.

"Hey, you came, and you brought pie." Peter held the door open and reached to take the pie from her. "You even made proper packaging and a logo." He grinned as he examined the pack.

Erin's head dropped. "I'm sorry. I didn't have time to make one."

Sneaking a look, Peter shrugged. "You'll just have to owe me. Come on in, everyone's here."

Peter pushed open the door that led into their dining room, and immediately everyone turned to see the new arrival. Erin smiled a hello as her gaze swept around the room, pausing as her eyes rested on an uncharacteristically bashful-looking Charlotte.

"I'm so glad you made it."

Erin barely acknowledged Ruth's welcome as her chest constricted. She was sure this time the pain had nothing to do with her ribs or the hours she'd spent in her truck. There was only one cause of the tightness, and it was sitting watching her carefully while folding napkins.

"Hi," she murmured, never taking her eyes from Charlotte.

"Hey Erin, how are the ribs?" Maddie asked, sweeping into the room.

Erin dragged her eyes from Charlotte finally and looked towards Maddie. Her brown eyes were full of encouragement. Finding her voice finally Erin nodded. "They're getting there, thanks."

Sully entered from the kitchen carrying a serving plate with a carved roast on it. "Hope you're all hungry cause the Doc has managed to carve up a treat today." He grinned towards Erin. "Glad you made it."

Lou placed a dish with vegetables down on the table. "Everyone best get a seat before this goes cold."

Erin watched as the group of friends moved around each other with ease as if performing a well-rehearsed dance. Each disappearing into the kitchen and returning with items for the table. She hesitated, unsure where to sit until Charlotte patted the seat next to her.

"I think they've put you here."

Nodding, Erin weaved her way past Peter and pointedly ignored Teddy's shit-eating grin as she slipped into her seat. She smiled a hello to Douglas, who was sitting next to Teddy and looking as awkward as she felt, thrust into this weekly ritual.

Finally, the table was crowded with the ten adults and Jessica. Ben sat between his parents, beating a spoon against the side of his high chair.

With a prompt from his wife, Peter raised his glass in a toast. "We're a little cozy today, but it's wonderful to be surrounded by those we love. I'm sure we all want to welcome Charlotte home again."

Erin watched from the corner of her eye as Charlotte laughed and raised her glass in response. As the table all toasted her and whooped their reply, Erin turned slowly and delicately clinked her glass against Charlotte's before quietly adding her own. "Welcome home."

"So I fully expected to you see you in the NFL Sully, or at least the draft pick?" Charlotte raised her eyebrows expectantly at Matt, as he wiped his mouth to reply.

She focused on Sully, trying desperately to ignore that she was sitting so close to Erin that their elbows brushed several times during dinner. She was so focused, she missed the glances and sad smiles from the friends around the table.

Sully placed his napkin down. "You an' me both. I thought I'd all the time in the world and passed on the draft to complete my senior year. But whaddya know, I blew out my shoulder in a tackle an' that was that. I got to complete college though, so that was something."

Charlotte gave him an apologetic smile and nodded. "Yeah, that was something."

"What about you?" Peter asked. "We kept thinking we'd see you at the US Open."

Shaking her head, Charlotte fiddled with the knife and fork she'd placed onto her plate after finishing eating.

"Similar story to Sully. I tore my ACL, so that ended my tennis hopes. Only I did it in my freshman year, and that ended my scholarship." She chewed on her lower lip then sighed. "I dropped out as I couldn't afford the medical bills on top of college. On the plus side, I ended up working at a gym, and the owner let me live in the apartment above rent free. Then when he wanted to retire, we worked out a deal, and I bought the business."

"So that's what you do now?" Alex asked, starting to remove plates.

Charlotte was unable to stop the look of regret that flashed across her features before she responded. "No, I sold up."

"It is so hard for small business owners these days." Ruth stood and started to collect everyone's plates. "The past six years have been tough." She squeezed Charlotte's shoulder as she passed.

Realizing Ruth had not only got hold of the wrong end of the stick, but she'd also run off with it waving it above her head, Charlotte opened her mouth to correct her. However, any words she planned to say stuck in her throat as she felt Erin's hand on her forearm.

"I'm confused. You never said anything about a scholarship. What happened to Cornell?"

Charlotte swallowed hard. "Cornell was on my parents' dime, and I didn't want anything to do with them. They'd already taken what I loved, and I didn't want to give them another chance to have a say in my life." She held Erin's gaze. "I let them think that was where I was going. I confided in my coach at school, and fortunately, she knew someone, and I managed to get a full ride at a private college in Queens."

"So everyone okay with mud pie for dessert?" Ruth asked cheerfully as she reentered the room holding up the pie Erin brought.

There were murmurs of agreement as the pie was placed on the table and plates distributed before they all leaned in to grab a slice.

The chatter stopped and was momentarily replaced with moans of appreciation while the pie was quickly consumed.

"You know I saw you play freshman year," Charlotte said, resuming her conversation with Sully. "I caught a game on ESPN."

"You did?" Sully grinned. "Did I play well?"

"You threw a twenty-yard pass that was like a missile."

"I was something special." Sully grinned, rubbing his knuckles against his shoulder and letting out a laugh as Lou popped him on the arm.

"Anterior cruciate ligament. They have to replace it with another tendon."

The adults all turned to look at Jessica, who had been unusually quiet during the meal.

"That's right isn't it?" She turned to look at Maddie for confirmation.

Maddie exchanged a quick glance and an apologetic look with Alex, then smiled broadly at Jessica. "It is, sweetie, but remember what we said about talking about medical things at the table? Not everyone finds them as interesting."

"I thought that rule was just about private parts?"

Teddy snorted into her glass of wine. Then coughed contritely as Alex glared at her.

"No, honey, it's anything medical really," Alex clarified. "It's not really what should be talked about at the dinner table."

Jessica sighed and shrugged. "It's not like I was talking 'bout Gregor White's piles this time."

Charlotte cleared her throat. "So, Sam was telling me about his training for the biathlon."

Everyone looked at her gratefully for the change in topic. Ruth rose from the table and started to collect plates. "Sully, you should tell her about the time with the luge."

Erin stood and took the plates from Ruth. "If you're going to discuss how my stupid brother almost got himself killed, I'll go take these to the kitchen."

Alex stood and gathered her family's plates. "I'll help you."

Watching, Charlotte couldn't help but smile as Erin gently cuffed the back of Sully's head as she passed. She followed Erin's every move with her eyes and hadn't realized she'd completely zoned out of the conversation again until Ruth placed a warm hand on her forearm.

"You know me and Peter are grateful for you paying the lumberyard's dues, but if you need it back then you'll let me know?" Ruth patted her arm, then sat back to listen as Sully regaled the table with the story of Sam and the homemade luge.

Alex watched as Erin cleaned off the plates and stacked them neatly to be washed. "Must be strange, Charlotte being back an' all."

Erin paused as she considered Alex's comment. She sighed softly then returned to her task. "It's like I've fallen into some sort of parallel universe. I never thought I'd see her again never mind sitting at Ruth's table."

"Sometimes life just likes to throw you curve balls or Teddy's somewhere in the mix," Alex said as she loaded the plates into the dishwasher.

Snorting, Erin shook her head. "Yeah, that sounds about right."

"She said you kissed her?"

"Teddy?"

"Charlotte!"

Erin stopped what she was doing and looked stunned at Alex. "She spoke to you?"

Alex thrust out her chin defiantly. "Now don't be getting your panties in a twist. She needed to talk to someone. I'm only mentioning it to you to make sure you're okay. If you want to know what's going on in Charlotte's head, you're gonna have to talk to her and find out."

Sighing Erin slumped against the wall. "I'm not sure I can deal with what's going on in my head never mind hers."

"So what is going on in your head?"

"I see her, and my heart reacts like we're seventeen. But my head, my head is screaming that we're not seventeen, and I should act my age."

Alex closed the dishwasher and smiled. "You know I stood in this very kitchen and had a very similar discussion with Teddy about Maddie."

Erin pushed her shoulders against the wall to stand up straight. "And?"

"My heart and other more southern areas of my body were sure Maddie was the one. While my head kept telling me, we barely knew each other, and she wasn't staying in town."

Nodding Erin sighed. "That's just how I feel. We don't know each other. I'm not the same person I was as a teenager. At least I hope I'm not" — She scrubbed her face in frustration— "and her life isn't here. She's got this whole other life in New York. I guess while I understand why she did what she did, I'm still a little pissed at her."

"Maybe you should speak to her about what she wants and figure out what you want from there?" Alex suggested as she opened the door back to the dining room. "You never know, maybe you both want the same thing."

Stepping back into the room they paused at the scene that greeted them. Harvey Mack stood rubbing the back of his neck awkwardly alongside Clinton Thorpe, the public health inspector, who looked like he'd rather be a thousand other places than in Ruth's dining room.

"Hey, Clint." Alex looked confused at the tableau before her. "You here to see me?"

Clint glanced up nervously at the sound of Alex's voice. "Um, no. Hey, Alex. I'm, um, I'm here for Sully."

Sully removed his arm from the back of Lou's chair where it had been resting and sat forward. "I don't recall having an inspection planned this month."

Clearing his throat, Clint clutched his clipboard to his chest and spoke with his eyes firmly fixed on the table and not at Sully. "You don't. We had a complaint we need to investigate."

Rising to his feet, Sully pointed towards Harvey. "You had to bring the Deputy Sheriff to tell me this?"

Harvey held his hands up in defense. "Now, Sully, it ain't like that. I was passing the bar when Clint came out and asked if I knew where you'd be. I'm only here 'cause I was hoping there was some of Erin's mud pie left. Peter was talking 'bout it this morning at church."

Peter grinned. "There's some in the kitchen, but it's not the homemade kind." He shot Erin a look before leading Harvey from the room.

Erin smiled apologetically at Harvey as he passed and whispered another apology to Peter.

"So what's the complaint?" Alex asked.

Clint checked the papers on the clipboard to buy himself some time before he spoke. "There's been a sighting of rats."

∞ ∞ ∞

"So that was interesting."

Erin turned as Charlotte joined her on Ruth's porch. They both watched as Sully and Clint climbed into Sully's truck.

"You think he really has a rat problem?" Charlotte asked.

"I'm sorry," Erin replied, taking a deep breath to prepare herself. Her conversation with Alex had struck a nerve, and finally, she knew what she had to do and say.

"I said, do you think—"

"No, I heard you." Erin sighed, flustered now her rhythm had been interrupted. "I meant, I'm sorry as in I'm apologizing, not that I didn't hear what you said."

Charlotte grimaced. "Sorry, I...God we used to be so good at this. Talking, I mean," she clarified, as Erin shot her a confused look. "We used to be able to talk for hours and never get bored and be so in tune with each other. Do you remember that? I've never had that since. That feeling of completely being in sync with another person—"

"Stop!" Erin yelled. She ran a hand through her hair as she watched Charlotte's bewildered expression. "Please, just stop. I need to say some things, and I need you to just listen."

Nodding her head, Charlotte leaned against the railing.

"I'm sorry I kissed you." Erin raised her hand as Charlotte opened her mouth to interrupt. "You promised!" When Charlotte closed her mouth and held her hands up in an apology, Erin continued, "I shouldn't have kissed you. It added confusion to something that is already hugely complicated."

She closed her eyes to compose herself. "Before you came back I'd realized I was too stuck in my past to let me really focus on a future. I've been living in limbo for

151

years thinking work and family and friends were enough for me. But they're not. I want to love. I want to be loved by someone and hanging onto the love I had for you was stopping that.

"I had so many landmines no woman could get close to me without setting one off, and I would barely even acknowledge that the landmines existed, never mind do anything about them. Then...then you came back" —Erin opened her eyes to look at Charlotte— "and I was so pissed at you. Because after I decided to move forward I see you and even after all this time my stomach flips, and I get this feeling of happiness that goes all the way to my bones."

She hesitated seeing a smile begin to appear on Charlotte's face. "And I feel like a teenager again. Only I'm not. I'm almost forty. Neither of us are who we were back then. You've been back twice in over twenty years an' both times have been this month. You have a home and a life back in New York, and I'm trying to build a better life here. I needed to work out what I wanted from you, and now I know."

She chewed on her top lip to stop herself crying. "I will always be grateful for what we had, and I'll probably always wonder what might have been. I'm thankful for you coming back and setting the record straight. But I need to leave the past where it belongs now. The people we are today, well, we're virtual strangers. So if you're staying in Grace Falls for me, then you should probably go home."

Without giving Charlotte a chance to respond, she stepped off the porch and strode to her truck without looking back.

$$\infty \quad \infty \quad \infty$$

"Teddy, you may want to go rescue Douglas from Jessica before she grills him about police procedure." Maddie stopped in the doorway and rolled her eyes. "Will you three come away from the window." She gave Alex a disapproving look.

"I think you might have bruised my kidney with your elbow." Alex slapped Teddy's shoulder.

Teddy shrugged. "Sorry, I was just trying to acknowledge the landmines."

"By giving me internal bleeding?"

Ruth spun around slowly, her face crumpled in confusion. "So wait. They were together?" she whispered, looking at each of her friends' faces for confirmation. "When we were at school. They were together?"

When Alex and Teddy nodded, Ruth flung her hands into the air. "How am I only finding out about this now?" She dropped down onto her sofa. "I just thought they were best friends."

152

"They were," Teddy replied, sinking into the sofa beside Ruth. "Only more so."

"You knew?" Ruth turned accusingly to Teddy.

Teddy held her hands up in defense. "Only recently. Alex has known for ages."

Ruth turned to Alex, who shrunk back under her glare. "I've only known for a couple of years. Sully knew all along."

Maddie shook her head. "Remind me never to commit a crime with you two snitches."

Ignoring her, Ruth continued to glare at Alex. "Yeah well he's not here right now, you are. I can't believe I didn't know this. Oh, my God, that was why you wanted me to tell Erin that Charlotte was back. I just thought you were being overly dramatic." She punched Teddy's arm. "You shoulda told me."

She returned her attention to Alex. "So you didn't know about them that time you and Charlotte got friendly on my mama's bed?"

Alex shook her head. "That was before they got together. I didn't even know Charlotte played on my team until I was laying on your mama's bed with her on top of me."

"Huh?" Teddy raised her eyebrows quizzically.

"What?" Alex asked.

Teddy shrugged. "Nothing, I just always had you pegged as an on top kinda gal."

Alex threw a flushed looking Maddie a triumphant look, which quickly turned into a frown. "You've thought about that?"

Teddy grinned at Alex. "Sure. Haven't you thought about what we all get up to? I mean I'm pretty sure Ruth—"

Ruth spun to look at Teddy. "If you finish that sentence, Claudia Roosevelt, I will boob punch you."

Teddy chewed on her lips meekly until Ruth was no longer looking at her. Immediately she mouthed 'doggy style' to Alex whose eye roll was enough to alert Ruth that her threat had been ignored.

In one fluid motion, Ruth turned and punched Teddy squarely on her right boob.

Maddie watched as Teddy clutched her chest and the friends continued their whispered fight. She glanced out of the window and spotted Charlotte still standing on the porch. Wordlessly she opened the door and snuck out of the house.

"You okay?"

Charlotte spun around, wiping at her red-rimmed eyes. "Yes. No. I honestly have no idea," she replied, giving Maddie a weary smile.

Maddie stood beside her, both looking out across Ruth's front yard. "You want to talk about it?"

Sighing, Charlotte patted Maddie's arm. "Not really. I'm gonna go home."

Maddie watched as Charlotte plodded down the steps. When she reached the bottom, she turned. "Can you thank Ruth for her hospitality for me?" Seeing Maddie's nod, she continued down the path.

"Charlotte!" Maddie waited until Charlotte turned towards her. "My mom says that things that are meant to be, have a way of working out."

Charlotte shrugged. "My mama said no matter if the glass is half empty or half full, there's always space for gin." She smiled and held up her hand in a wave. "I'm inclined to test out my mama's saying before believing yours."

Chapter Twenty-Four

ranky. All morning Cindy tried to find a better word for Erin's mood. Cranky pretty much seemed to sum it up best. Thanks to Erin's ribs, Cindy had spent the morning squeezing anal glands while Erin hid in the cupboard under the pretense of stocktaking.

"If anyone has grounds to be cranky it's me," she muttered, leaning on the reception desk.

Erin's head appeared from behind the desk. "What?"

Cindy jumped back and clutched her chest. "What the hell you doing back there? I thought you were in the cupboard still."

"I was, and then I came to find a pen and ended up clearing the mess back here."

Cindy peered over the counter and took a sharp intake of breath as her chaotic looking desk had been decluttered and reorganized by Erin. "I'm never going to find anything now," she wailed in frustration.

"I have no idea how you found anything in the first place." Erin stood up and winced at the pain the movement caused.

Cindy grabbed her by the sleeve and pulled her from behind the desk. "This is my workspace. I don't go into yours, and you don't go into mine. That's the deal." She moaned as she surveyed the damage Erin wreaked on her desk.

"Yeah, well maybe you should keep your workspace tidier."

Pulling herself up to her full height, Cindy shook her head. "Okay, what the hell is wrong with you?" You're acting like a wet hen in a tote sack." She glared at Erin waiting for her response.

Erin's eyes narrowed. Cindy was tempted to take a step back as she sensed an impending outburst of anger. It didn't happen often, but when Erin did lose her temper, it was a sight to behold. It was like a cloudburst on a sunny day. One minute the world is as you'd expect, then all of a sudden all hell breaks loose. Then as quick as it appeared it was gone. Faced with the possibility, she summoned her inner Mack and crossed her arms. With a cocked eyebrow, she glared right back at Erin.

"I'll tell you what's wrong." Erin placed her hands on her hips. "In the space of forty-eight hours, I have had the sum total of four hours sleep. I have ribs that hurt like hell when I move or breathe, and if that wasn't enough, I kissed the only woman I've ever loved and then promptly told her to leave town."

"Charlotte Grace?"

"Christ! Does the whole town know my business?"

Cindy shrugged, her attention only partially on Erin as a car pulled up outside the clinic. "No secrets in this town, but I do know one thing. Your whole 'this town ain't big enough for the both of us' speech didn't work."

"What do you mean?"

Nodding towards the door, Cindy smirked. "'Cause she's about to come through that door."

A look of panic spread across Erin's face as she sprinted towards her office. "I am not here!"

The door to Erin's office closed just as Charlotte opened the front door.

"She in?" Charlotte pointed towards the rear of the vet's office, barely waiting for a response as she strode through the office.

Cindy held up her thumb in the direction of Erin's departure. "Third door on the left."

She smiled sweetly as Charlotte passed, then looked back at her desk. "Mess with my workspace, you mess with me."

Erin pressed her back against the door and exhaled slowly. She was in no state to deal with Charlotte today. Last night when she'd made her declaration she'd been sure it was the right course of action for them both. However, in the early hours of the morning, doubts plagued her. She rested her head against the door and took a calming breath. She was still inhaling when she was thrown forward as the door to her office was flung open with force.

"What the hell, Cindy!" She managed to grab the exam table to stop her fall. The pain in her ribs caused specks of light to appear in front of her eyes.

"Oh my God, I didn't know you were behind the door."

Erin spun as she heard Charlotte's voice. "Why are you barging into my office?"

"I was trying to make an entrance," Charlotte said sheepishly.

Standing up, Erin smoothed her hands down her plaid shirt and strode to the door ready to let rip at Cindy. She stuck her head out of the door and scowled at

Cindy, who stood holding up the full trashcan Erin had filled with the clutter from her desk.

"Seriously!" Erin shouted.

With a smirk on her face, Cindy dramatically emptied the contents back onto her desk. "My workspace," she trilled, before disappearing behind her desk to return it to its previous state.

"You okay?" Charlotte asked.

Erin thumped her forehead lightly against the door frame a couple of times before retreating into her office. "I'm fine." She moved around Charlotte to the sanctuary of her desk. "I don't have anything else to say. I said everything last night."

"Good," Charlotte replied, flopping down into the seat opposite Erin's.

Sensing that Charlotte was not going to be deterred Erin sighed and dropped wearily into her own seat. "Charlie—"

"No. It's my turn." Charlotte stood up and started to pace. "I think I'm proof that one of us making decisions that affect both of us doesn't work." She stopped pacing and turned to look at Erin. "I listened to what you said last night, and you were right. We don't know if we have anything in common now other than our past. But I do know I want to find out more about the woman you've become.

"I totally get you have worries about me going back to New York, but just one of the fascinating facts you'll find out about me is I don't have anything keeping me there. So"—Charlotte sat back down, crossed her legs and looked challengingly at Erin—"I'm not going anywhere."

Before she could respond the door to her office opened, and Cindy's face appeared. "Sorry, Caleb Sutton is on the phone wanting you to go out to the farm for a consult on Junior. They're still having problems. You want me to refer him to St Anton?"

Erin turned slowly to look at Charlotte as if considering something. A slow smile broke out across her face as she shook her head. "Nah, tell him I'm on my way. I have an assistant."

∞ ∞ ∞

Erin glanced over as she fastened her seatbelt. Her hand paused in mid-action as she took in the expanse of skin visible thanks to Charlotte's cut-offs and vest top.

"You okay? Are your ribs hurting?" Charlotte noticed Erin's hesitation. "Should you even be working?"

Erin shook her head part in response and also to rid herself of the thoughts seeing Charlotte's long toned legs had created.

"I'm fine." She leaned over to the glove compartment and retrieved the sunblock she kept there. She tried to ignore the butterflies in her stomach as she inhaled Charlotte's fragrance in passing. "You should put this on if you're not already wearing some" —She reached across the console to snag her battered ball cap—"an' this."

Charlotte took the hat and threaded her hair through the back. She was oblivious to Erin's growing stares as she applied the sunscreen to her arms and exposed shoulders.

"So maybe we should ask each other questions?" Charlotte returned the tube of sunscreen to the glove box. "You know, to get to know each other. Maybe start with—"

"How come you didn't come home for your daddy's funeral?"

Charlotte cocked her head and held back a smile as Erin nervously tapped the steering wheel as she waited for a response. "I was going to say start with the easy stuff, hobbies, favorite movies, but we can do it your way." She released her smile as Erin looked at her apologetically.

"Sorry, what hobbies you got?" A matching smile appeared on Erin's face.

"I didn't know he died."

Erin's smile slowly disappeared, and she looked at Charlotte in confusion. When the penny dropped, she had to stop herself from snarling in rage.

"She didn't contact you?"

Charlotte reached out and placed her hand on Erin's thigh. Her touch immediately soothed Erin's rage while simultaneously eliciting an altogether different reaction.

"I'm not sure she knew how to. I cut myself off from them both after high school. Although Ruth managed to track me down. So I guess where there's a will there's a way."

"Ruth used Alex's daughter Jessica to find you." Erin tried to ignore the heat on her leg where it felt as though Charlotte's hand was burning through the fabric of her shorts.

"She's just a kid!"

"A really bright kid." Erin reached down and patted Charlotte's hand, which still rested on her thigh. The action seemed to remind Charlotte where her hand was, and she removed it.

"By the time Ruth got me, the funeral had passed."

"It was a nice service."

Charlotte swallowed and tipped her head back.

"So hobbies? You still play tennis?" Erin asked with forced levity in an attempt to lighten the atmosphere.

"Occasionally. I run more than I play sports. Not having to change direction is less stress on my ACL."

Erin looked over at the slight scarring on Charlotte's right knee. As if feeling her gaze, Charlotte's fingers traced the white marks.

"What about you?"

"Nothing specific. Work takes up most of my time." Erin pulled off the road and onto the track leading to the Sutton farm.

Charlotte reached over and flicked the turn signal. "I see you still don't know what that's for."

Erin frowned and flipped the lever off. "The noise bugs me." She pulled to a stop, turned to Charlotte and stuck her tongue out.

"Hey, Doc."

Erin rapidly rearranged her features and turned to the driver's window where Caleb Sutton stood smiling in.

"Miss Charlotte, is that you?"

"Hey, Mr. Sutton." Charlotte greeted him with a small wave. "Hope you don't mind me tagging along with Erin." She opened her door and climbed out of the truck.

Caleb opened Erin's door. "No problem at all. Doc, we've got Junior tethered up over in the front paddock."

Erin winced as she climbed out of the truck, and her pain wasn't lost on Charlotte. "You sure you're okay to do this?"

Waving her hand in response, Erin went to the rear of the truck to gather the supplies she needed.

"Seriously, you let me know if there's something I can do," Charlotte said. The genuine nature of concern in her tone was evident as she watched Erin collecting items.

"Oh don't worry, you'll be lending a hand," Erin replied, walking briskly from Charlotte.

"I can't believe you made me do that!" Charlotte said watching as Erin waved a cheerful goodbye to the Suttons and steered her truck out of their yard.

"You wanted to help."

Hearing a smile in Erin's voice, Charlotte turned in her seat. "Do you think it's funny? Yes, I wanted to help. I thought I could maybe hold your stethoscope, maybe pass you pliers. That sorta stuff." She huffed as she turned back and glared out of the passenger window.

"I'm a vet, not a mechanic! You're the one who demanded to spend time with me, to find out more about the woman I've become."

Charlotte spun back to face Erin. "You made me hold a bull's penis!"

Erin biting down on her bottom lip was almost enough to make Charlotte forget about her righteous indignation. Almost. "While you stuck something up its ass and zapped it 'til it came!"

Erin's laughter exploded from her. She glanced across at Charlotte whose disgusted expression only made her laugh more.

"It's not funny." While a huge part of her was still outraged and somewhat horrified by what Erin made her do, a small part of her brain rejoiced at hearing Erin's unbridled laughter. "I will get you back," she added, a smirk finding its way onto her lips.

"Oh God, my ribs."

"Yeah, well that there"—Charlotte pointed her finger towards Erin's side—"is Karma and Molly says 'Karma's only ever a bitch if you are.'" Glancing over at Erin, she caught the flicker of hurt on her face. "Shit. I'm not calling you a bitch." She reached out and tentatively touched Erin's leg. She could feel the anxiety coming off of Erin, and her heart almost broke that her presence had that effect. She frantically tried to recover lost ground.

"When Molly says it to me she's all sassy and funny. Holy crap, I didn't mean to call you names. I'm getting this all wrong."

Erin chewed on her bottom lip. When she eventually spoke she didn't turn to look at Charlotte. "Thank you."

"For apologizing?"

"For staying."

The grin on Charlotte's face showed no signs of dimming until they approached the outskirts of town.

"Where we going?" Charlotte asked, twisting in her seat to look back at the turn she'd assumed they'd take.

"Figured we'd make a stop."

Charlotte's eyes narrowed as she attempted to work out where Erin was taking her. With the very next turn, they took, their destination became apparent. Charlotte's heart started to thump faster in her chest.

"Erin, please."

"It's time, Charlie. You should go pay your respects." Erin pulled the truck to a stop, put it into park, and switched off the engine.

Charlotte pulled Erin's ball cap lower. She slumped in her seat and fixed her eyes on the still windshield wipers, refusing to engage with Erin or her surroundings.

They sat in silence. Charlotte knew Erin was giving her time to come to terms with where they were. Despite the passage of time, Erin could still anticipate her emotions. Five minutes passed before Erin pulled the keys from the ignition and placed them on Charlotte's lap.

"I'm gonna go say hi to my pop. If you're planning on going, just come back and get me in a half hour."

Charlotte transferred her gaze from the wipers to the keys that lay in her lap. The metal was cool against her exposed thighs. She heard Erin's quiet groans as she climbed out of the truck, followed by the click of the driver's door.

Several more minutes had passed before she removed Erin's cap, slowly opened the passenger door and climbed out of the truck.

She entered the cemetery and walked with her head down towards where Erin stood.

"Hey, Daddy, you remember Charlotte Grace," Erin spoke in quiet tones towards her father's headstone. She turned, and a small smile tugged at her lips. "I come about once a month just to say hi and let him know Sam's not managed to maim or kill himself."

"Hey, Mr. Hunter." Charlotte lifted her hand as if to wave and then stopped as she realized the absurdity of the action. Erin caught the gesture and reached for Charlotte's hand.

"You wanna go see your daddy?"

Gripping Erin's hand Charlotte nodded. Erin tugged gently and led Charlotte to where her father was buried.

"Did you see much of him after I left?" Charlotte blinked rapidly to clear her eyes of the tears gathering there.

Erin squeezed her hand in support. "To be honest, I was a bit chicken-shit. It was bad enough seeing your mama's death glare. I didn't want to face the wrath of a father pissed off 'cause I..."—she lowered her voice—"de-flowered his daughter."

Charlotte choked back a laugh. "Technically, Sully did the de-flowering."

"So what did I do then?"

"You made things blossom."

A blush appeared on Erin's cheeks. "To be fair to him, when I did speak to him he never let on he was pissed at me. In fact, a few months before he died, he cleared off what was left of my debt from school."

Charlotte looked up in surprise. "Did you find out why?"

Shaking her head, Erin knelt down to clear some leaves from the grave. "Nope, but he did tell me one day he was proud of what I'd achieved. So maybe that was it."

The words hit Charlotte like a sucker punch. The one thing she craved to hear from her father were words she would never hear from his lips.

Seeing Charlotte's body curl as if to protect itself from her words Erin rose and pulled her into a tight hug. "He was proud of you," she whispered against Charlotte's hair.

"You don't know that."

Erin gripped Charlotte's shoulders and gently created enough space to allow her to look into her eyes. "I'm sure of it. Why don't I give you two some time alone?"

Charlotte gazed into the hazel eyes studying her. A slight wariness still keeping away the warmth she knew they could convey. She nodded and turned towards her father's grave. Knowing, without looking, when Erin had left her.

At one time there wasn't a thought Charlotte could have that Erin didn't already pre-empt or share. However, that all ended abruptly in the hallway of the Grace house, and Erin was no longer sure of her ability to read Charlotte. Witnessing Charlotte's reaction earlier allowed her to see a vulnerability she was sure so few had ever seen. Erin felt both protective and incredibly blessed.

She looped back towards the Grace Family plot, hoping the time she'd given Charlotte had allowed her to find some peace. As she neared the headstone, she couldn't see Charlotte but could hear her voice.

"Daddy, you remember how I was best friends with Erin. Well, she was always more than my best friend an' I know you didn't approve, but you need to know I never set out to hurt or disappoint anyone. All I did was fall in love.

"I hope you can appreciate that now and also understand I don't care about our family name or reputation. I have never stopped loving Erin. Leaving her was the hardest thing I've ever done. I've never felt complete since. I've blocked people from getting close to me and buried myself in a terrible relationship to punish myself for denying how I felt.

"It's been over twenty years. Yet I spend a moment with her, and she makes me feel as though I'm whole again. I don't know if she'll ever trust me or love me back, but I am going to do my damnedest to prove she can."

Charlotte stood up and dusted off her legs. As she straightened, her eyes met Erin's.

"Did you mean that?" Erin stepped forward hesitatingly to stand in front of Charlotte.

"I did. It's what I should have said back then."

Erin's lips curled into a smile. As Charlotte attempted to mirror her smile, she felt another section of the wall that sheltered her heart crumble. Without thinking she leaned closer and grazed Charlotte's lips with her own. She allowed them to rest there for a moment, reveling in Charlotte's softness, before pulling away.

"Please don't." Charlotte's voice was ragged with emotion. Seeing the questioning look on Erin's face, she continued holding both of Erin's hands. "I have a lifetime of memories of you kissing me then running away. Don't run this time, please."

Erin's confused look gave way to a smile. "I wasn't going to run, I promise. It's just making out in the town cemetery..."

"Oh." Charlotte looked around as if suddenly remembering where they were. She looked back towards her father's grave and blushed. She turned towards Erin. "I promise. I will do anything you ask of me if only you'll give me a chance."

Erin smiled widely. "Well, I do have some neutering work. I could use an extra pair of hands on."

Charlotte flinched. The hopeful look she wore was momentarily replaced with one of horror before she managed to muster a look of resolve. "As you wish."

As Erin directed them back towards the entrance, she could almost hear the cogs turning in Charlotte's head wondering whether she was serious about the threat. Finally, she took pity.

"Stop worrying. I'm not going to make you remove balls," Erin said, without looking in her direction.

The sigh of relief filled Erin with a warmth that had been missing since her teenage years. It appeared that her ability to read Charlotte remained intact.

Chapter Twenty-Five

*E*rin hummed softly to herself as she saved the update to a patient's record. Her time with Charlotte the day before had been unexpected and at times fraught with emotion. However, hearing Charlotte's speech at her father's grave almost obliterated Erin's softening resolve. That said, there was still a part of her terrified of allowing Charlotte full access to her heart again.

As she lifted her coffee cup to her mouth, she replayed the gentle kiss Charlotte had bestowed on her when she'd dropped her back at the Anderson house. She imagined the cool ceramic pressed against her mouth were Charlotte's soft lips. It was only when she took a sip of cold coffee that the image withered from her mind.

She sighed, stood up and crossed her office intent on replenishing her coffee from the pot in reception. As she opened her door, she heard Cindy's voice.

"She's good, but she's not a miracle worker. She can't Lazarus a dead animal!"

Erin exchanged an exasperated look with Cooper, who was completely disinterested in her personnel issues. She stepped out to apologize to whoever Cindy was no doubt upsetting, when she heard Sully's voice in response.

"I don't need her to bring it to life. I just want her to have a look at it." Seeing Erin, Sully shot Cindy a glare. "Hey, Erin can you have a look at this for me?" He picked up a box from the counter and stuck his tongue out at Cindy when Erin said she would.

"So what have you brought me?" Erin asked, holding the door open for Sully.

"A dead rat." Sully set the box down on the examination table.

Erin's eyebrows raised as she walked over to peer into the box. "You know flowers or candy are usually the way to go if you want to woo me."

Sully smirked. "I think Charlotte's got the wooing sewn up if what I saw last night outside the Anderson house is anything to go by."

Furrowing her eyebrows, Erin looked up at Sully's smug expression. "I hate you."

"You love me."

"I hate you!" She pointed to the box. "So why are you bringing me a Fancy rat?"

Sully looked into the box. "It's not fancy, it's just dead."

Erin shook her head. "Fancy with a capital F. It's the domesticated breed of rat."

"A pet?"

Nodding her head, Erin pulled on a pair of gloves to pick up the rat to examine it further. She turned it over to look at its underside. "If I'm not mistaken it's a black cap. See the coloring around its head?"

"A pet?" Sully repeated, looking at where Erin was pointing. "You sure?"

"It's hard to be absolutely sure. Typically, their behavior sets them apart from wild rats. But with this one being dead its behavior is kinda the same as a dead wild rat." Seeing Sully start to lose his temper she coughed and returned her attention to the rat. "The coloring of this one would be extremely rare to see in a wild rat. Where'd you find it?"

Sully pointed to the rat still in Erin's hand. "That there is my rat problem."

"Why would a pet rat be in your bar?"

"That's what I want to know," Sully replied with a clenched jaw.

∞ ∞ ∞

Charlotte walked through the deserted school halls looking for the right room. Although the color on the walls was different, the school still had the same smell. However, everything seemed smaller somehow. She held back a laugh as she opened the door to Teddy's classroom and saw the group of assembled adults huddled into the chairs designed to host Teddy's third-grade class.

"You're late." Teddy flicked her hand out towards the classroom. "Take a seat."

Biting her cheek to avoid apologizing, Charlotte took a place beside a bemused looking Erin. "What are we doing here?" she whispered.

Without taking her eyes from Teddy, Erin responded out of the side of her mouth. "At the moment I'm contemplating repeating grade school 'cause I'm not sure my ass will get out of this seat ever again."

Charlotte hastily smothered her snort as Teddy glared in her direction.

"Thank you for coming." Teddy clapped her hands together to gather everyone's attention. "As you all know Sully"—she nodded in Sully's direction, who held up a hand and waved apologetically at everyone—"has had his bar closed due to a rat problem. The only problem with his rat problem is that evidence would suggest this is not a natural problem!"

"Seriously?" Ruth turned to Sully for confirmation.

165

Sully nodded. "Looks that way. Erin says the rat I found in the bar is more likely a pet rat than wild."

"Seriously?" Alex turned to address Erin. "People keep rats as pets?"

"They're actually quite intelligent and affectionate," Erin replied, ignoring the incredulous looks on her friends' faces.

"Focus people!" Teddy yelled, bringing their attention back to her. "So since it's a pet rat, we can assume someone put it in the bar on purpose." She turned to the whiteboard she used for her classes. "So I've put some names up as possible suspects."

Charlotte's eyes widened as she spotted her name on the list. "Why am I on there?"

Teddy crossed her arms. "Just because of the timing. You appear, and the rats appear."

Charlotte was about to object further when Sully stood up and wiped her name from the list using the heel of his hand. "It's not Charlotte."

"Thank you, Sully." Charlotte smiled and nodded before returning her gaze to Teddy and narrowing her eyes. Satisfied she'd made her point, she returned to the names on the list and let out a soft snort as she read her mother's name. "You honestly think Virginia would handle rats?"

Teddy looked at her contemplatively before shrugging and removing Virginia Grace's name. "Good point. Although she could have got someone else to do her dirty work." Teddy underlined Brett Ford's name with a flourish.

"Who's he?" Charlotte whispered to Erin.

"The man your mama hired to run the lumberyard." Erin turned to look at Charlotte for the first time since she sat down. She smiled shyly. "Hi."

"Hi."

"When you two lovebirds are done. Can we focus on why we're here?" Teddy rapped her pen against the desk to get their attention.

Reluctantly both turned to face the front of the classroom again. "Is it likely he'd do it? Do y'all know him at all?" Charlotte huffed as she attempted to sit forward on the small seat. The pain of the seat digging into her thigh muscles made her give up and sit back again.

Ruth glanced at Peter, who shrugged then raised a hand motioning her to go on. She cleared her throat before speaking. "I don't think there's too much love lost there. I overheard Virginia giving him a dressing down a while back when the wages were missed at the lumberyard."

At the mention of wage issues, Charlotte ignored the discomfort and sat forward in her seat. "They've not been paying folks?"

"Just that once I think," Ruth added hastily. "I think maybe cash flow's been a problem of late."

"People!" Teddy barked. "Less lumber talk, more rats!"

"Anyways, I'm not sure he'd do what Virginia asked," Ruth concluded.

Sully seemed to consider the conversation for a moment before speaking. "What if he's doing it on his own?" All eyes in the room turned to look at him. "He's always drank up a storm at the bar. But he never appeared the type to be an angry drunk, more just beaten down by life. But that whole scene about ladies' night seemed to spark a rage in him. He's never been back in the bar since. I figured he'd just found somewhere else to spend his dollars."

"I think we might have just spotted our prime suspect." Teddy circled Brett Ford's name. "Now we just need proof. What we should do is — "

Teddy halted at the sound of Charlotte's cell phone ringing, sheepishly she rushed to pull it from her pocket. Seeing Molly's name flash on the screen, she apologized and hauled herself, with the help of a gentle push from Erin, out from the seat. She turned to thank her and smiled at the blush on Erin's face.

"Thanks, I owe you one."

Her smile turned into a wide grin when Erin's blush deepened. She ignored Teddy's death glare as she left the room and answered the FaceTime request.

"So you're alive!" Molly yelled before Charlotte had the phone up to her face.

"Sorry, Moll."

"You don't call. You don't text. I've been out of my mind with worry."

"Really?"

"No, not really. I used that 'find your phone' thing and saw where you were. Figured you would contact me eventually. However, since that started to look unlikely..."

"I've just been so busy since I got here."

It was a surprise to Charlotte that it wasn't an excuse. Her life back in Manhattan felt like an entire lifetime away and much to her chagrin, she hadn't given her friends back there a second thought since her return to Grace Falls.

Molly let out a huff and rolled her eyes.

"Honestly, I'm sorry," Charlotte said pitifully, giving Molly her best puppy eyes.

"Oh, stop with the eyes." Molly groaned, placing her hand over the screen to avoid looking at Charlotte. "You done?" She lifted her hand and peeked. Seeing Charlotte was now grinning at her, she took her hand away completely. "So I suppose you've been too busy to even check your email?"

Charlotte winced. "I'm sorry."

"You want the good news or the bad news?"

"Good news?" Charlotte replied warily.

"You look really relaxed." Molly grinned. "Now I'm going to give you the bad news which might impact that whole relaxed Big Easy thing you've got going on."

"That's New Orleans," Charlotte correctly absently. She briefly considered Molly's observation and was surprised. She did feel relaxed.

"What's the bad news."

"Grace Timber. Being a private company, there's not much we can get our hands on officially to make an assessment of the accounts. The company's too small to even register on the databases we usually use. However, we have been able to do some data mining." Molly hesitated, biting her bottom lip.

Charlotte recognized the facial expression and immediately caught onto Molly's use of 'data mining.' This meant that the channels Molly had gone down may not be strictly legal. "And?"

"Not good," Molly concluded. "Up until your father died the business was growing. It looked like they were producing good quality products, and a wide range too. Just like you thought. They had bulk contracts with some big builders in the state. Your father had it sewn up from the felling, cutting and finishing. The reputation was good."

Charlotte barely had time to acknowledge that Molly must have been doing her homework on all aspects of the lumberyard before the 'but' that had been lurking in Molly's tone finally appeared.

"But since your father...well, they've lost some contracts with house builders, which made up the bulk of their income. They have some low-level debts, much like the one with the mechanic you paid off. Nothing too major. Their wage bill caused them to go into a credit line at the bank, which they'd never done before. While it's not terrible, it's just not sustainable the way they're going." Molly winced as she finished her assessment of the current situation.

"How long they got?" Charlotte asked.

"The way they're going. A year. Eighteen months tops," Molly surmised. "That's not all. The guy running the business..."

"Brett Ford?"

"That's him. His resume is a crock. He's never managed on this scale, and his last employer sacked him for drinking on the job. Apparently, he went off the rails when his wife ...wait for it."

"Ran off with another woman?"

Molly's face fell. "Holy shit, is that a gaydar thing?"

"Nope, it just explains a whole lot."

"What do you want me to do about Grace Timber?"

Charlotte took in a deep breath. "Make her an offer."

Molly leaned closer to the camera. "Did you just hear what I said?"

"I did, and I didn't hear anything that wasn't insurmountable."

"You honestly want to make a go of it there, 'cause this isn't something you're going to be able to manage from here." Molly waved her arm around to indicate the city behind her.

"I do." Charlotte chewed on her lower lip. "I can't describe it exactly, but it just feels right. I had no idea how lost I felt until I came back here."

Molly's eye's widened. "You're serious? You're considering not coming back? You do realize how crazy this sounds, right?"

Charlotte thought back to her conversation with Maddie and what she'd given up for Alex. While nothing was guaranteed with Erin, Charlotte couldn't help but hope that staying in Grace Falls would at least provide them with the opportunity to explore whether they had a future.

"I know you're worried, but honestly, this feels like it's what I was meant to do." She knew what would make her friend realize she was serious. "I deleted the folder with Tina's photos. I'm ready to move on."

"Get me the details of your mother's lawyer, and I'll get something drawn up. I'll send it over so you can review before we submit."

"It's important this can't be traced back to me. Otherwise, she'll never agree."

"Leave it with me."

Charlotte could see how unhappy Molly was with her revelation. However, she felt content with her decision.

"You know I love you!" Charlotte said, smiling at her friend.

"Yeah, I love you too, assface," Molly grumbled. "An' just so you know, absence doesn't make the heart grow fonder, 'cause I love you more when you're here to help me manage Joanne."

"I'll be back soon to help you with her and get things sorted." Charlotte laughed. "I'll call soon."

Molly nodded and ended the connection. Pausing, Charlotte looked at the screen of her cell. During the call, she'd come to the conclusion about her future that had been eluding her since she sold her business. The smile on her face grew as she became excited at the prospect. Putting her phone back in her pocket she reentered the room.

"So we're all clear?" Teddy looked at each of her friends in turn and ignored Charlotte rejoining the group.

Erin held her hand up to speak, then dropped it and rolled her eyes as if realizing she'd automatically fallen into school habits. "You know he might not have bought them local."

Waving her hand to dismiss Erin's point, Teddy shook her head. "We have to start somewhere and where we're starting is with Ruth. She will snap a photo of him, and you and Charlotte will go to the suppliers of rats. Peter and Sully will start surveillance tonight on Ford's home to see whether he tries something else."

Sully grinned towards Peter. "I'll bring the coffee. You get the donuts."

Teddy clapped her hands together. "Okay then. Let's be careful out there." Fully engaged in teacher mode, she turned and started to erase the names from the whiteboard.

"How come we didn't get anything," Alex grumbled as she stood up, ignoring Maddie's shushing noises. "I'd be great at this. I wanna chase him down and do that ass slide thing over the hood of the car."

Maddie grinned and spoke quietly into Alex's ear. "I'll let you be Cagney to my Lacey tonight."

A slight blush appeared on Alex's cheeks as she laced her fingers through Maddie's. "Okay, that sounds like more fun." She waved a hand towards her friends. "Let me know how you get on and, Peter, I'll have the donuts in the coffee shop waiting for you."

Charlotte watched as the friends slowly dispersed. She felt envious of Alex and Maddie and their relationship. She wanted that easy banter, and the ability to make her lover blush just from her words. Turning to face Erin, she smiled. "So we're going to check out rat suppliers?"

"Looks like it. I've got a list of breeders back at the office. We can start with them once Ruth gets the photo." Erin glanced in her direction. "Do you want to come with me?"

"Let's do this! Rat breeders here we come," Charlotte said, following Erin out of the classroom.

Chapter Twenty-Six

"So how we going to do this?" Charlotte browsed Erin's office while she waited for her to find the list of breeders.

Hitting print, Erin sat back in her chair and watched Charlotte as she studied her certifications mounted on the wall. The blonde highlights were more evident in her auburn hair than Erin's memory recalled, but her green eyes and sensual mouth were just as she remembered. The most recent memory of those lips pressed against hers had Erin calling upon every ounce of resolve she possessed not to grab Charlotte and continue where they'd left off the night before.

"I guess we just take it slow and get reacquainted." She tugged absently on her earlobe as her eyes traveled over Charlotte's profile.

Charlotte turned her head and grinned. "I was talking about the rat breeders."

Flustered, Erin ran her hands through her hair and stood up to collect the list from the printer.

"But," Charlotte continued, "I like that you were thinking about us, and it's not just me preoccupied with thoughts of us."

Smiling, Erin looked at the paper in her hand. "We have four to check off that are within a two-hundred-mile radius of town. You up for a road trip?" she asked Charlotte, who had resumed investigating. She was now assessing the shelf where Erin kept her display of vintage veterinary instruments. Erin watched in amusement as Charlotte picked up one made of thick glass, in the shape of a horn. She pressed on the thick rubber bulbous end and made a honking noise. Taking the instrument from Charlotte, Erin stifled a chuckle.

"Not really what it was designed for." She placed it carefully back on the shelf.

Charlotte stuck out her bottom lip. "Shoulda been."

"Yeah, it was used more as an enema pump than a horn." Erin waited for the inevitable reaction from Charlotte.

A shudder went through Charlotte's body. "Okay, not going to touch anything else in here, ever."

Moving into her personal space, Erin cocked her head to the side. "Really?"

"Is this what you had in mind when you said reacquainted?"

Reluctantly Erin stepped back. "A large part of me, well the brain part wants to go slow. My more southern parts want to reacquaint now."

Charlotte moved forward, so they were breathing the same air. "I get it. If I'm honest, I'm not ready. I don't want to mess this up. I want to take it slow. We have time."

"Yeah, you being so close when saying that doesn't help. It sorta makes me want you more." Erin grazed her bottom lip with her teeth.

Charlotte's green eyes darkened as her gaze moved between Erin's eyes and her lips.

Erin leaned forward. She hesitated when her lips were seconds away from capturing Charlotte's. Smiling as she spoke she could feel her breath caressing Charlotte's lips. "You know if you deny yourself something you'll only crave it more. So I'm doing this for the good of both of us. One kiss and then we get on with the whole slow reacquainting thing."

She brought her hands up to the back of Charlotte's neck, her fingers trailing into the soft hair at the nape. With the slightest of pressure, she brought their lips together. The soft tender kiss grew quickly as both women desperately took what they needed from the brief moment.

Charlotte placed her hands on Erin's hips and tugged her towards her, her greedy mouth seeking out Erin again and again. Neither was sure who moaned at the point their tongues touched, and neither cared. They simply lost themselves in the familiarity of each other.

A vibration from Erin's pocket was enough to bring them back from the brink. They pulled apart half-heartedly both breathing heavily, their lips swollen.

"Good plan," Charlotte said breathlessly.

Erin tilted her head and placed a chaste kiss on Charlotte's lips before pulling away entirely and pulling her cell from her pocket. She rolled her shoulders as if the action could somehow relieve the tension in her body.

"You think, 'cause I'm not so sure it was my brightest idea." She checked the screen of her phone. "We've got a photo. Looks like we're hitting the road."

"You honestly think he drove two-hundred miles to get some rats?" Charlotte climbed into the driver's seat of her rental.

Erin paused before cautiously entering the vehicle. Her ribs still ached from her accident. "I don't know, but I do know if we don't check them out, Teddy will have something to say about it."

Charlotte laughed as she started the engine. "And we're not just calling them, why?"

"Something about seeing the whites of their eyes. If you don't tell Teddy, I won't, 'cause we're gonna skip one. I can call the one breeder who's north. I know her. She has kin in the area. That way we can focus on the other three in the south without doubling back on ourselves."

"Okay, so point me in the right direction." Charlotte put the car into drive and pulled out of the parking lot at the office.

"East of Livingston is our first stop. Which means we have a whole hour and a half for reacquainting purposes."

Grinning, Charlotte shook her head. "Not while I'm driving! That's only gonna end in a crash."

"I meant the other kind of reacquainting." Erin gave Charlotte's thigh a playful slap.

"So where do you wanna start?"

"The relationship you mentioned at the cemetery."

Charlotte blew out a breath and settled in her seat for the drive and the explanation. "While I had one relationship that lasted six years, she had several in the same time period." Charlotte smiled sadly. "It wasn't the healthiest of relationships. We used each other. She wanted a nice lifestyle, and I guess I wanted a relationship where there was little chance that I would cause any emotional hurt. I knew she was sleeping around but chose to ignore it."

"She the reason you said you had nothing back in Manhattan?"

"No, that's all down to me. I have an apartment in Chelsea and the grand total of three friends." She glanced over at Erin before continuing. "Not exactly the greatest list I'll admit. It wasn't until all this stuff about home came up that I realized even my friends didn't really know anything about me. I never told them anything about home. It was all too painful. So it was easy to hide in work until that wasn't fun anymore."

"Okay, we're going to take these in order of appearance. Tell me about your friends."

Smiling as she thought about them, Charlotte navigated the roads leading them away from Grace Falls. "Well, there's Molly. I've known her longest, almost fifteen years. God that makes me feel old," she snorted. "Molly used to come into the gym where I worked. She was fresh out of law school and climbing the corporate ladder. When the owner agreed to sell the gym to me, it was Molly that acted as guarantor for the bank loan and did all the legal work for free.

"Then there's Joanne. She's Molly's sister. Her bark is worse than her bite, and she and Molly seem to have this thing where they're never happy unless they're pushing each other's buttons. And Ellie. Ellie's the peacekeeper. She and Joanne are getting married soon. She's got this real gentle nature, and you can't help but be calm when she's around."

"Ah, 'Karma Molly,' was she the one that refused to be treated by me?"

Laughing, Charlotte nodded. "The one and same."

"What about work? You sold your gym?"

"Gyms, plural," Charlotte corrected. "What's the one thing you love about your job?"

"Helping animals and their owners," Erin replied without hesitation.

"Okay, now imagine your practice got so big, you only got to do that thing you love two percent of the time."

Erin shifted uncomfortably in her seat. "That would suck."

"Yeah, it did. So I sold up, and since then I've been waiting for something that gets me excited again. I don't want to jinx it, but I think I may have found it."

"An opportunity in Manhattan?"

Charlotte could hear Erin's trepidation as she asked the question. She chewed on her lip unsure of how much to share. She really didn't like counting her chickens, and there was absolutely no guarantee the offer Molly was pulling together would be accepted by her mother. However, she also wanted Erin to know she was serious about wanting more. In the end, she opted for a cautious reply.

"The opportunity would be much closer to Grace Falls."

Releasing her breath in a whoosh, Erin nodded. "Well, that's a relief."

"Is it?" Charlotte asked, risking a look across to Erin. She was still nervous Erin wasn't on the same page, and she could be turning her life upside down, only to lose the one woman she'd ever really loved.

"Of course it is. The whole reacquainting thing works better if we're in the same state. Plus, Sam will love a local gym."

Charlotte smiled, leaving Erin in the belief that the opportunity was related to her previous business experience.

Several hours and two rat breeders down, they were driving towards Mobile. Their conversation ranged from the serious to the nonsensical and despite so far drawing a blank on their quest, neither felt the time wasted.

"Last one." Erin typed the directions to the breeder into the car's GPS system. "You still okay to drive?"

"Yup. Although I am regretting not using the facilities at that last gas station." Charlotte squirmed in her seat. "I've had a thought. Do you have any reason to get back tonight?"

Erin moved slowly in her seat so she could face Charlotte. "Just Cooper, he's with Cindy. I'm sure I can ask her to keep him overnight. What do you have in mind?"

Charlotte shrugged. "Just that it's a long drive back, and it might be better if we do it tomorrow."

"Uhhuh." Erin smirked and raised an eyebrow.

"Honest. Gulf Shores is only another hour or so away. So maybe once we've seen the last guy we could get somewhere for the night."

"Separate rooms?"

Charlotte made a cross over her heart. "I promise."

Their final call turned out to be the jackpot. The breeder identified Ford immediately from the photo and was annoyed when he heard what his rats had been used for. As Erin called Sully to give him the news, Charlotte used her phone to find them somewhere to stay. She dug her credit card out of her back pocket when she found the ideal accommodation and smiled as she tapped the numbers into the screen.

"Please don't do anything stupid, Matt. Call Harvey and let him know what's been going on, and let him deal with it," Erin pleaded with her enraged friend. "It won't do anyone any good if you end up in jail."

Charlotte tried to listen in to Matt's response, but it appeared to be a whole lot of expletives and not much else. Waiting for Erin to finish, she opened her email and saw a summary of the offer Molly was proposing for the lumberyard. In her heart of hearts, Charlotte knew she was less interested in paying a fair price for the business. She just wanted to own it.

Left to her own devices, the offer would have been a ridiculous one her mother would not refuse. She knew though Molly would have taken the time to research and the price offered would be a realistic one. Replying back with the details of her mother's lawyer, her excitement increased again.

"If you don't promise me you'll call Harvey, I'm gonna hang this phone up and call Mack. And then you can deal with both the sheriff and her," Erin yelled.

The threat seemed to have the desired effect as Erin nodded and spoke at a normal volume. "Let me know how you get on." She ended the call and looked at Charlotte. "Phewwweee, he's madder than a wet hen in a tote."

Charlotte started the engine. "You blame him?"

"Not a bit." She tossed her phone into the side pocket of the door. "So what were you up to while I was trying to keep Sully outta trouble?"

"I found us somewhere to stay."

∞ ∞ ∞

"What the hell, Charlie?" Erin ignored the pain in her side as she sat forward to get a better view of the large property. Similar to all the houses in the area, it was raised on stilts. Its pristine white trim stood out in sharp contrast to its cool gray siding. "This is where we're staying?"

Charlotte drove into the carport beneath the house and put the car into park. "It is. You like?"

"I love." Erin took off her seatbelt and moved from the car as if in a trance. She practically ran up the white wooden staircase that led to the main door. Her sneakers shedding traces of sand on each step. Waiting impatiently at the top for Charlotte to catch up she used her toes to slip off her shoes. Letting her feet luxuriate on the sun-warmed wood, she huffed as Charlotte finally put a foot on the top step.

"What took you so long?"

"Had to get these from the security box." Charlotte grinned, holding up a set of keys. "Thought you might want to get into the property. But if you want to sleep out here at the front door, we can do that too."

Grabbing the keys, Erin quickly unlocked the door and entered the property and gasped. Ignoring the living areas, she walked straight through to the windows which made up the entire back wall. Pushing open the doors she stepped onto the balcony that lined the whole rear of the house. The increased height meant the views out across the beach and water were more spectacular than Erin had ever experienced before.

"Yeah, this was the view that made me choose this one," Charlotte said, coming out to join Erin.

"It's gorgeous. It must be costing you a fortune. Let me pay half."

Charlotte shook her head. "Nope, this is my treat. Next time we come down, it's your choice, and you pay. Deal?" She held out her hand.

"Deal." Erin took Charlotte's hand, and instead of shaking it, she stepped closer and pulled her closer, wrapping Charlotte's arm around her.

Charlotte rested her chin on Erin's shoulder. "I can't quite believe we're here."

"Me neither. I'd ask you to pinch me, but if I am dreaming, then I don't want to wake up."

Smiling, Charlotte started to pepper Erin's neck with kisses. "I could bite you instead?" she said against Erin's skin.

"Now that's an offer." Erin laughed. "But you should stop that."

Charlotte moved to pull away, but Erin held on.

"I didn't mean stop everything." She turned and enclosed her arms around Charlotte's waist. "Sun will be setting soon. We should get something to eat."

"I thought maybe I could order in a pizza for tonight. There should be some sort of welcome basket in the kitchen for anything else."

"You've thought of everything."

Charlotte pulled her closer. "Aside from a change of clothes, we're good."

Later, they sat watching the sunset. Pulling slices of pizza directly from the box and sipping the white wine left in their basket, neither could think of a more perfect end to a day.

∞ ∞ ∞

"So what room do you want?" Charlotte leaned lazily on the doorframe of the master bedroom.

Erin lay spread-eagle on the king-size bed. "Oh, I was thinking maybe this one." She grinned, propping herself up on her elbows.

Charlotte stuck out her bottom lip and nodded. "Good to know, 'cause I wasn't sure."

"That okay?"

"Of course it is! Anything you want. I'm gonna go grab a shower." She hiked a thumb over her shoulder towards the second bedroom.

Erin smiled. "Yeah me too. I spotted fluffy robes. I may be in heaven."

Charlotte pulled the door closed. "I'll see you in the morning."

Erin's reply was muffled by the door Charlotte now leaned against. She willed her feet to move and take her to her room and away from Erin.

∞ ∞ ∞

Waves crashed gently against the sand. The moon bathed the room with soft light and despite how relaxing the surroundings were and the exhaustion of the long drive, Charlotte felt too pent-up to sleep.

She lay on the bed, almost in the same manner as Erin had jokingly lain on her own earlier. With still damp hair, she opened her robe and allowed the breeze coming through the open window to dry her.

Erin was under the same roof as her.

Across the hall.

Fresh from the shower.

Rising up, Charlotte wrapped her robe around her, opened the door of her bedroom and crossed the hall.

∞ ∞ ∞

Erin stood in her bathrobe watching the perpetual motion of the ocean. Its movement was the only thing keeping her from going to Charlotte. She thought she'd imagined the soft knock on her bedroom door until she heard the door open. Keeping her focus on the moon reflecting off the water, she took deep breaths to slow her now rapid heartbeat.

"It's perfect here," Erin murmured as the heat from Charlotte pressing her body against her back did nothing to slow her heart rate.

Charlotte wrapped her arms around her. "You're perfect," she whispered into her ear. "I know we said we would wait, but I've waited for you for so long. If you want me to stop, you only need to say, and I'll go."

Erin made no sound.

Tugging gently on the belt of Erin's robe, Charlotte loosened the knot allowing the garment to fall open.

Erin's breath quickened as Charlotte's lips caressed her neck. Her hands glided beneath the fabric of the robe. The sensuality of her touch was entrancing. She stood motionless as Charlotte slipped the robe from her shoulders, revealing her nakedness.

The gown pooled in a heap between them and Charlotte stepped onto it. Using the height gain to her advantage, she continued placing soft kisses on Erin's skin as she caressed her shoulders, allowing Erin to become accustomed to her touch.

Erin felt the same gentle touch trace patterns on her back as lips continued to press lightly on her neck. Without conscious thought, her eyes closed and she let her head fall to the side, welcoming Charlotte's exploratory touch.

Erin was so lost in Charlotte's caress she didn't register when one of the hands exploring her back disappeared. Her breath caught in surprise when it gently cupped her breast. Her breathing came in shallow gasps as the hand lightly kneaded her breast. When a thumb tenderly swept over her nipple, sparks flew behind her closed eyes, and her body jerked in visceral response to the touch. She'd barely regained her composure when Charlotte's free hand slipped around her hip and traced the contours of her pelvis. When an arm tightened around her chest, and soft fingertips flamed her desire, Erin's knees buckled.

As if supplying her at least some chance at self-preservation, her mind flashed back to their earlier agreement to take their time. For a split second, she fought against her every other desire, rebelling against the sensations generated by the woman pressed tightly against her back.

A gentle voice whispered in her ear, "It's okay, I've got you."

She finally surrendered. Lunging forward, her hand pushed against the cool glass for support, as her hips matched the rhythm of Charlotte's movement. The cry wrenched from her body as she climaxed was a mixture of joy and profound relief, which reverberated as her muscles twitched their pleasure.

"Oh my God." Erin turned around, her breathing still labored. "I have missed you, so much. No one has ever come close to making me feel the way you do."

She took Charlotte's face in her hands and pulled her closer, kissing her thoroughly. She could feel her body respond again to the closeness of Charlotte, and needing more she frantically pulled at the tie holding Charlotte's robe closed. Pushing the robe roughly from Charlotte's shoulders, she started placing desperate kisses along Charlotte's collarbone. She was fueled by an unbridled desire to claim what was rightfully hers, and always had been.

"Bed now!"

With a catlike smile, Charlotte obeyed immediately. Walking over to the bed she lay down. A small growl rumbled at the back of her throat as Erin grabbed her thighs and pulled her towards the edge of the bed. All consideration of her injuries were smothered by her longing to possess Charlotte.

Erin looked down and faltered. This was Charlotte. Her Charlie.

She was panting lightly now. The sight of Charlotte laying on the bed, presenting herself was almost too much. She reached out and was astonished that her hands were trembling.

"It's okay," Charlotte said breathily. "It's just me."

"It's a bed." Erin slowly sank to her knees. "It's our first time in a bed."

Charlotte sat up and cupped Erin's face. "The first of many."

Smiling, Erin kissed her. A languid passion replaced the desperation. Safe with the knowledge there was no need to be quick. They were no longer seventeen and desperately clawing at each other to frantic climaxes before anyone disturbed them. Erin pulled away from the kiss and gently pushed Charlotte's shoulders to encourage her to lie down again. Satisfied, she started to make a slow ascent with her mouth up Charlotte's leg, pausing at her right knee to place light kisses on the scarring there.

Making her way up Charlotte's thigh, she hesitated. Looking up, her eyes locked with green eyes urging her to finish what she'd started. Never taking her eyes from Charlotte's, she delicately placed her mouth on hot skin and felt Charlotte's thigh muscles constrict around her head.

She placed light kisses around the folds of skin, feeling her own arousal surge as finally, she allowed her tongue to sweep over Charlotte. She licked slowly upwards, eventually bringing her tongue onto Charlotte's swollen clit, her touch causing Charlotte's hips to involuntarily jerk. Erin groaned as her own arousal rose. She pressed more urgently with her tongue creating a steady rhythm, which Charlotte rocked gently to.

When Charlotte's breathing became faster and her moans louder, Erin lifted her chin and plunged two fingers into her. She could feel her start to lose control as her muscles clenched. With one loud guttural grunt, Charlotte shuddered into her climax. Erin slowly removed her fingers and kissed her way back up until she was lying on top of her smiling. "So are we fully reacquainted?"

"Not by a long shot," Charlotte retorted grinning.

∞ ∞ ∞

Charlotte woke to the sensation of fingers mapping an intricate pattern on her back. She smiled into her pillow and let out a satisfied sigh.

"Did I wake you?"

Turning to face a wonderfully disheveled looking Erin, she nodded. "You did! How am I meant to sleep with you touching me?"

Erin's brows furrowed and she removed her hand. Charlotte caught it and brought it up to her lips, peppering Erin's fingertips with kisses. "Don't ever stop."

Erin's concerned expression faded into a wide grin, and she relaxed her head back into her pillow.

Charlotte's gaze lazily drifted down Erin's exposed body. In the morning sunlight, she was able to see the discoloring on Erin's side better. She sat up quickly. Her fingers tentatively reached towards the bruised area.

"Are you okay? I totally forgot your ribs. Did I hurt you?"

Erin captured her hand and repeating Charlotte's actions, pressed her lips against her fingertips. "I'm fine. It was totally worth it." She pulled Charlotte down and snuggled against her. "I needed to touch you to make sure you were real."

Charlotte placed a small kiss on the top of Erin's head. "I know what you mean. I never thought I'd have this again."

"Me neither. It's as though we've never been apart." Erin looped her leg over Charlotte.

Feeling the heat of Erin's arousal against her thigh, Charlotte moaned. Her body automatically twitched towards Erin, trying to increase their connection.

Erin slowly lifted herself and moved to lay on top of Charlotte.

"I missed you. I missed us." Erin placed gentle kisses on Charlotte's breast. Charlotte closed her eyes as Erin's mouth surrounded her hardened nipple. She raised her hips, desperate to feel more of Erin.

She felt Erin's lips stretch into a smile against her skin as a lone finger slipped effortlessly inside her. Charlotte writhed with pleasure as Erin moved her hips, painting her thigh with slick warmth. They moved in unison, each encouraging the other to increase the pace.

Charlotte wanted desperately to delay her orgasm, but the sensation of Erin was all-encompassing. With a long, loud groan, her muscles tightened, and the air left her lungs. She hadn't had time to recapture her breath when Erin let out a resounding moan and collapsed bonelessly onto her.

"I missed you too," Charlotte said, brushing Erin's hair away from her forehead.

Chapter Twenty-Seven

"So where are they?" Teddy stood motionless, ignoring Alex's huffs as she worked around her.

"They spent the night down at the Gulf somewhere," Alex replied, completing her morning tasks at a marginally slower pace thanks to Teddy continuing to get in the way of her movements. "Will you please go stand over there, so I can get my prep done." She pointed over to the corner of the kitchen.

With a sigh, Teddy snagged a fresh Danish tossing it back and forth in her hands until it cooled enough for her to hold it.

"You think they did it?"

Alex stopped slicing bread and slowly turned around, pointing her knife in Teddy's direction. "How much and who with?"

Teddy opened her mouth to deny the accusation but seeing that Alex was unlikely to believe her innocence she rolled her eyes and shrugged. "Ten bucks and Ruth."

Shaking her head, Alex resumed her cutting. "When will you two grow up and stop betting on stuff?"

Unable to provide a response that would mollify Alex, Teddy just ignored the question and changed the topic. Pulling the now cooled Danish to pieces and she popped them in her mouth one by one. "Did Sully say what happened with Ford?"

"Harvey went round with Matt last night to speak with him. Matt said he denied everything but reckoned that just going there saying they knew it was him might be enough to stop him doing anything again. Matt said he looked like he'd been rode hard and hung up wet."

"There oughta be something else that gets done. Can't Harvey charge him with something?"

Alex shrugged and shook her head. "The only thing is harassment, but the evidence is pretty flimsy."

"Someone should go tell Virginia Grace about what he's been up to. That would sort him out. She'd make earrings outta his man sack."

Shuddering, Alex glared at her best friend. "And now we have today's image that I won't be able to shake."

∞ ∞ ∞

Two days. It had been two whole days since their return from Gulf Shores, and Erin could scarcely believe she was able to feel this happy and content. Over the years, when she wanted to torture herself with what could have been, she'd often daydreamed about what her life with Charlotte would have been like. Not in any of her imaginings had she thought it would be like this.

For two days they'd holed themselves up in Erin's home, continuing to get reacquainted. Her cheeks flushed.

Reacquainted. That word would forever increase her heartbeat and make her blush with the images it brought to mind.

They'd taken the time to talk, but despite Erin's best efforts to find out more about Charlotte's plans to open a gym, she was still holding back on sharing her plans for the future. Any frustration Erin felt had been dampened by her assurances that whatever the plans might be, she was firmly placed within them.

Shifting Cooper from her lap, she stood up from the sofa. Standing she noticed the twinge from her side was definitely lessening. Her antics with Charlotte over the past forty-eight hours had done nothing to aid the speed of her recovery, but they had certainly taken her focus away from the discomfort.

Through the window, she watched Charlotte pace back and forth on the porch. She was talking animatedly into her cell phone. Despite exploring every inch of her body during their reunion and being confident she could map every freckle and blemish that adorned it, the sight of her in denim cut-offs and tank top offered a tantalizing view. It was a view she was certain she would never tire of. She made a note to remove the items at the first opportunity, to expose what they so carefully hid.

Sighing, she turned from the window and looked down at Cooper laying on the sofa. The spaniel occasionally opened one eye to check she was still there, and he hadn't snoozed through the opportunity of a walk or a treat.

"She's turned me into a sex addict, Coop." Erin flopped back down onto the sofa and tousled the loose skin of Cooper's ruff. "I've probably had more sex in the past two days than I've had in the previous two years and I still want more."

Cooper raised his head. With a soft sigh, he unfurled his legs and stood up. He gave Erin a cursory glance before shaking and jumping down to relocate to his bed.

"Okay, duly noted. You're not interested in my sex life."

"He may not be, but I surely am."

Erin jumped at Charlotte's voice. "You near gave me a heart attack!" she said, as Charlotte pulled her close.

Charlotte nuzzled her lips against her neck. "That would be counterproductive to what I have in mind for you."

"Everything okay?" Erin felt a panic rise in her chest as she prepared to ask her next question. "Do you need to go back to New York?"

Charlotte stopped and pulled back to look into her eyes. "Everything's fine. There was an unexpected bit of negotiation, but it should be okay. The only place I'm going is upstairs." She slid her hands down the outside of Erin's arms until their hands connected. "Do you want to join me?" She cocked her head to the side, smiled a sultry smile, and backed up a couple of steps.

"Well, since you asked so nice 'n all," Erin replied, pulling her bottom lip between her teeth. Her increased heart rate caused by the panic of Charlotte leaving had been quickly replaced by arousal.

Charlotte let out a low hiss. "You know what that does to me."

Erin managed her features into her most innocent face. "I have no idea what you're talking about."

Pulling her along, Charlotte navigated the pathway to the stairs. "Sure you don't."

Hand in hand, they took the steps two at a time to get to Erin's bedroom as fast as they could. They'd almost reached the door when Charlotte's willpower gave out, and she trapped her against the wall.

"I need you." She captured Erin in a searing kiss. Her hands already working their way under Erin's top. Her fingers danced over smooth skin until they cupped her breasts. Her thumbs slowly teasing her nipples until they hardened against her touch.

Erin pulled her mouth away and let out a moan. "Bed, we need the bed."

Charlotte's lips pulled back in a smile. "Still can't get over the novelty of that, can you. You know some folks would be turned on by the spontaneity of sex in the hallway."

Extracting Charlotte's hands from under her top, Erin gently pushed her back far enough so she could make her escape. She quickly tugged her T-shirt over her head, promptly losing eye contact with Charlotte, whose attention was now firmly on her chest.

She turned and started to walk into her bedroom. "And some folks would be turned on by the fact that in two seconds I'm going to be on my bed, naked, and waiting. Go figure."

Charlotte didn't need telling twice.

∞ ∞ ∞

Ruth frowned as she pushed the stroller along. "So how do we work out who won?" She glanced over towards her mother's home, where she knew Charlotte and Erin were. Their brief honeymoon period in Erin's home had been interrupted by Sam. Who, while recovering from the shock of seeing things no brother should, had alerted Peter. This being Grace Falls, Peter had casually mentioned it to his wife.

Shrugging, Teddy pulled a face at Ben making him giggle. "Ask 'em!"

"You can't just walk up to them and say excuse me, but we'd like to know exactly when the bow chica bow wow happened 'cause we have a bet."

Teddy stopped and looked thoughtfully towards the Old Anderson place that Charlotte was renting. "Sure we can an' thanks to Sully an' your sis, we have the perfect reason to be calling on them." She strode off, ignoring Ruth's muttered comment about 'brain fart ideas.'

She skipped up the steps, knocked on the door and with a triumphant grin turned to watch a reluctant Ruth walk up the path. She heard footsteps on the hardwood floor and turned expectantly as the door opened to reveal a disheveled Charlotte.

"Afternoon," Teddy said cheerfully.

"What can I do for Y'all?"

"Well we were just passing, and it occurred to us that you may not have heard the news. What with you and Erin getting all reacquainted for the past, what is it four, five days?" Teddy raised her eyebrows hoping Charlotte might correct her assumptive timeline.

Blushing, Charlotte shifted her gaze between the two women standing at the door. "What news?"

Teddy huffed at the lack of response and opened her mouth to attempt again when she was halted by Ruth's voice.

"Sully's got the go-ahead to open again. He's having a party tonight to celebrate and have a belated engagement party. We thought we'd make sure you and Erin were there." Ruth ignored the wide eyes and encouraging head jerks she was getting from Teddy.

"That sounds great," Erin replied, stepping into the doorway behind Charlotte and wrapping her arms around her waist. "We'll be there."

Charlotte relaxed into Erin's embrace. "What time do we need to show?"

Ruth smiled at Erin's appearance. "Six. We're starting early, so Jessica gets to celebrate with Sully."

With the conversation now seemingly concluded, the four women stared at each other awkwardly until finally, Ben let out a yowl from his stroller. Ruth sprang into

185

action. "We should get going. We'll see y'all later." She yanked on Teddy's sleeve to get her moving before she embarrassed them both further.

As they retrieved the stroller from the bottom of the steps, they looked up and waved goodbye to Charlotte and Erin who were watching them from the doorway.

"Ask them, she says," Ruth muttered under her breath. "Claudia Roosevelt, sometimes you let your mouth overload your butt."

"Kiss my grits," Teddy responded snarkily. "Didn't see you chime in an' ask."

They were part way up the path still bitching at each other when Erin called after them. Both women wheeled around, the broad smiles on the faces giving no indication of their muttered conversation.

"We know 'bout the bet. Alex told us. So you can both stop wondering who won," Erin yelled, laughing as Teddy stomped a foot down on the ground in temper. "But thank you 'cause you coming over today won me ten bucks with Maddie."

Teddy and Ruth watched as Erin and Charlotte disappeared, and the door closed. Chewing on the inside of her mouth, Teddy shook her head. "Goddammit."

$$\infty \quad \infty \quad \infty$$

Charlotte drew the shower curtain closed. "Nuh-uh, you're not getting back in here. If you distract me again, we'll miss the party. And I'll lose the hot water, and I have no idea how to work Ruth's mama's boiler."

Erin pouted. "I'll be good. I promise."

Poking her head around the curtain, Charlotte snorted. "We both know that's a big fat lie."

Taking her opportunity, Erin placed her hands on Charlotte's cheeks to stop her disappearing back into the shower. She leaned forward and placed a gentle kiss on her lips. Pulling back, she smiled and tapped her playfully on the nose.

"I'm gonna go downstairs to avoid temptation."

Clearing her throat, Charlotte nodded. "Yeah, you should probably do that."

Hearing Erin leave the bathroom, Charlotte sighed contentedly. Finally, she had everything she had ever wanted. She could barely contain her excitement; Erin was back in her life, and Molly's email had confirmed her purchase of the lumberyard was complete.

She hadn't expected the sale to be easy. The terms her mother had demanded had surprised her, but that was all in the past. Her present and future were slotting into place. Soon she could share her news with Erin while they were surrounded by friends at Sully's party.

She'd managed thus far to deflect Erin's inquiries about her business plans, allowing her to continue to believe she was going to open a gym. But now it was finalized, it was time to come clean.

∞ ∞ ∞

Erin skipped down the stairs two at a time. Her foot had barely touched the bottom step when there was a knock at the door. Grinning, she pulled the door open fully expecting to see Teddy standing on the threshold. The smile froze on her face as a familiar scent wafted in with the warm evening air, and she found herself face to face with Virginia Grace.

If she was surprised to see Erin answer the door, Virginia Grace's face showed no sign of it. Her eyes darted around unable to stay on Erin for any length of time. "Is my d..." She faltered, before closing her eyes as if to fully compose herself. "Is Charlotte available?"

Torn between closing the door in Virginia's face and calling for Charlotte, her manners won out. She stepped out of the doorway and indicated towards the stairs. "Charlotte's in the shower, but you're welcome to wait, and I'll go get her."

Hesitantly, Virginia stepped into the house. She looked around, and a small smile ghosted on her lips. "This place looks just the same as when I used to drop Charlotte here for her piano lessons." She turned and looked at Erin fully for the first time since the door had opened. "You'd be hiding around the corner waiting for me to leave."

"You knew that?"

"I knew more than I admitted to," Virginia replied, "and less than I should."

"I used to sit under the window an' listen to her practice. I always wished I could play."

"God had other, bigger plans for your hands than playing the piano." As if surprised by the gentleness of her own words, Virginia hastily added in a brisk tone. "My Pearl is much better thanks to you."

Erin was reminded of the almost vulnerable woman she'd glimpsed in her exam room earlier in the year. "That's good to know." She turned, intent on fetching Charlotte so she could deal with this new and unnerving version of her mother. Virginia's voice halted her.

"This was rude of me. I shouldn't have stopped by without an invitation." She started to fuss with her purse. "Perhaps you'd be so kind as to let Charlotte know I called and give her this." She handed Erin a folded piece of paper. "Tell her this isn't to make up for what I took from her. But it is what her daddy would have wanted."

"I'll be sure to tell her." Erin took the paper, held it up and nodded. She watched as Virginia Grace rolled her shoulders back as if assuming her usual persona again. With a brisk nod in response, the older woman swept out of the door, leaving Erin wondering what the hell had just happened.

∞ ∞ ∞

Charlotte padded down the steps. The sound of Erin tentatively picking out the notes of 'Twinkle Twinkle' on the piano made her smile. She quietly made her way across the room to where Erin stood, thankful for once she'd managed to avoid each and every hardwood board that creaked. She wound her arms around Erin's waist and started to pepper her neck with kisses. The novelty of being able to touch and kiss her whenever she wanted had not worn off and seemed unlikely ever to.

"I missed you," she whispered into her ear.

Erin stopped tapping on the keys and pulled Charlotte's arms tighter around her. "It's been twenty minutes!" She turned in Charlotte's arms and ran her fingers lightly through her damp curls. "Not even enough time for your hair to dry."

"I don't want to waste a minute when I can be with you, I'm still stunned that I get to do this" —She placed a quick kiss on Erin's lips—"and that you don't smack me."

Smiling, Erin extracted herself from Charlotte's embrace. "I'll be honest with you, me too." Seeing a wounded puppy dog look appear on Charlotte's face, she grinned wider. "I'm just happy we're here now and that I've moved on from our past."

"We've moved on," Charlotte corrected.

Erin stepped away and leaned against the back of the sofa. Tilting her head to the side, she regarded Charlotte. "I think it's just me for now." She held up a hand, stalling any comeback. "I think there's still some things you need to sort out."

Immediately knowing what she was talking about, Charlotte sighed. "Virginia."

"Do you plan on speaking to her?" Erin paused, chewing on her lips and looking terrified at what Charlotte's response might be to her next utterance. 'Cause if you're gonna stay in Grace Falls, you can't avoid her forever."

Knowing Erin was still hesitant about her intentions made Charlotte's heartache. She vowed there and then to ditch her plans for later and come clean with her plans for the future.

"When I came back, I intended to speak to her. Having it out with her was definitely on my to-do list. It's just that sorting things out with you came first."

"Good to know I'm high on your to-do list," Erin quipped. "So now that you've done me…"

"That sounded all wrong. I meant you were my priority." Charlotte stepped closer to Erin and placed her arms on Erin's shoulders. "You still are. I won't make that mistake again. I want to speak to her. I want to try and understand why she did what she did."

She looked up towards the ceiling as if using the white space to rearrange her thoughts and emotions adequately so she could speak. "I want to be the bigger person and forgive. I'm just not sure I can, and that makes me feel ashamed. She's never given me a reason to want to."

Smiling, Erin tucked a loose strand of hair behind Charlotte's ears. "She stopped by earlier. I reckon she's giving you a reason." She held up the folded paper Virginia had given her. "To be accurate. She's given you seven million reasons."

Taking the paper, Charlotte's nose twitched at the smell of her mother's perfume. She slowly opened it, and her eyes widened. "I've gotta go talk to her."

"Now?"

"Yeah now." Charlotte turned towards the door, intent on finding out what exactly her mother was up to.

Erin shook her head. "At least put some shoes on!"

Charlotte slammed the car into park and took a deep breath to calm down. Seeing Erin holding a check from her mother had turned her plans on their head. She was no longer sure the deal was in place. Molly wasn't answering her calls and so the only place to confirm whether her dreams of owning her father's legacy was with her mother.

It had taken several more breaths before Charlotte felt able to open the car door and step out onto the gravel drive. She looked up at the imposing house built by Ebenezer Grace twenty years before the town adopted his name. Ever since its construction, it had been handed down to each generation to maintain for the next. Despite her trepidation, Charlotte had to admire her childhood home. The crisp evening sunlight made the large white columns, and wooden siding appear pristine. The black shutters that adorned each window looked as though they'd been painted recently. It was only when her eyes reached the front door she realized it was open, and her mother was standing watching her.

Before Charlotte could move, her mother nodded an acknowledgment and disappeared into the house, leaving the door open for Charlotte.

"Well here goes," Charlotte muttered and climbed the steps up to the imposing porch wrapped around the house.

The unmistakable scent of lilies filled the entrance hall. Their sweet smell immediately transported Charlotte back to her childhood. She fully expected to see her father wandering through with the newspaper wedged under his arm and a welcoming smile on his face. A dull ache settled in her chest. It wasn't a sight she would ever experience again, and the smell of the flowers suddenly lost their comforting properties, becoming cloying and sickly.

She quickly moved through the hallway. She was sure she would find her mother in the parlor room. Despite the gray walls, the room was bathed in sunlight. The furniture had been updated, but the room still held a timeless quality; aided by the ancestral paintings on the walls. The eyes of various Grace family members watched dispassionately as the latest generations met for the first time in decades.

"I have some sweet tea if you'd like some?" Virginia didn't wait for Charlotte's response before pouring a glass.

Charlotte noted the slight tremor in her mother's movement and felt comforted. Perhaps she wasn't the only one nervous about their interaction. She accepted the glass and perched awkwardly on the seat indicated by Virginia.

She felt too taut to sit. She needed to pace at speed to help dispel some of the energy that made her limbs feel as though the muscles and tendons were about to burst from her skin. Instead, she focused on breathing in and out. After all that happened, and all the years that had passed, Charlotte almost had to stifle a snort at the absurdity of the situation.

Virginia cleared her throat, and Charlotte realized she hadn't uttered a sound since arriving at the house. She took another drink and licked at the sweet taste on her lips before finally speaking. "Erin gave me the check. Why are you giving me this money?"

"I sold the business, and it's right that you should have the money. Your father wanted you to take over from him, but I don't want to saddle you further with my failures."

Surprised by her mother's candor, Charlotte was speechless.

"I failed you as a mother before, and I don't want to fail you again. After your daddy died, the man I hired has made a meal of running it. According to the new owner's lawyers, almost everything that man had on his resume was a lie. Yet another example of my poor judgment. I'm trying to make things right, Charlotte."

Virginia's voice caught. "I've asked the new owners to remove him and ensure Ruth Campbell is put in as manager. They've also agreed that there will be no job losses."

"Is that all you want to make right?"

With unshed tears in her eyes, Virginia shook her head quickly and then composed herself. "I have no excuse for the mistakes I made with you, and I won't offer one. You deserve more than some trite 'I'm from a different generation.' I failed you, and I'm sorry."

Charlotte choked down the lump that threatened to burst from her. "I lost everything. You took everything that mattered from me."

"I know. I didn't understand you and Erin. I'm not sure I do now for that matter."

"What's to understand? We love each other. That's all that matters."

Virginia stood up quickly and moved to the window. Wrapping her arms around herself, she spoke as if only to herself. "That's exactly it. I'm not sure I fully understand love. I've not experienced a great deal of it."

"What about Daddy? He loved you."

Charlotte could see a small smile appear on her mother's face as she stared out. "He did, but I ruined that."

She turned to face Charlotte and looked squarely at her daughter for the first time since she'd entered the house. "I never told him about seeing you with Erin. At first, I told myself I was sparing him. But in reality, I knew if he were to make the choice on who to support it would be you. Then later I was ashamed" —seeing Charlotte bristle, she held up a hand—"of how I dealt with the situation. I was so angry all the time. I couldn't seem to control it. Everyone got the brunt of it, Erin especially. It was like having my shortcomings thrust into my face each time I saw her. To her credit, she can give as good as she gets.

"We tried to find you over the years. I tried myself after he died. It seems I should have just hired Alex Milne's daughter and saved a whole lot of money and effort. I did eventually tell him the reason you left, and I was right in my assumption. Rightly, he blamed me. He paid off what Erin owed the foundation, practically lived at the yard and we barely spoke after that."

Wiping angrily at tears, Charlotte stood up. "Why now? Why after all this time do you decide to be honest about things?"

"Because you're here. Because in a while I won't be and you deserve my honesty. It's all I have left to give you."

"What do you mean you won't be here?"

Seeing the shocked expression on her daughter's face, Virginia let out a soft laugh. "I'm sorry. I'm being melodramatic. I'm not dying if that's what you hoped. I'm retiring to Florida. I have too many memories in this town, and frankly, I'm tired of my reputation as the wicked witch of Grace Falls. I'm not saying I don't deserve it, or that at times I've relished it. I'm just weary, and while I'm not sure I can be anything else, I do know that whatever else I want to be I won't be it here."

Charlotte dropped back down onto her seat. "When are you going?"

"Soon. Now the business is sold, I have little to keep me here."

"It's mine."

"What's yours?"

"The business."

Virginia sat down on the sofa and reached a tentative hand across to pat Charlotte's leg. "The money is yours, but the business is already sold. I'm sorry this has probably been a lot for you all at once."

Charlotte managed to control her surprise at her mother's continued uncharacteristic behavior. "No, I mean I own the company that bought it."

"You bought your daddy's business?"

Charlotte nodded.

Virginia's face hardened. "Have you got enough money to burn a wet mule? Didn't you learn anything from your daddy?"

Charlotte opened and closed her mouth. This was the mother she was used to.

"You paid far too much. I'm not sure I should give you that money back if you can't be trusted to not spend it frivolously." Virginia's stern expression melted into a smile at Charlotte's befuddled expression. "Your daddy would be so proud of you, and for what it's worth, I am too."

"For what it's worth, it means more now than it did before."

"Then it's a start," Virginia replied, nodding.

Chapter Twenty-Eight

U pon first sight, Erin smiled at the number of people swelling out of Sully's bar. It was only as she got closer and saw the anger on their faces, that she considered there was something other than celebrating afoot. She pushed past people, ignoring their protests. She spotted Teddy and Ruth standing at the bar with their arms crossed and looking like they were ready to wage war.

"What the hell's going on?" Erin asked, shouting over the din.

Teddy leaned closer to her. "Virginia's sold out all the Grace businesses. The yard. The lodges. Everything."

Erin's eyes widened as she realized the significance of the check she'd held earlier. She almost missed Teddy's continued explanation.

"They turned up 'bout twenty minutes ago, led by Ford, who is whipping them up into a frenzy."

"I can't believe Sully let him in the bar," Ruth said, shaking her head.

Teddy shrugged. "It's not like he gave him much choice."

Erin's cell vibrated in her pocket.

"If that's Charlotte, I'd tell her not to come here." Teddy signaled towards Erin's phone.

Nodding, Erin quickly read a text message from Charlotte, which said she was heading their way. She hastily typed out a reply, warning her what would greet her if she came and telling her to go back to the Anderson house and wait.

She started to pay attention to Ford's rhetoric, which consisted mainly of scaremongering that jobs would go and repeating that Virginia Grace was a stuck-up entitled bitch of a woman. She jumped as a warm hand squeezed her shoulder. She turned to see a worried looking Sully standing behind the bar.

"How you holding up?" she asked, giving his hand a squeeze.

He smiled wearily, as he leaned over the bar to speak with her. "Yeah, I'm good. I've called for Harvey to come help calm this mob down and get them out. I'm past my maximum occupancy, and I don't want to get closed down again. Plus, I'm not making any money, 'cause I sure as hell am not about to add alcohol into the mix. You okay? Haven't seen much of you around."

Erin blushed and rubbed her neck. "I'm more than okay."

Whatever smart-assed reply Sully was going to say stalled on his lips as he spotted Harvey's hat cutting a swathe through the throng of people. Erin turned to see what had caught Sully's attention. She saw a stern-faced Harvey move people out of his way, either physically or by a look borrowed from his wife. The small sense of relief at his appearance disappeared almost immediately as Charlotte's auburn hair became visible behind him.

She watched as the two made their way towards the small stage occupied by Ford, who seemed oblivious to the fact that the yells in support of him had quelled with the Deputy Sheriff's appearance.

"Oh crap," Teddy muttered, "does she have a death wish?"

Erin looked at Teddy in alarm and then towards Charlotte, who was leaning over and whispering something in Brett Ford's ear. Nudging people out of her way, Erin made her way to the front. She was anxious to offer Charlotte some protection should she need it.

By the time she made it there, with Teddy and Ruth at her elbows, Ford was no longer on the stage. Charlotte stood alone. Erin watched as Charlotte held her hands up to quieten everyone down. Then, with a quick clear of her throat, she started to speak in a confident voice.

∞ ∞ ∞

"I appreciate you've all heard the news about the sale of the businesses owned by the Grace family. I can assure you this is not the way that you were meant to hear of this."

A voice rang out, "How come you're the one up there telling us this? Where's your mama?" A grumbling noise of agreement came from the crowd.

"I am here speaking on behalf of my mama," Charlotte replied. She looked out across the sea of faces looking up at her and had to stop a grin appearing when she saw Erin's raised eyebrow.

"I know I've been away a long time, and you have no reason to trust me. But I want to reassure you my mother's actions have been in all of your best interests."

The rumblings were quieter in response this time.

"It is true my mother sold all Grace businesses to a company from New York. She negotiated the following terms with them. There will be no job losses, and the lumber business must remain in Grace Falls for a minimum of ten years. Effective immediately, Brett Ford is no longer an employee. Anyone who believes that this decision is wrong is welcome to resign. However, you should know he has mismanaged the yard's finances, stolen from the company, and gained the job under false pretenses."

There was muttering from the crowd as they digested the information. "Ruth Campbell will be appointed manager, should she accept the job." Charlotte smiled at Ruth, whose eyes were wide as saucers.

Charlotte allowed them a moment to process while she composed herself for her next announcement. She looked down to Erin and tried with every ounce of her being to transmit an apology to her. "There is one more matter. While those terms were agreed to, I know some of you are probably concerned about the new owner and whether they'll stick to them." Her heart thumped in her chest. "I want you to know all terms will be met."

A voice to Charlotte's right yelled. "How can you be so sure?"

Charlotte glanced in the direction the query came from then turned her attention back to Erin. Her eyes locked on Erin. "I'm one hundred percent positive because I'm the new owner."

Erin saw the uncertainty in Charlotte's eyes as she made her announcement. She knew Charlotte was worried that keeping something so big from her had damaged them as a couple.

She did the only thing she could think of to let her know they were okay.

Lifting her hands, she looped her fingers together.

"I can't believe we missed it all," Alex grumbled, only slightly mollified by the hug she received from Maddie.

The friends sat around a table in the now much quieter bar, finally enjoying the celebration they set out to have.

"It was amazing." Ruth's words slurred thanks to the celebratory drinks she'd consumed.

"You're only saying that 'cause she's your boss. Suck-up," Sam said, taking a swig from his beer.

Peter prodded Sam in the arm, causing him to spill beer down his T-shirt. "Maybe you could learn a thing or two on sucking up to your boss."

"So you bought the businesses, and then your mother gave you the money back?" Maddie asked, still trying to catch up.

Ruth frowned. "How'd you buy them in the first place? Your gym went bust."

Charlotte shook her head. "I never said that. You did that all by yourself."

Maddie sat forward. "So you didn't lose your gym?"

"Nah, I sold them."

"Them?" Ruth halted her husband's movement as he attempted to remove the drink in front of her.

"In 2012, Elliot Enterprises sold its interests in LifeFit's thirty gyms, ten health clubs, and two tennis centers, situated throughout the Eastern Seaboard. For sixty-five million dollars."

The adults all turned towards Jessica, who was sitting reading from her father's cell phone screen.

"What?" Jessica shrugged, waving the phone "It was just sitting there unlocked."

Alex reached over and removed the phone from her daughter's hands.

"LifeFit," Maddie said, impressed. "I was a member in Atlanta." She held up a finger. "Sully, I swear if you make one comment about me in lycra I will throat punch you." She paused to see if her threat was enough. Seemingly satisfied, she continued. "I joined in January, went until February and then kept paying until I could get out of the contract. I kept the towel though."

"You're not alone." Charlotte laughed. "Many did that, and I thank you for it."

"So basically you're richer than God," Sam joked.

"Not quite, but I did okay." Charlotte bit her lip. She wasn't uncomfortable with her wealth. She'd worked damned hard to create her business, but she knew sometimes it changed how others were with her. Erin squeezed her thigh in support. "That gonna cause an issue with anyone?"

Sam shrugged. "Nope, you're still you. Money don't make no difference. You still squat to shit like the rest of us."

Jessica spun around to face her mother. "How come that's okay, but I can't talk medical stuff at the table."

Alex glared at Sam. "It's not okay."

"So, Charlotte what exactly did you say to Ford to make him scuttle off the stage?" Teddy interrupted to save Sam while signaling another round was required.

"I told him if he left quietly that Virginia wouldn't pursue charges for theft."

Sully sat back and placed his arm around Lou. "I can't believe you let him off so easily."

Grinning, Charlotte tweaked Sully's nose. "Who said I did? I just wanted him off the stage. Virginia might not charge him, I, on the other hand, had Douglas waiting outside to arrest his ass."

Disentangling himself from Lou, Sully grabbed Charlotte's cheeks and planted a sloppy kiss on her lips.

"Hey big guy, wind it down." Erin playfully reached around Charlotte to swat Sully on the back of the head.

"Before I forget." Charlotte picked up her now replenished drink. "There is one more announcement. The Grace Falls Foundation and Elliot Enterprises are sponsoring Sam Hunter to allow him to train in Norway."

"What?" Erin spun around to look at her younger brother. "What is this and why am I only hearing about this now?"

Both Charlotte and Sam muttered 'shit' in unison.

"You, little brother, I will deal with later." She turned back to Charlotte. "You're just full of surprises today."

"Fifty bucks he breaks something in the first month," Teddy yelled, capturing Erin's attention away from a sheepish looking Charlotte.

Sully slapped his hand on the table. "I'm in. I'll take two months."

"Guys, I'm right here," Sam whined.

Erin leaned over, her breath on Charlotte's neck causing a delicious tingle up and down Charlotte's spine. "You have a lot of explaining to do."

"I promise I'll make it up to you when we get home."

She felt rather than saw the smile on Erin's lips as she replied. "Home?"

"Home."

Epilogue

A year later

With a sigh, Erin rested her forehead on the reception desk. "Please tell me we're done."

Cindy tapped the back of Erin's head lightly with her pen. "We're done. You're free to go."

Straightening up, Erin grinned. "Thanks, boss."

"Don't you forget it," Cindy replied without looking up from her screen. "While it's your name on the door, we both know who's really in charge here."

Erin was already on her way back to her office, shrugging out of her white coat as she went. She tossed it into the laundry hamper and pulled her cell from the back pocket of her jeans. She smiled as she read the text from Charlotte.

'Meet me after work at our usual place.'

She typed back she was on her way before switching off the light in her office and heading back to the reception area.

"Don't stay too late." Erin paused beside Cindy on her way out.

"I'm just about done."

Erin waved a goodbye as she slipped out of the air-conditioned office and into the warmth of the evening. Driving her car through town, she smiled as flags were hung outside Sully's to celebrate the town's one hundred and fifty-first birthday.

It was hard to believe a year had passed since Charlotte returned for the previous event. Sam was still in Norway training and would miss the party. The bet on his breaking something had been won eventually by Maddie when he dislocated his thumb six months in.

Sully and Lou were now married, and to everyone's surprise, Teddy and Douglas followed suit shortly afterward. Maddie and Alex were, unbeknown to most of the group, attempting to become pregnant.

Charlotte was firmly embedded back into life in Grace Falls. However, every couple of months they would take a trip north to allow Charlotte and Molly to have their friends fix. Erin also accompanied Charlotte to Joanne and Ellie's wedding, throwing the seating plans into disarray.

Charlotte and her mother were attempting to forge some sort of relationship. It wasn't proving to be the easiest of tasks as Virginia could be just as ornery as ever. But some progress had been made.

She parked her car and stepped out onto the trail that led to their rock. It was a warm summer evening, and honeyed rays of sun glinted through the trees as she walked the short distance to where she knew Charlotte would be waiting. Approaching their spot, she wasn't disappointed. Charlotte lay spread out on the rock. Her red hoodie was bunched under her head as a makeshift pillow.

Erin approached as quietly as possible, smiling as she almost reached Charlotte before green eyes sprang open.

"Hey, you." Charlotte quickly sat up and propelled herself from the rock to capture Erin in a hug.

"You've got sawdust in your hair again." Erin picked small particles of wood from Charlotte's auburn hair. "If you've been 'helping' in the saw room again Molly will have a fit about your liability insurance."

Charlotte snuggled her face further into Erin's neck. "What she doesn't know won't cost me anything."

"So how come we're meeting here?"

Charlotte pulled back and placed a gentle kiss on Erin's lips. The tenderness quickly developed into something more passionate as she clutched Erin's ass and brought their lower halves closer together.

Before things went too far, Charlotte started to take the heat out of their kisses until eventually, Erin's heart rate was back somewhere normal.

Pulling apart, Charlotte smiled shyly. "I thought maybe we could go for a swim."

Not letting Erin respond, she held onto her hand. Grabbing her hoodie as she passed, she started to walk them towards the Grace family property.

When they reached the boundary fence, Erin stopped. "What happens if we get caught?" she asked, echoing her teenage concerns.

"We're not gonna get caught," Charlotte replied, climbing over the fence.

Erin cast a glance up towards the large colonial style property. "You're sure?"

"Positive." Charlotte reached for Erin's hand to help her over. "Look all the lights are off. There's no one home."

Erin quickly stripped off her clothes and dove seamlessly into the water, treading water until Charlotte joined her. A dog barking from the house broke the silence of the night.

"They've got a guard dog." Erin looked towards the noise.

Charlotte swam closer and pulled her into an embrace. "I'm not sure Cooper can ever be classed as a guard dog."

Erin smiled, wrapping her legs around Charlotte's waist. "Don't disparage our dog. He could save your life one day."

"I would never disparage him," Charlotte replied, reaching her hand around Erin's neck to tug her into a kiss. "Besides, I don't need saving. I'm already saved."

About the Author

H.P. Munro lives in London with her wife and a wauzer named Boo. She started writing in 2010 when a new job took her away from home a lot, and she found herself in airports, on flights and in hotel rooms with room service for one. The job didn't last, but the love of writing did.

Her début novel Silver Wings won the Golden Crown Literary Society Historical Fiction award in 2014. Her novels Grace Falls and Stars Collide were published in 2014 and quickly became lesbian romance bestsellers, with Stars Collide selected as a finalist in the Goldies 2015 Traditional Contemporary Romance category.

You can connect with HP through:
Email: munrohp@gmail.com
Facebook: www.facebook.com/munrohp
Twitter: @munrohp
Website: www.red-besom-books.com

Other Titles by Author

SILVER WINGS

WINNER - 2014 Golden Crown Literary Society – Historical Fiction
ISBN-13: 978-1482023572
ASIN: B00FXY3LTU

When in 1942, twenty-five-year-old Lily Rivera is widowed, she finally feels able to step out of the shadows of an unhappy marriage. Her love of flying leads her to join the Womens Airforce Service Pilots, determined to regain her passion and spread her wings, no suspecting that she would experience more than just flying.

Helen Richmond, a Hollywood stunt pilot, has never experienced a love that lifted her as high as the aircraft she flew...until she meets Lily. Both women join the W.A.S.P. program to serve their country and instead find that they are on a collision course towards each other, but can it last?

GRACE FALLS

Amazon Best Seller - #1 Lesbian Romance, #1 Lesbian Fiction
ISBN-13: 978-1495400544
ASIN: B00I5UVVN2

Dr Maddie Marinelli is looking for a fresh start; she's leaving behind the ghost of a failed relationship and looking forward to starting a new job and life in San Francisco...what she didn't count on was car trouble and the colorful residents of Grace Falls.

Alex Milne has spent most her adult life putting other people's needs first. She is busy raising her daughter in her hometown while running her business and the last thing she expects is to be attracted to Grace Falls' newest, albeit reluctant, resident.

Sometimes you don't know what it is you're looking for, until it comes along and finds you.

STARS COLLIDE

FINALIST – 2015 Golden Crown Literary Society –
Traditional Contemporary Romance
Amazon Best Seller - #1 Lesbian Romance, #1 Lesbian Fiction
ISBN-13: 978-1499357776
ASIN: B00KHAEHTI

It's tough growing up in the spotlight, and Freya Easter has had to do just that, being part of the Conor family, who are Hollywood acting royalty, has meant that every aspect of her family's life has been played out in the spotlight. Despite her own fame Freya has managed to keep one aspect of her life out of the public eye; however, a new job on hit show Front Line and a storyline that pairs her with the gorgeous Jordan Ellis, may mean that Freya's secret is about to come out.

In a world of glitz and glamor, Jordan Ellis has come to the conclusion that all that glitters is not gold. She has become disillusioned with relationships and is longing for a deeper connection, and is surprised when it comes in the form of the most unexpected package.

While their on-screen counterparts begin a romantic journey, Freya and Jordan also find themselves on a pathway towards each other.

Printed in Great Britain
by Amazon